LAKELAND
HEATWAVE

Riding the Ether

K D GRACE

Published by Xcite Books Ltd – 2012

ISBN 9781908262189

Printed and bound in the UK

Cover design by
The Design House

Lakeland Heatwave: Body Temperature and Rising
is dedicated to the Natural World, the
true source of magic and mystery
beyond imagining.

Thank you, with all my heart!

THE LAKELAND HEATWAVE SERIES

9781908086877

9781908262789

9781908262202

Acknowledgements

Very special thanks to Brian and Vron Spencer for all of their guidance and help in Lakeland lore, and for some of the most amazing walks I've ever had. Your boundless love and enthusiasm for the Lake District is contagious. Thanks for all you've taught me, and thanks for your help in exploring and experiencing, and I hope, bringing to life on the page, the magic of the English Lakes. You two are the best!

As always, thank you, Renee and Jo and all of the lovely Ladiez at Sh! You've been a bright spot in my writing journey almost from the beginning. Not only are you a fount of information, fun and encouragement, but you're an endless source of inspiration to me. Hugs and kisses and my deepest gratitude.

Thanks to the indomitable Hazel Cushion, and all the fabulous people at Xcite Books for making the *Lakeland Heatwave Trilogy* a reality.

Thank you, Lucy Felthouse, for cracking the PR whip, when necessary, and for staving off more than one panic attack for this neurotic writer. Thanks for letting me bend your ear when I just needed to talk. I couldn't have done it without you, EP!

Thank you, Kay Jaybee, for just being there for me and being your fabulous self. The journey has been so much better because we've shared it. You're amazing!

Thank you, Raymond, for putting up with me when I'm not my charming self and loving me anyway. Thank you for believing in me and being proud of me and easing the journey. There's no one I'd rather have by my side. Volim te mnogo!

Chapter One

'THERE WILL COME A time, my dear Tara, when you must let him use his gift.' Anderson nodded to Tim Meriwether, who sat naked and meditating on the edge of the dream bed in the cave. 'You have said it yourself that he is ready. He has progressed even more quickly than we had hoped now that he has made peace with the difficult circumstances in which he finds himself. In which we all find ourselves.' He lifted his high priestess's chin, forcing her to meet his gaze. 'And it is possible that I may not always be here.'

She pulled away and continued to loosen the plait of her hair. 'You're my high priest. What, are you planning early retirement, maybe a holiday away from all this fun?' As was common when he broached the subject of permitting Tim Meriwether to perform the task that fell to their masculine sex in the coven's dream magic, she made no pretence of hiding her irritation. In truth, he knew this irritation was focused inward. Irritation was the most effective disguise Tara Stone could manage for her fear of becoming too attached to the living. In fairness, Tara had done all in her power to see to the proper training of Tim Meriwether and Marie Warren, since they had been added to the coven. And they were quickly becoming formidable witches because of it.

But on this one subject, she would not be moved. Tara Stone would not have intercourse with the living. She allowed herself sexual congress only with ghosts. And though Anderson, being himself a ghost, benefited greatly from what Tim Meriwether referred to as Tara's sexual neurosis, he worried about her still, worried about her as he had the entire

150 years they had been together. The burden she bore would have broken anyone else long ago, and yet she shouldered it. His heart ached for her at the thought. He brushed a dark lock of her lush hair away from her cheek.

'I have heard that Tahiti is lovely at this time of year, and I think I should quite enjoy a bit of warmth after the long Cumbrian winter.'

She gave him a look that told him she neither believed him nor was she impressed. 'You're a ghost.'

'A ghost who is at this moment fully in the flesh, and I assure you, my darling, my flesh does not appreciate the cold any more than does yours.'

She forced a smile. 'And yet your flesh is doing a lot more complaining about it than mine is.'

'My dear Tara, you have once again successfully directed our conversation away from the topic I endeavoured to broach.'

She shook her head slightly, and the last of the plait collapsed into a soft torrent of deep auburn that reminded him of the peaty waters in the fast-moving streams on the fells. 'Clearly not as successfully as I'd hoped,' she said, 'or you wouldn't be bringing it up again.' She took him by the hand and led him toward the dream bed. 'Now, do you think we could focus on the magic we're here for instead of my choice of sex partners?'

He thought it wise not to remind her that the magic had been precisely the topic of their conversation, aware as he was that in her heart she knew that fact even if she could not bear to admit it. And in truth, his timing had been poor. But Tim Meriwether was truly gifted in dream magic, while Anderson had come to practise it only by default – being, before Tim Meriwether's arrival, the only member of the coven equipped with a penis.

Anderson was more at home in the Ether. He was trained in ethereal magic and, in truth, it had been many long years since he'd had need of what was now referred to as REM sleep, that sleep in which dreams occurred, that sleep which kept the living sane and healthy. Not for the first time he wondered if it might be more expedient simply to allow him to journey into the Ether and seek out with more direct methods the information they desired. But Tara had forbidden it as too dangerous at the moment. And in spite of the unease he felt, he would do his high priestess's bidding.

He brought his attention back to the circle that had been cast earlier, and let the full weight of the magic rest against the flesh he wore as comfortably as the living wore theirs. He immediately felt his manhood stiffen and tense with the growing urgency of the rising magic. He became aware that Marie and Tim Meriwether were now entwined around each other, naked and sheened in perspiration in spite of the winter outside the cave. Through their act of pleasure, their task was to prepare the way for the magic that was to be worked. Sitting next to them with their arms around each other in a caress of their own were Sky and Fiori, theirs the responsibility of witnessing all that was to happen.

Anderson watched as Tim Meriwether positioned himself between Marie's pale thighs. She moaned softly and lifted her legs to his hips. Tim's buttocks clenched with his first thrust, obscuring for a brief moment the lovely back hole with which Anderson had grown quite familiar in the passing of the eight months since they had fought the demon together.

Could it really have been such a short time since Deacon had been bound in the flesh, in the strange lifeless limbo in which Marie and Tim Meriwether had trapped him? Anderson's stomach clenched as he thought of how very close he had come to losing the two he had so grown to love.

He knew them both intimately, and memories of making love with them served only to tighten the growing weight of desire in his own loins, as he knew it did with Tara and Sky and Fiori, as it was intended to do. It was the foundation set in motion, the drive to rut, the ancient need that brought humanity to the very edge of ecstasy while at the same time driving it to the brink of its own destruction. And in between ecstasy and destruction, the next generation was birthed into existence. And there, on that knife-edge in between, the magic happened as it could happen nowhere else. Again and again Anderson had experienced it, always new, always wild, always almost beyond his control.

With the weight of the magic pressing in on him along with the desperate need it created, he shrugged off his robe and eased aside Tara's, then drew her down onto the bed of cushions, kissing each of her heavy nipples before beginning his descent to the gateway. He nibbled at the base of her sternum where her ribs yielded to the rise and fall of her belly, which tightened with the touch of his lips and teeth. The caress of his tongue forged the path to her navel, sinking in, darting, probing in sympathy with what his penis would soon do. He traced the soft, goosefleshed skin down to the pillowed curls of her pubis, down to the very bud of her pleasure. In his mind's eye he could see clearly the gateway as he reverenced it with a kiss to the keystone. He worshipped at its entrance with long lavings of his tongue, preparing the way.

Tara curled her fingers in his hair and spoke words, ancient words, words that could be understood in no other context than that in which they now found themselves. Words that would never be uttered in any other space but the space they now created in their intimate act.

And when he was certain the gateway was fully open, fully inviting, he rose on his knees and positioned himself, one hand on his member, the athame in flesh, the other bracing himself. Then he entered the gateway with a shifting of his hips and a sigh of pleasure laced with fear of the unknown, fear of the Dream World, which was always unpredictable, never completely safe in its revelations.

From a long distance, he heard Tara moan, heard the rush of her breath, felt her legs tighten around his hips, but he was already through the gateway, speeding forward with each thrust, deeper and deeper into the dream. It was familiar territory, a journey he had made with Tara many times before. He found himself poised there on the threshold of the unconscious, waiting to be drawn under, waiting to uncover

4

secrets. He felt a slight tightening in his chest, an acceleration of his heart, and the scraping of flesh against stone, solid and bruising. His pulse accelerated further. The hair on the back of his neck rose. Someone called his name from a long way off, but it was not Tara. His last thought before he was catapulted from the flesh with a force violent enough to take his breath away, if there had been breath left, was that he was no longer in the Dream World.

He was unsure if he had lost consciousness but Anderson knew immediately, when he had gathered himself enough for the knowing, that he was in the Ether, though how he had got there he could not tell. Immediately, he cast the counting spell his mother had taught him when, at last, she had agreed that even though he was no daughter, he had wit enough and was gifted enough in the Old Ways to walk safely in the void.

He had already crafted his own counting spell, for until she had relented, he had visited the Ether in secret without her permission. More efficient than his, her spell allowed him to set a small clock in the back of his mind, a clock that kept track of time in the World of Flesh, the only way to mark the passing of time in the Ether. If the counting spell were not cast, one could very easily die. While starvation set in, and the comatose body withered away in the World of Flesh, no time passed at all in the Ether. Time was simply not a concept in the void.

And though he did not remember casting the special enfleshment spell, the one he always cast for himself in the Ether, he was fully in the flesh, albeit flesh that only had substance in the Ether. He was completely naked, and fully – nay, outrageously – aroused. The pressure in his groin was both agonising and exquisite. He reached for his manhood, knowing full well he was in need of wit that he did not possess when his lust was so great. But before he could stroke himself to release, a voice spoke out from the void. 'That belongs to me.'

He was not startled that the woman appeared out of

nowhere – after all, this was the Ether. He was, however, very startled, if most pleasantly so, that she was as naked as he, and it was no hardship for him to look upon her. Before he could utter even a cry of surprise, she knelt next to him, slapped his hand away and took his member into her mouth.

'My dear woman,' he gasped as her tongue snaked up the underside of his manhood. 'I do not believe we know each other.'

She stopped pleasuring only long enough to reply. 'We will very soon.' Then she returned her efforts to his great need.

'I fear this shall end quickly if you do not stop what you are doing.' He tried, though only half-heartedly, to push her away. After all, what manner of man saw to his own release before the pleasure of his lover?

'I know you.' As she spoke, she continued to stimulate him with her hand. 'It may be over quickly this time, but then –' she lifted her head enough to brush a quick kiss against his lips, enough for him to catch the tiniest glimpse of dark cinnamon eyes. 'When it's over we'll begin again, and then –' she gave his cock a squeeze '– then I'm sure I'll be well compensated.'

She spoke no more, but took the length of him deep into her throat and tightened her grip until there was nothing else for it. He shuddered the weightiness of his release into her throat, and she drank it back like fine brandy. And when she had drained him as surely as if he had been the glass containing her drink of choice, she slipped up next to him, so that her tight, roseate nipples pressed against his ribs. And when she kissed him, he tasted himself on her lovely tongue. This time she kissed him with all of her mouth – nay, with all of her body if that were possible – and he felt lust already returning to his loins.

When she pulled away, he spoke in one breathless sentence, fearful that if he did not find his voice immediately, the lady's own greed for the pleasures of the flesh might make him forget that he even possessed the power of speech, might

6

make him forget why his voice would even be of importance. 'My dear woman, might I at least enquire who it is that pleasures me so well and in such unusual circumstances?'

Once again, she held him with the deepest, darkest eyes he had ever seen on a woman so pale of complexion. 'I'm Cassandra, Cassandra Larkin, and I've been waiting for you.'

'Then it is clear you have most definitely found me, Cassandra Larkin.'

Though it was usually fear and uncertainty that drove those who rode the Ether to complete the task for which they had come and then return to the World of Flesh as quickly as possible, those who were more adept at journeying in the Ether knew that passions and desires were always more difficult to control in that vast space. Therefore, even though he had never taken his pleasure in the Ether before, it came as no surprise that his desire should return with such intensity. He was certain other practitioners of ethereal magic would not approve but at that particular moment on his internal spell-induced clock, he could think of nothing in the Ether he would rather be doing than sharing pleasure with Cassandra Larkin.

He was much more in control of his manhood after she had so deliciously emptied him, but he would most definitely be the first to agree with modern theories on human sexuality, stating that the brain is the seat of desire. And this slender woman, pale of flesh and hair and dark of eyes, was truly intoxicating. He wondered if her appearance in the Ether was as her appearance in the World of Flesh. Some, he was aware, chose to appear differently when riding the Ether.

He felt her hips shifting and rocking with her unsatisfied need and as he lifted himself onto one elbow, rising above her, for the first time he became aware of the bed on which they lay. It was devoid of colour, like the emptiness in which they found themselves, but it was a bed nonetheless. Anderson could not help but admire the woman's attention to function, much more important in ethereal magic than form. And at this moment, hers was the only form in which he was interested, though he wondered why that should be when there was important coven magic in which he ought to be participating.

She guided his hand to the soft warmth between her legs, and he eased a middle finger into the slippery wetness of her ardour. His thumb caressed the heavy node of her pleasure and she trembled like a leaf on water, honeyed eyelashes fluttering over dark eyes. She opened herself to him, shifting her buttocks until he could see the heavy folds and hillocks of her womanhood pouting open before him, until he could smell the heat of her rising up from below her belly at the seat of her desire.

She lifted her arms around his neck. 'Anderson,' she pressed his name up through her chest and past her lips with laboured breath. 'Anderson, it's all right for me to have you here in this place, and I need you. Please. I need you.'

His own need grew with the feel of her beneath him, and he did not deny her the release she so needed. He cupped her buttocks, felt them tighten in his grip, felt the strain of her anticipation as he positioned himself, the head of his erect member tight against her womanhood. 'Please,' she whispered again.

He pushed into her until the sigh of her breath was a sob, then she wrapped herself around him and pulled up to meet him, pressing her mouth to his, whispering against his lips. 'Ride it with me, Anderson. I need you to ride it with me.'

The power of first contact drove fire up his spine and up into his head until the very fabric of the Ether sparked with it. Then, as he thrust, it was as though she had inhaled all of him into herself, right up through the very core of her womanhood, all the way to the beating of her heart. And then she gave it all back to him again, each time driving the fire up into him hotter and brighter than the time before.

His bliss was such that he wondered if it were her intention to burn him until he was but ash to be blown away into the nothingness of the Ether. But he was too far gone for his possible destruction by fire to matter, and when she began to shudder with her release, driving her heels into his kidneys, digging her nails into his back, he allowed himself to tumble into the abyss with her. The bed she had created quite literally vanished and they were falling, endlessly falling into the heat of their release.

For a time, they floated in the nothingness, wrapped around each other. The clock in his head warned him that he had been gone too long, that there were important responsibilities he must return to, but still he clung to her.

'Are you all right?' she whispered against his ear.

He chuckled softly at such a question. 'As ecstatic as the experience of sharing pleasure with you is, my dear Cassandra, it was only *la petite morte*. And surely you are aware that I am already dead, and therefore undamaged by even the power of your great ardour.'

To Anderson's surprise she wept, only a little, but he appreciated the ways of women. Their ease with their own emotions was a thing much to be envied. And she did indeed weep, and hold him even closer to her, if that were possible.

'Only *la petite morte*,' she sighed. 'Of course.' She moved a hand down to rest against his heart. 'I have to go now, Anderson, and so do you.' She kissed him and in that startling moment, colours flashed before his eyes. Steamy sunsets, nights dense with stars, an older woman with a cascade of white hair falling over a black robe. Ghosts, memories, wild places. And the sharp crack of a bullwhip and fire that was cold and unnatural, and yet familiar in a way that chilled him even in his ethereal body. Then, as inexplicably as he had come to be with Cassandra Larkin in the Ether, he fell away from her into darkness.

When the darkness broke over him, he awoke on the dream bed, looking up into the concerned faces of the rest of the coven.

Chapter Two

'WHAT THE HELL JUST happened?' The anger in Tara's voice could not disguise the fact that her lovely skin was porcelain pale and her pulse beat against the tender spot in her throat as though it would explode from its confinement.

Anderson recognised the fear in the coven leader's face before he was even aware she had spoken. He had seen that fear before, and it turned his very insides to ice. A quick glance around him reassured him that every member of the coven was present and safe, though every one of them looked somewhat shaken. And then the events that led him to be in this position, reclining on the dream bed beneath their anxious gaze, came back to him in a rush of memory. The Ether, the sex, Cassandra Larkin – and, just before he had fallen back into the cave, back into the arms of his high priestess, something much more sinister.

He sat up carefully, not wanting to disgrace himself. Even in his created body, returning from the Ether too quickly could result in the disgorgement of one's dinner. Though, in truth, he could never recall his body feeling such bliss after riding the Ether. He wasn't sure he could ever recall his body feeling as it did at this moment, even when he had lived. And yet this experience should not have happened. He knew it far better than anyone else here. And he knew it would be the cause of great consternation for Tara, and for the rest of his coven. And for him, once he felt less … ecstatic.

'Anderson?' The concern in Tara's voice forced him back to the moment.

'I believe I was riding the Ether,' he said softly.

'Goddamn it, Anderson!' Tara cursed, making no effort to hide the fact that she was trembling. 'I strictly forbade you to go there. You know what's been happening. Do you want to come back witless and insane or, worse yet, not come back at all? What the hell were you thinking?'

He reached around her, found her robe and pulled it up onto her shoulders. 'My dear Tara, I assure you I did not ride the Ether against your will. I am as astounded as you. In truth, I cannot explain how I arrived there, or how I returned.'

'What do you mean, you can't explain?' Tara asked.

Fiori took advantage of the opportunity to bring out a large picnic basket with a steaming flask of lamb stew and home-made Irish soda bread. Food after magic, always. Even though she and Anderson and Sky no longer required food, since they were no longer numbered among the living, they all still took pleasure in it. It was Fiori who always made sure there was food after magic and that it was always good food.

Wrapped in blankets and shawls, they sat in a circle on the big pallet of duvets and cushions that served as the dream bed and partook of Fiori's feast while Anderson shared his experience in as much detail as he could remember it.

'It has to have been a dream,' Tara said, after she had heard his whole story. 'You weren't prepared. You'd done none of the ritual involved in entering the Ether.'

'My dear Tara, I am a ghost. Whatever ritual I do to enter the Ether now is for the benefit of those who ride with me who are still in the flesh. And, my love, you are the only living member of this coven family skilled enough in ethereal magic to accompany me on those journeys.'

She shoved a bite of soda bread into her mouth and swallowed without chewing. 'Are you sure it wasn't a dream? I mean, is there any way it could have been a dream?'

'Perhaps we should ask Tim Meriwether. He dreamed with us. He would have sensed a lost dreamer.'

They all turned their attention to the young farmer, who sat wrapped in a Mackenzie plaid blanket, staring down into his tea. He shook his head and looked up, a lock of unruly

11

brown hair falling over his face. 'You weren't a lost dreamer, Anderson. You flat out weren't there. Oh, your body was, but you weren't, at least not anywhere in the dream I could see.'

'And the woman you were with, this Cassandra Larkin, you said you heard the crack of a whip and saw fire when she kissed you?' Fiori said. She brought her hand unconsciously to rest on her throat. Even dead as she was, even with the demon safely bound, the magical flesh she had created for herself paled and sheened with the perspiration of fear when she spoke of him or thought of what he had done to her. 'Do you think she has something to do with Deacon?' Her voice wavered slightly at the mention of her tormentor's name.

He shook his head. 'It was only a flash, only for the tiniest of instances and, in truth, my attention was otherwise occupied. It could have simply been that the lady prefers sexual congress to be more painful than what I was equipped to provide at that time.'

Tim Meriwether chuckled softly. The women offered the poor man a withering gaze in unison. He returned his attention to his tea.

Anderson smiled to himself. It had been his desire only to ease the tension, but of course the women would interpret his behaviour and Tim Meriwether's response to it as proof that a man's mind is controlled by his member. They were right, of course, and the very thought of Cassandra Larkin made him uncomfortably heavy beneath the wool blanket he now wore.

'As happy as I am for the pleasuring of your cock, Anderson, I'm wondering how you got into the Ether from the dream bed, especially considering the importance of the magic we were attempting to do.' Tara's voice was no louder, no softer than it usually was, and yet in it at that instant was power, magic. Old magic. Magic that made the fine hairs rise along the flesh, magic that ached deep into bone and sinew. And with that power sheathed in the soft voice of a woman, no one could ever doubt her rightful place as head of the coven.

All eyes were averted, and Anderson knew all hearts,

12

including his, were beating just a little faster. Once she was sure she had their full attention, she continued. 'The two are mutually exclusive. There are no gateways in between, no secret passages.'

'There are no passages of which we are aware,' Anderson said. 'No one, living or dead, has ever journeyed to the boundaries of the Dream World or the Ether.'

'But Deacon is neither living nor dead,' Marie said softly.

'That is true,' Anderson replied, recalling how Marie and Tim Meriwether had bound the demon with a spell that held him in the flesh, neither living nor dead, as she said, but in a strange limbo in between. 'I will not deny the possibility that Deacon has found that secret passage, if there is one. But I do not believe that Cassandra Larkin has any involvement with Deacon.'

'Why?' Sky asked. 'Because she pleasured your cock? That's a distraction, Anderson,' She flashed him a succulent breast from beneath her robe as proof of her point. 'Not evidence of this woman's purity.' She offered him a knowing smile, well aware of how his manhood would respond to a glimpse of her lovely bosom.

'Perhaps you are right, my dear Sky, but of one thing I am certain. If indeed my experience was only a dream, then it was more like the Ether than the Ether itself. If, however, it was, as I believe it to have been, the Ether, then upon my honour I swear to you I do not know how I came to be there, nor do I know whence came the magic Cassandra Larkin used upon me. In truth, it was a strange magic, indeed, such as I have never, in all of my substantial years, experienced.'

Tara laid a hand on his wrist, and he felt instantly calmed. 'You're certain that it was the Larkin woman's magic that brought you there?'

He held his high priestess's gaze, careful to hide nothing from her. If he did, she would know, and as always, he wanted no barriers between him and his oldest, dearest friend. When he spoke, it was to her, knowing that somehow she would understand more than his words, perhaps more than even he understood, as was so often the case. 'The magic she possessed was strong enough to have brought me there, of this much I am certain. And that, my dear Tara, is astounding.'

'I'm not really comfortable with this. Is it absolutely necessary?' Alice Hartley shifted on the sofa in the therapist's office and glanced out of the window at the falling snow, trying to avoid the woman's pointed gaze. She bit her lip gently, raked her teeth across it and tasted vanilla lip balm. 'It's worse during meditation. That's why I stopped.'

The psychologist looked at her over the top of horn-rimmed glasses, glasses Alice suspected the woman really didn't need, but wore only to make her look older and wiser. 'If there is something in your meditations that frightens you, Alice, then the only way to overcome that fear is to confront it.' She gently tapped the end of a very expensive pen against the desk pad. 'However, if you're not comfortable with a guided meditation, we can certainly put that idea aside until you are.'

For a second, the two women sat in silence. Alice fondled the tiny silver pentacle at her throat with icy fingers. Ms Barrows – Kate, as she kept reminding Alice to call her – studied her with unreadable eyes. At last she spoke above the quiet whir of the electric heater. 'Tell me, Alice, this man you encounter in your meditations, is he like your ex-husband?'

The question was so ridiculous that at first Alice thought she was joking, but the sincere blink-blink of her pale blue eyes was not humorous. 'Of course he's not like my ex-husband. My ex-husband never wanted to fuck me. He wanted to fuck everyone else, not me. But this man …' She felt her stomach tighten with nerves and something more. He's … well, he's not like any man I've ever known before.' She forced an embarrassed laugh. 'But then, why should he be? He only exists in my imagination, which is why all of this is so totally ridiculous.' She puffed out a heavy breath and folded her arms across her chest, shrugging the thick wool cardigan she wore tighter around her against a sudden chill.

'Alice –' if the woman leaned any farther over her desk, she'd be sprawled across it '– have you had sex since your divorce?'

It was Alice's turn to blink. She felt the heat rise in her cheeks and mentally kicked herself for being embarrassed about sex. For fuck's sake, she was an adult. 'If you mean with a man, no.' She paused. 'But I do have a vibrator … several actually, and I use them.'

Dear Goddess, she hoped the woman wouldn't ask how often. Since her imaginary friend, as she had first called him back before her fantasies gave him a name then started to turn frightening, since he had arrived in her life … well, she was going through batteries like water, and she was only using the vibes part of the time. She couldn't seem to keep her hands out of her knickers, and she knew exactly what to do with them. And then there were the thick candles and veg and other things that she would have never imagined could feel so good up inside her fanny. She shifted again on the sofa, this time with a different kind of discomfort.

Still, she didn't want a man. The fact that she didn't was something else that frightened her. She'd been divorced well over a year now; she should at least be craving male companionship. And yet she couldn't picture herself with any man other than him, the one she imagined. And sometimes she could almost imagine him making love to her. She could almost feel him, feel him against her skin, feel him inside her. But at those times, he was more than just inside her … so much more … And that's when she had stopped meditating.

'Well, I can certainly understand you not being anxious to have intercourse with a man after your marriage dissolved,' the therapist was saying. 'And I think it's a big step forward that you're taking responsibility for you own sexual needs. It's a very important step for you, for every woman. But I am going to encourage you again to let me lead you on a guided meditation, just a very short one for now, and once you're comfortable with it, we'll consider longer ones.

'Many women find guided meditations helpful, and I think

15

you might also, Alice.' She glanced around her. 'You're in a safe place here with me. No one can hurt you, and just having someone witness for you, share the journey with you, may go a very long way toward your healing. If you're willing.' Her smile was genuine, but then it always was. The woman was trustworthy, sincere, had come highly recommended. And yet, Alice was reluctant.

Ms Barrows, Kate, said nothing, only held Alice's gaze, held it until Alice squirmed in spite of her effort to stare her down. Then the therapist offered her a smile that was calm and sympathetic, and Alice released a long, shaky breath. If she were ever going to get past this, here was the place to do it, with this woman, and it wasn't likely to get any easier the longer she put it off.

She rubbed sweaty palms against the legs of her trousers, not surprised to see that her hands were shaking. 'All right, then. What do you want me to do?'

The therapist straightened in her chair and folded her hands together on top of her desk blotter like she was about to say a prayer. 'Just get comfortable, Alice, like you normally do when you meditate. That's it, just relax. Feet flat on the floor. Shoulders soft. Deep, even breaths. And when you're ready, I want you to go to that place where you meet this man of your imagination. Go there just as you are, relaxed, comfortable, unafraid. Go there and just be in that space and just …'

And she was. She was there, surround by … well, surrounded by nothing. Just empty space. How could there be just empty space? But it was all right. Empty space she could handle. Empty space was all right, as long as she was there alone. But there was barely time for a mental sigh of relief before her blood chilled in her veins and it was as though a shadow had crossed over her consciousness. She couldn't hear him, she couldn't see him, but she knew. Dear Goddess, she knew! He was there.

'I've missed you, my darling. Why have you stayed away so long?' His voice was in her ear, like he was right behind her – no, more like he was inside her, right there with her. Her skin crawled, like it wanted to escape her flesh. Her throat ached with a scream it couldn't quite form, a scream for help from Kate. Her nipples were suddenly painful, and she was wet. Oh dear Goddess, she was so wet and swollen. She whimpered desperately and tore at the fly of her trousers.

'Oh, my poor little witch, my poor little darling, do you see how you suffer when you stay away from me?'

She clawed at her pentacle for comfort, but found none. He only chuckled softly. She could feel his voice deep in her chest, making her nipples even harder. 'But all of your suffering is over now, my beauty. I shall make you feel better, and that is what you want, isn't it? You want me to make you feel better.'

Great Goddess, yes! That was what she wanted, what she had always wanted, to feel better. Her fingers sank into her pussy, her thumb raked at her clit, and she sobbed.

And then there was no time, there was nothing but the burning ache of lust unsatisfied, in sharp contrast to the icy breath of fear tearing at her lungs. *Thrice bound and once released, thrice bound and once released, thrice bound and once released.* The strange chant filled her head, then filled the whole world. *Thrice bound and once released, thrice bound and once released.*

An eternity later, someone shook her. She woke with a start on the rug in front of the sofa with Ms Barrows gripping her shoulders hard, shaking her, calling her name over and over.

She sat up quickly and pushed the therapist away.

'Are you all right, Alice?' The woman was trembling, at least as badly as Alice was, as though she was struggling mightily to remain calm. It was then that Alice noticed the scratches on the therapist's face, the dishevelled blonde hair that had been perfectly coiffed when the meditation had begun. But mostly she noticed fear. She smelled it, felt it, saw it like some physical apparition, settling cold and clammy over the room, sheening across the woman's damaged skin,

17

raising rough goose-flesh against her own.

'I'm fine.' Alice forced the words up through the raw-meat ache of her throat. 'What happened?' As she spoke, she realised her trousers and knickers were down around her thighs and her shirt was torn. The cord on which she'd worn the pentacle lay shredded on the floor, and beneath the edge of the therapist's desk, the pentacle itself lay snapped in two pieces. And the fear tightened like a noose around her neck. 'Oh dear Goddess,' she sobbed. 'He was here. He was here, wasn't he?'

Chapter Three

CASSANDRA WOKE TO THE cold mist of her own breath rising in the room above the mattress and pulled the thick duvet up tighter around her. She had expected the fire to be out by the time she returned, though she had banked it as best she could. It was then she realised she had the tiniest bit of a headache. The fact that she had a headache at all caused a clench in her stomach that was far more painful than her head.

She never had headaches unless she had taken too much. And she never, ever, did that. Not any more. She hadn't done since she was in uni, and then she hadn't known any better, hadn't known what would happen, hadn't known how to control herself. And once she did know what would happen … She pushed that thought out of her head. Still, how could she have taken too much? She had been so careful with her research, so careful with her training. Anderson was a ghost, and they'd been in the Ether, and he had seemed fine, had said he was. He'd certainly seemed all right when she had left him. More than all right, actually.

Suddenly, the clench in her stomach and the ache in her head were both overshadowed by the rhythmic thrumming between her legs that buzzed up her spine. It was the feel of him. The feel of his energy still on her, still in her. She reached between her legs and felt his wetness still there. Even though they'd been in ethereal bodies, sometimes a bit of the Ether escaped back into the World of Flesh. Fooling the Ether, her grandmother used to call it.

Even the feel of his semen against her fingers tingled. She brought it to her mouth, strangely scentless for semen, but that

19

was the curse of ghosts who wore the flesh. They could generate no scent. She wondered if he had been able to smell her scent on him after they'd left the Ether. There was always a scent on her when she came back from the Ether. It was the scent of high- altitude cold and metallic bite. She hoped it was more than that that lingered on him when he left. But then it would be, wouldn't it? Much, much more, though she wasn't sure about scent.

She licked his juices from her fingers and instantly she knew that he was indeed all right, if a bit confused. He was very all right. She slid her hand down for more, feeling the buzz of energy relax the knot in her stomach and clear her headache until her whole brain felt like a window, open to all she needed to see, to feel, to experience. And fuck, it was amazing! It had always been amazing, like a drug she dare not allow herself for fear of becoming addicted to it, but this was bloody awesome! It was more than her research had ever prepared her for, way more!

With little more than a stroke, she came, trembling all over as she reached between her legs for more of his juices, unable to hold back shudders that led to moans and, embarrassingly, nearly to bellows that vibrated her whole body. With each clench and tremor, her pussy forced out more of his delicious essence, and she wiped it, rubbed it, slathered it all over her body. Great Christ, she wondered what the man must have smelled like when he lived. He was … He was a rider of the Ether. And he had been for damn near ever. He was power and virility and physicality in ways she had only dreamed of. And she could make love to him. She *had* made love to him. Great Goddess, how she had made love to him!

With her orgasm mellowing to ripples, she sent out her fetch, that magical part of her that was, in itself, almost like a ghost, her essence, sent forth to explore beyond her body, sent forth whenever she rode the Ether.

She could have never breached the protective magic of Elemental Cottage before. But now she was connected to Anderson. She wore his essence inside and out. She passed through those boundaries and protective spells like water. And she would be able to find him anywhere, in the flesh, or not. She paid no attention to the house, took no time to marvel at the domain of the witches she so admired. She was sure it was amazing, but she had no time for that. She had sent her fetch out for one thing, and one thing only, and that was to find Anderson, to look, just look at him, to reassure herself that she hadn't dreamed such a man, such a coupling.

And he was there, exactly as she knew he would be. He slept in the arms of his high priestess, slept the deep, even sleep of dreams, dreams which he didn't need – and yet he chose to have them, in the vulnerable act of sleep that he also didn't need. He slept wrapped around her. They had had sex. Though Cassandra could not smell him, she could smell the woman, earthy and slightly piquant from the labour of lovemaking. He slept, but the woman, Tara Stone, did not.

She could sense the woman's worry, her restlessness, but that didn't concern her at the moment. It was Anderson in his unnecessary sleep that interested her, fascinated her, drew her. He was erect. In a thought she felt was worthy of a teenager with a crush, she wondered if he was excited by dreams of her. She could find out easily enough, but she never invaded people's dreams on purpose. She never entered people's private places.

She ran her hand along his flank, feeling her own essence against his flesh as surely as she felt his on her. She could take him now while he slept and he would never know it. She could give him such sweet dreams of her, such passionate dreams that he would come in his sleep, and she would wear the energy of his release, the energy of his dream, like a tight-fitting skin – a skin that would nourish her, give her strength in a way her own never could. That she could do such things frightened her. That she still wanted to do such things frightened her even more. She bent over him and pressed her mouth against his parted lips, breathing a kiss against them, and he sighed softly.

The woman started and sat up, looking around the room.

Cassandra couldn't imagine that she was able to sense her presence, but she knew Tara Stone's reputation so just in case, she quickly pulled her fetch back to herself, back to her own bed, and her flesh felt all the more vibrant, all the more alive for having been with him, even if it had been from a distance.

Her clit felt heavy. Her nipples ached, and she masturbated again. It was in the receding tremors of orgasm that she noticed the ghost watching her, peeking around the edge of the hanging blanket that separated Cassandra's sleeping space from the rest of the bothy.

When she caught her breath, she sat up, no longer noticing the cold in the room, and not bothering to pull the duvet over her breasts. After all, the ghost had just seen her having a wank. 'What do you want, Serina?' she asked, trying to keep the irritation out of her voice. The woman was still adjusting to being dead after a very traumatic fall off Raven Crag only eight months ago. Demonic forces, the little ghost claimed, and no matter how much Cassandra wanted to chalk it all up to the delusions that sometimes affected the newly deceased when they were still in denial, in her gut, she feared Serina spoke the truth.

That being the case, she wished Serina Ravenmoor would just stay away from her. She didn't want attention drawn to herself, especially not the attention of some pissed-off demon. Still, Serina was really not the kind she could imagine a demon pursuing beyond the grave. More likely the demon had used her until it had no further need of her, and had then driven her crazy and she'd killed herself. Cassandra hadn't asked. She didn't want to know. And yet, that was ugly enough, and sad enough to keep Cassandra sympathetic in spite of her irritation at having her ruminations disturbed.

The little ghost stepped forward. 'I'm lonely.' She looked as though she had been crying. Not for the first time, Cassandra wished she couldn't see all the things she saw. 'Can I sleep with you?'

She knew the woman could no longer sleep, which made the horror of her death and bodiless wandering all the more dreadful. To suffer with not even the respite of sleep was something Cassandra would have wished on no one. She pulled back the duvet with a soft sigh. 'Do you want flesh?'

'If you don't mind. That would be nice,' the ghost said. 'I can tell you're aroused. I practised sex magic when I was alive, you know. I can take care of you.'

'I know, you told me.' Cassandra reached out her hand and touched the ghost, who shuddered as the enfleshment spell enveloped her. 'But as you saw, I just came. I can do you, though, if you want me to.'

'I'd like that,' Serina said, as she crawled onto the mattress next to Cassandra, and kissed her slowly with soft probings of her tongue. When she pulled away breathless, she spoke. 'Do they know you can do that?'

'Do what? The enfleshment spell?' Cassandra pushed up the edge of the thin satin negligée Serina wore, moving her hand up inside the woman's thighs, gently teasing them open, then shifting until her palm cupped the ghost's mound and she squirmed beneath her touch.

'Any of the stuff you do. Ride the Ether, give ghosts flesh, and –'

Cassandra covered her mouth with a kiss, not wanting to continue the conversation, and slid her finger down to caress Serina's clit and press up into her pussy, already slick and grasping at her fingers. 'They don't know anything about me,' she said when she came up for air. 'And I like it just fine that way.'

'Then why did you fuck their ghost in the Ether? You know they're saying it's not safe to go into the Ether any more, and they're right. Don't you know he's there?'

Cassandra kissed her again, and when Serina pulled away, she bit her lip. 'Shut up, Serina, and let me make you come.' She kissed her again, and when she was certain the ghost would make no more comment, she pushed aside the strap of the negligée and cupped the small breasts. They were mostly nipple, pale-peach nipples that rose up from the tight stipple of areolae, sensitive nipples that made Serina's breath hitch, the breath that was on loan to her temporarily until Cassandra fell asleep and the spell was broken. Sharp little whimpers that were nearly soundless, but not quite, escaped the ghost's throat. Her hips rocked and shifted with a tension that made Cassandra's own hips rock in empathy. She sucked each lovely, high nipple in turn, then whispered into the bony striations of Serina's sternum, 'Shall I lick your pussy for you? Would that make you feel better?'

'Yes,' the little ghost breathed. 'Yes, it would help, I think.'

With kisses and lovebites, marking flesh that would be gone in a few hours as though it had never existed, Cassandra moved down over Serina's thin belly, then, with a stretch, reached for an extra pillow and pushed it beneath the ghost's bottom, elevating her hips and exposing her cunt like jewellery in a display case. Then she buried her face in the scentless wet heat of the woman's pussy, driving her tongue along the splay of her until she probed the tight central hole that gripped creamy-slick with need.

With her arms pressed low over Serina's abdomen, she held the ghost in position so that the flat of her hands rested on her mound and her thumbs took turns raking the exposed hillock of her clit. Serina thrashed against the mattress, making little grunting sounds that could have been either pain or pleasure. She forced herself upward onto one elbow and fisted her fingers in the tangle of Cassandra's hair. Her feet pressed down on Cassandra's shoulders for leverage, and Cassandra forced herself on to her knees, arse in the air, legs wide apart, still not feeling the bite of the cold room. Instead, she felt her exposure with an aching need for Anderson, whose ethereal semen still warmed her, and she drove her face still deeper into Serina's cunt, biting and sucking and licking until she felt the woman's orgasm break, felt her hips buck. And Serena keened, 'Oh dear Goddess, I'm coming!' And just as Cassandra felt her own orgasm building low between her hip bones, the little ghost pulled harder on Cassandra's hair and gasped, 'Take me, Cassandra, please take me. It's all right. I want you to.'

It was as though ice water had suddenly backwashed into her veins. Cassandra pushed Serina away and tumbled off the edge of the mattress, sliding her bare arse across the cold stone floor, sending a precarious stack of books avalanching around her. For a second, she sat blinking, the sight of the ghost on the bed more like a hunter's view through night-vision goggles. She blinked again and shook her head hard. 'Don't ask me that, Serina. Don't ever ask me that, or I won't give you flesh ever again. Do you understand?'

'I'm sorry.' Serena was now sitting on the mattress with the duvet pulled over her exposed breasts. Her eyes were welling with tears. 'I only wanted to give you something in return, a gift for being so kind to me.'

'Please don't cry.' Cassandra ran a hand through her hair and blew out a sharp breath. Her vision slowly began to clear. 'It's not your fault. It's just that you don't know what you're asking, and trust me, it's not something you really want me to do.' She forced a smile and clambered to her feet. 'Now, I'm starving, and I bet you are too. How about I get a fire going and, I haven't had a chance to shop, but I think there's still a can of potato-leek soup in the cupboard. Would you like a bowl? I know I would.'

By the time the kettle had boiled and the soup was heated, the wood fire had warmed the shepherd's bothy to a more comfortable temperature. The relish with which Serina ate her food gave Cassandra pause to wonder about all the things the living took for granted. She knew how wonderful everything solid, everything that could be touched, smelled, tasted, felt seemed after a sojourn in the Ether. But she had always been able to return at will. She had a tendency to inhale her food so she could get back to her research, get back to her studies, but as she sat opposite the ghost, she forced herself to eat more slowly, to savour. She had just poured them each another cup of tea when she noticed Serina was staring at her.

'What?' she asked, tearing off another piece of the stale baguette she had scrounged from the larder for them.

'You won't be angry if I ask?'

'Maybe, I don't know. But ask anyway because I hate being stared at.'

Serina lowered her gaze to her half-eaten bowl of soup. 'Why would you take him, but not me? I mean that ghost, Anderson?'

Cassandra felt the heat in her face, and fought back the urge to tell the ghost to mind her own fucking business. She took a gulp of tea to calm herself, and burned her tongue in the process. 'We were in the Ether. Our bodies were conjured bodies and besides, I didn't take him.'

This time, Serina did not look away. 'You had sex with him. I know you did. I felt it.'

'That's pretty rude, hanging around watching other people fuck, don't you think?'

Serina toyed with her spoon. 'I didn't say I was watching. I said I felt it.' She leaned over the table. 'And if I felt it, he felt it.'

'I didn't take him, Serina. I don't do that. I'm not like that.' Cassandra suddenly found it hard to find the right words, and she was amazed to realise that she really wanted, even needed the ghost to understand.

'Then what?' Serina asked.

'Anderson's different. Surely you know that? He doesn't need anyone to give him flesh. He wears the flesh whenever he wants and he rides the Ether freely, more freely than anyone living could. And he's the only male, as far as I know, to ever ride the Ether at all.'

Serina nodded. 'That is amazing, I have to admit. I never really believed he could do it. When I was alive, I tried several times to enter the Ether. I never got past the threshold, and I always ended up very ill afterwards.' She shivered and chafed her arms.

Cassandra nodded to the pegs full of jackets and cardis next to the door, and Serina chose a pale blue cardigan which, tiny as she was, hung on her in great folds.

'Very few people who weren't born to it go willingly into

26

the Ether,' Cassandra said. 'And as far as I know, Anderson is the only man ever born to it.'

'How do you know all of this?'

Cassandra found herself blushing again. 'I do my research.' She returned her attention to her soup. She could tell Serina was studying her, but she pretended not to notice.

'*He's* not a rider, but he found a way in somehow.'

Oh fuck, here it came. Cassandra ground her teeth and tried to hide her irritation – it was the Deacon thing again.

Serina leaned over the table. 'Cassandra, please believe me, if I know you were with Tara Stone's Anderson, then Deacon knows it too. Don't you understand? That's what happened with Maybell.'

'The witch you were staying with before you …'

'Before I died, that's right. She has some skill at riding the Ether – though it's not her gift, she can do it. Things were happening, things that shouldn't be. She thought she could help. I don't know, maybe she felt bad about what happened with me.' She fell silent, staring into her now lukewarm tea. 'Of course, there was nothing she could have done. Deacon would have had me. I was already dead, really.' She looked up again, her eyes misted. 'That's why I was there with them, that's why I saw him. I wanted her and Verity to know that it wasn't their fault, what happened, that there was nothing they could have done. And I saw what he did to her.'

'Jesus!' Cassandra pushed back from the table, nearly upsetting her chair. 'I don't want to know this, Serina. This Deacon of yours.'

'He's not my Deacon!' With a sweep of her hand, Serina knocked the teacup onto the floor where it shattered, bleeding out its contents over the stone. 'I'm dead because of him and my death wasn't pretty, and neither were the few weeks before. Do you understand?'

Cassandra took a step back until she felt the edge of the counter against her hip. She was prepared to disenflesh the crazy woman if she needed to, but she did outweigh her considerably so that probably wouldn't be necessary. 'OK.'

She kept her voice even and calm. 'So why are you telling me this?'

Serina found the rubbish bin and knelt to clean up the broken mug. 'Because I saw him. I saw him at the threshold waiting for Maybell that day. I saw him. He was there, and he dragged her back through, and held her there. It was him. I know you think I'm crazy, but I swear to you it was him.'

Cassandra paced back and forth, feeling the fine hairs along the tops of her arms rise. 'That has nothing to do with me. He has nothing to do with me.'

Serina stood with the rubbish bin in her hand. 'Of course it does. I told you. If I can feel it, he can feel it. He never misses anything. I promise he knows you were there.' She worried her bottom lip with her teeth. 'He knows everything that in any way concerns Tara Stone and her Elementals.'

'But I don't have anything to do with them.' Cassandra shivered involuntarily. 'I'm a nobody. Why would he care about a nobody?'

The ghost looked her up and down. 'You're an extremely powerful nobody, Cassandra.'

'No. No, I'm not. I'm just a horny witch, that's all.' She watched while Serina began to wipe the spill with kitchen roll. 'Anyway, why did you come to me if you know all this stuff that affects them? Why aren't you warning them?'

The woman blushed and scrubbed until the paper disintegrated in her hand. 'They don't like me very much. They'd never believe me.'

Chapter Four

AN IMPROMPTU GATHERING IN the formal sitting room at Elemental Cottage never boded well. That Tim Meriwether had been called from his farm duties on an evening he would have otherwise not been at the cottage boded even less well. Tara poured tea and Fiori passed around a plate of home-made shortbread. Even under the worst of circumstances, civilised behaviour and hospitality were always practised at Elemental Cottage. When everyone had been served, Tara spoke.

'Maybell is dead.'

There was a murmur among the other coven members, and Anderson detected a sniffle among those who had known the witch well.

'What happened?' Sky asked.

Tara shifted on the sofa and looked down at her hands, folded in her lap. 'She was hit by a bus.'

The murmuring grew to gasps of surprise. 'But she's been in a coma ever since she was trapped in the Ether,' Marie said. 'That makes no sense. How could she have been hit by a bus?'

'When the nurses went to check on her, she was gone,' Tara said. 'No one saw her go, no one heard anything. One minute she was in a coma with no change and the next, she was running out in front of a bus in her hospital gown. The nurse swears she hadn't been alone for more than five minutes.'

The room erupted and everyone spoke at once.

'There's more.' Tara's voice rose above the din and, just

as quickly as the hubbub had begun, the room returned to silence. 'Apparently, she literally threw herself in front of the bus.' She swallowed hard. 'Then she got up, and kept getting up.' She took a deep breath. 'And Verity saw the whole thing.'

'Oh dear Goddess,' Sky breathed.

'Fuck,' Marie said, gripping the arms of her chair with white knuckles.

For a long moment, Tara said nothing. Anderson could see the fine muscles along her throat struggling against her pulse.

'There is more, is there not, my darling?' he said. 'Please tell us.'

Tara blinked twice, composed herself and continued. 'She spoke as she was dying, as she kept struggling to get up. She said …' She looked around the room at her coven and her eyes became hard, cold. 'She said, "It doesn't matter, you stupid bitch. I'll find another way back. I'll find another stronger than you."'

A strangled cry escaped Fiori's throat, and Tim Meriwether moved quickly to her side, pulling her close, stroking her hair, speaking softly to her until she was calmer. Then he returned his attention to Tara. 'Then Deacon's found a way back.'

Tara nodded slowly. 'We dare not assume otherwise.'

'Fuck,' Marie whispered again. 'How could this have happened?'

Tara stood, moved to the window and looked out into the lush back garden, now buried under snow. 'Clearly he's found access through the Ether, just as we expected. I don't know how. It makes no sense. But, as Anderson said, no one living or dead has ever been able to explore the boundaries of the Ether or the Dream World, nor do I know of anyone who's tried, unless his Cassandra Larkin has somehow managed it.'

'It is possible that she has done this, I suppose,' Anderson said. 'Though I think it unlikely. I am certainly willing to find out, and I am the logical choice for the task since I am the only one who can safely go there.' He paused, then continued.

'Because I am dead, it is unlikely that Deacon may harm me. I cannot see how we can fight him when we do not know how he has managed such a thing, and if Cassandra Larkin knows how this can be, then we must find her.'

'I agree we need to find her,' Tara said, turning back to face her coven. 'And it may come to sending you into the Ether to see what you can learn. But I want to exhaust every other possibility first.'

Before Anderson could respond, she raised a hand. 'I'll hear no argument. This is not up for debate until, as I said, we've exhausted all other possibilities. I will not put any of you in unnecessary danger. Is that clear? I said, is that clear? Anderson?'

Everyone nodded their agreement, but all eyes were focused on him.

'Anderson?' Tara's voice now made the hairs on the back of his neck rise, and he knew if he argued with her directly, he would most definitely lose. He released a long, slow breath that, though not necessary, certainly felt appropriate at that moment. 'Yes, madame. You have made yourself quite clear.'

For a blistering moment she held his gaze as though she were trying to read him, as though he might keep secrets from her. He made an effort to be offended by her doubts, but he could hardly take offence at the fact that she knew him almost as well as he knew himself. He nodded his acquiescence once again and lowered his gaze, as much out of fear of what she might see in his face as in deference to her position.

She turned her attention back to the coven. 'Now,' she said, pausing to finish her tea in a single gulp. 'I need to be with Verity. Blessedly, Maybell's ghost hasn't lingered among the living. I'll light candles and do the passing rites with her. We owe her no less.'

'If that stupid Ravenmoor woman would have stayed out of it, she'd still be alive,' Marie said.

The force of Tara's essence suddenly filled the room, making the space crowded and tight, making skin prickle and pulses race. 'I will hear no ill spoken of the dead in this

31

house, Marie Warren. You of all people know Deacon's power, and Fiori more so.' Delicate china cups rattled softly against their saucers, the chandelier trembled overhead and the room felt uncomfortably hot, as though it were bathed in intense sunlight. 'Serina Ravenmoor was a victim of his vileness, as have we all been, and more to be pitied that she lacked the skills to fight back.'

'I'm sorry,' Marie whispered, lowering her eyes. 'I'm very sorry.'

Suddenly, the air in the room softened and calmed, and breath rushed back into the lungs only now aware they had been without. Tara gazed down at her. 'You are young in our ways, Marie, and your heart is tender. That is the very best of your gifts. In the journey of a witch, compassion is above all, and above all to be most treasured.'

It was always a bit of a surprise, even after all these years, when Tara resorted to the more formal speech of the era whence she had come. Unlike Anderson, she had chosen the speech of each era as her own. It was not that he could not imitate the clipped, flavourless parlance of the Twenty-First Century, it was simply that he chose not to. And since he had no affiliation with the herbal apothecary she owned and operated with Sky and Fiori, and his wealth was his own, he found himself in less need of blending into Cumbrian society.

She looked down at her watch. 'I have to go. In the meantime, the rest of you strengthen the protection spells, all of them, and find out who this Cassandra Larkin is. The woman is either very dangerous or the answer to our prayers. We need to find her.' She walked out of the room and within a few minutes, they heard her Land Rover pull out of the driveway.

Sky guided Fiori to the kitchen to prepare food to be taken to the grieving Verity. Fiori always found solace in the kitchen, and Sky was quite used to being her sous chef. Anderson was left with Tim Meriwether and Marie. When he was sure everyone was out of hearing range, he spoke quietly to the two. 'If it would not be too much of an imposition, I am of a mind to return to Lacewing Farm in your company.'

Marie and Tim Meriwether shared a meaningful glance and it was clear to Anderson that they understood he was accompanying them for reasons other than the pleasure of their very enjoyable company. They consented.

'Let me get this straight,' Tim Meriwether said. 'You want us to do dream magic with you?'

Anderson had enjoyed the spaghetti carbonara the two had made. The conversation had been congenial and as pleasant as could be expected given the circumstances, and it continued as they shared a bottle of claret. They were all three settled on cushions in front of the warmth of the fireplace at Tim Meriwether's cottage, the cottage he now shared with Marie Warren, an arrangement they had enjoyed for the last four months. 'Does this surprise you?' Anderson asked.

'Not really,' Tim Meriwether replied, sipping his wine. 'I suspected as much when you offered your company for the evening.'

'What exactly do you have in mind?' Marie said.

Anderson scooted forward on his cushion. 'It is not so much dream magic as it is sexual congress, after which we three sleep together when we have relieved our needs. I believe you may refer to it as post-coital bliss.'

'In other words, dream magic,' Tim Meriwether said. 'Go on.'

'It was while practising dream magic that Cassandra Larkin was somehow able to pull me into the Ether, and it was when she released me back into the dream and into the presence of my coven that I saw the images of Deacon. And though I had hoped they were otherwise, I am persuaded that I now no longer have that luxury. I am persuaded that they were truly images of the demon.'

'And you think this Cassandra chick will pull you back into the Ether again?' Marie said. 'What if she won't let you out this time?'

'My dear Marie, I beg you to have a little faith in me. I

33

assure you I at no point felt that I could not have escaped the Ether if I had chosen to, nor was there any time in my sojourn with Cassandra Larkin that I felt anything from her but goodwill.

Half-giggling, Marie asked, 'Is that what you're calling it these days, Anderson? Goodwill?'

Both men chuckled and Anderson continued. 'While I will not deny that the sexual pleasure of the woman's company was, indeed, sublime, I assure you that I am still in possession of a very finely honed sense of intuition, even being dead as I am, and Cassandra Larkin means no harm. That she is benign is yet another reason why my journey to her is paramount. Not only may she be able to help us discover a way to Deacon and to prevent him from committing further atrocities in the world of the living, but she may very well be in danger from him herself and unaware.'

'I had thought about that,' Marie said.

'I'm sure Tara has too,' Tim Meriwether added. Then he shrugged. 'Still, as far as I know, we've always been encouraged to practise and refine our magical skills at every opportunity, and since Marie and I both are such novices to magic, I can't see how Tara could object to us practising a little dream magic, especially when we do it under the kind supervision of a superior witch. How shall we proceed?'

'Well, you two are the dreamers,' Marie said. 'It's clear to me that I should be the witness.'

'But then there's no gateway,' Tim said. 'How can the magic work without a gateway?'

Anderson leaned forward and kissed Tim on the mouth, pausing to let the farmer return the favour with his very exquisite tongue. Then, gently, he touched Tim's temple with his index finger. 'My dear man, the magic is in the dream, and the dream itself is generated here, and here.' He touched his own temple. 'Much more so than here.' He laid a hand against the place where Tim Meriwether's trousers restrained his now expanding manhood.

'If you think she can get to you through the dream alone,

then why do you need us?' Marie asked. 'Not that we're not willing, of course.'

'Sex always strengthens the magic, my darling,' Anderson said. He reached to slide his other hand inside her blouse and caress the fullness of her bosom and the press of her delightfully responsive nipples, barely restrained by the lace of her thin brassiere. 'As well as the dreaming.'

Tim Meriwether was already opening Anderson's trousers, and Marie's fingers quickly and agilely dispensed with the buttons of her blouse and the clasp of her brassiere. As Anderson settled in to nurse at her lusciousness, he decide not to tell them that he was quite certain Cassandra had visited him two nights ago while he slept. It delighted him that she had come to him, more than it should have considering that she had breached the boundaries of protection and had come to him as an intruder. It was only her fetch, he was certain, but had Tara not sensed that something was amiss, he would have gladly endured such an intrusion and followed her fetch wherever it led him. He was not sure why he kept the visitation a secret, but neither could he feel remorse for holding this small bit of pleasure to himself.

He lifted his buttocks to allow Tim, who was already naked, to remove his trousers and undergarment. Anderson marvelled at what a quick study the young farmer was as his skilled tongue made warm, insistent undulations against his receptive nether hole. Marie quickly kicked her way out of the rest of her garments and lay back, lovely thighs opened wide to offer Anderson her exquisite womanhood, an offer he could never have refused. He reverenced her dewy gateway with tongue and lips and teeth. And he had barely pushed into her, and Tim into him, when he felt the harsh pull of his essence from his flesh, and the room and the fire and his lovers and Lacewing Cottage all disappeared in an instant, as though he had been exhaled out of the world of the living.

At the same instant, he was inhaled into a world surrounded by his own reflection and nothing else but the emptiness of the Ether. He was hard. Painfully hard. As difficult as it was to think of anything other than the weight of his lust, he set the time spell in motion and reached down to caress his penis. 'Cassandra? Why the mirrors?' He spoke between slightly parted lips, knowing that if she did not arrive quickly, he would spill his seed without her.

'Because I wanted to watch us fucking.' From out of nowhere, she spoke next to his ear, and he was amazed at the depth of his delight at being in her presence again. He felt the caress of her hard nipples against his back, a sensation that forced him to press his thumb to the tip of his manhood to hold back the tide.

'I think that said fucking must happen quickly,' he breathed, as she ran a hand down his chest to stroke his belly, 'or all you shall see is me emptying my manhood into the void.'

'Another time, Anderson. I'd love to watch you jizz the void, but not now.' She moved from behind him and stood above him, naked and exquisite, the scent of her intoxicating in her need. She slid a hand down over soft, tight curls to splay her womanhood before his eyes, her inviting gateway slick and trembling and swollen deep red with her lust. 'As you can see, I'm in as much need of you as you are of me.'

'For this fact, my dear woman, I am thankful to all the gods.' He placed his hands on her hips and guided her to squat over his anxious member, and with a single thrust he emptied himself into the trembling grip of her womanhood, and her whole body convulsed with her own release. She bit his shoulder in the throes of her pleasure, a pain that was exquisite in its own right.

'Sweet Goddess!' she grunted, sucking breath between her lovely full lips. 'I needed that, Anderson, I needed to come all over your cock. I needed to feel you emptying your load way up deep inside me. I haven't been able to think of anything else.'

'I confess that you also have not been far from my thoughts, since we last had intercourse. Your heat lingered on me long after our tryst, lingers on me still, I believe, though I

do not know how that may be. I have never felt such magic.'
He eased her back onto the colourless bed and held her there,
impaled as she was, his manhood throbbing and swelling
again inside her.

'Are you always hard?' she asked when he began to move
and shift within the gripping of her flesh.'

'I am seldom soft.'

She grunted and tightened her caressing womanhood still
further. 'I can't tell you how much that pleases me.' She
wrapped her legs tightly around him and thrust up to meet
him. 'Is that because your body's magical?'

He lowered his mouth to suckle her exquisite nipples in
turn. 'It is because, as Tara so eloquently states, I am a randy
bastard.' He bit her nipple. She flinched and he felt the flood
of her pleasure along his shaft.

'I know your parentage well, Anderson. You're most
definitely not a bastard.' She tightened her grip around him
until he was fearful that he might lose control before he had
brought her to her pleasure again. 'But you can be as randy
with me as you like, and I promise you I'll never get enough.'

He pulled his member from her and repositioned her on
her hands and knees, and she cried out her surprise as he
nibbled the seat of her pleasure and inhaled her lusty scent. 'I
shall consider it a personal challenge, then, to satiate you,
Cassandra Larkin. To bring you to such heights of pleasure so
often that in the end you shall tremble beneath me, weak as a
kitten and as docile and affectionate in my embrace.'

'Fucking hell,' she grunted as he raked his tongue up
between her swollen lady lips and suckled once again at the
node of her pleasure. 'I'm no kitten, Anderson, and it'll take a
hell of a lot to satiate me.'

'Then I accept your challenge.' He eased her down onto
her side and, as he was about to push his face in between her
thighs to indulge in her sweetness, she reached for him.
'Sixty-nine me, Anderson. I want to suck your cock.'

'As you wish, my darling.' He positioned himself so that
his head pillowed on her thigh, his face close to that exquisite

landscape that is a woman's treasure. Then, at the first nip of her clitoris, the catch of her breath, she took his member deep into her lovely throat, one hand caressing the weight of his testicles, and he was in ecstasy. She ran her other warm hand over his flank and found her way into the cleft between his buttocks, and he grunted and caught his breath.

She pulled away from his penis, spat on her finger and pressed it into his nether grip. 'You're very sensitive in the arse. Did the Meriwether bloke fuck you well?'

Again he nipped at her pearl, delighting in the tremble and the swell of her. 'The poor man was only just beginning his ministerings to my sensitive backside when you very unceremoniously interrupted.'

'Mmm,' she breathed, tugging at his manhood with one hand and fingering his tender bottom with her other. 'That was very rude of me. Please give the farmer and his woman my apologies when you return.'

'We would have happily welcomed your company into our little tryst,' Anderson said.

'I'm not very good in crowds,' she replied, taking him back into her mouth with such gusto that he shuddered with the tactile pleasure of it.

'I am sure you would be enchanting in any situation.' He gasped his words into the lush valley of her womanhood, his face wet with her excitement, and it entered his mind – what little mind was left to him in the embrace of such bliss – that perhaps he should be wary of such powerful magic as was hers, and yet he could not but trust her. Indeed, how weak was the will of a man in such fleshly ecstasy? The rhythm of her mouth against his penis was synchronous with the beating of his heart, with the beating of her heart, which he could feel so deliciously against his mouth. How could it be that he had never experienced such as this before in all of his years of physical pleasure? How could it be that he had never felt another's body as though it were his own, as though he could gladly let himself be taken, emptied to the very dregs, until nothing remained of him but the ecstatic celebration of such a sweet emptying?

He felt Cassandra shudder against him, nay, convulse, flooding his face with her sweetness, and in so doing, her exquisite mouth sheathed him still tighter, and he was undone. In the place of emptiness that he had walked so many times before, there was suddenly colour and sound and sensation such as he had never felt in life nor in death.

'Oh sweet Goddess! Anderson, do you feel that?' It was Cassandra's voice, up inside him, pressed tight to the very core of him, for she had not physically spoken, still feasting so on his manhood as she was. And his response was much less eloquent than he would have hoped, but then she had left him so little with which to think and consider and contemplate. She had left him only enough of his wit to utter a startled, ecstatic affirmation as he filled her throat again and again with his release, as he dived deep into the tide pool of her trembling sweetness, swallowing down her own ecstasy in great hungry gulps .

'What have you done to me, dear woman?' he sighed when she released him.

'It doesn't matter,' she breathed. 'Whatever it is, it's good, isn't it? You like it, don't you?' Breathing as though oxygen were rare and precious, she rearranged herself, giving him another lovely glimpse of her well of delight before she sheathed him to the hilt, seated atop him. And with such a lack of dignity as would have made him blush in different circumstances, he cried out his ecstasy as she consumed the length of him into herself.

'I like it very much indeed,' he breathed, reaching to cup the sway and dance of her bosoms as she undulated and shifted against him. 'If I were not already dead, death by your tender ministrations would be a very welcome death, indeed.'

The sudden shudder of cold that passed through him, the sudden sensation of heaviness as she rolled off him made him feel as though the weight of his own body might crush him. She pushed away to the very edge of the bed she had magically created, and it wavered beneath her as though it might be consumed back into the nothingness whence it was created, but it held. Cassandra, however, sat trembling, arms wrapped around herself, the strong lines of her face drawn tight, the flush of arousal now gone, leaving her lovely skin pale and translucent.

'What is it, my darling? What troubles you?' He moved to take her to himself, to comfort her, but she jerked away as though the touch of him was too hot to bear.

'I would never hurt you, Anderson, please don't say such things.' Her voice was thick with emotion he could not understand.

'Of course you would not hurt me, my darling. Not for a moment did I think that you would. My dear Cassandra, oh do forgive me. Humorous comments about the death which has so inconvenienced us are common among those of us who no longer live.'

He eased closer to her, as though she were some extraordinary wild animal he wished not to frighten away. 'It is, in the early days, I believe, the way we cope with the loss which we would not have wished, the loss of our bodies, the loss of a thing so personal and wondrous, and yet so intimate that we seldom think of its value until we no longer possess it.'

She let him place his arms around her and pull her close, then he continued. 'I am blessed among the dead who wander the earth, in that I possess the magic to create for myself a body. Though not as wondrous as that within which I lived, it is still a vessel not without its merits, and one in which I am only too delighted to share pleasure with you. Please calm yourself, my darling. And forgive my remark. I meant nothing untoward – surely you must know that?'

She came fully into his arms and rested her head against his chest, and he stroked the softness of her hair, the tops of her lovely ears, the place at her throat where her pulse trembled and shuddered. And she pulled him to her in such an embrace as would have crushed ribs and banished breath had they not been in the Ether, had he not been flexible in his physical condition.

'You came to me on purpose,' she said at last. 'That's why you were with the farmer and his woman, isn't it? So you could come to me.'

'Yes, that is the reason, though I often take pleasure in their company.'

She brushed her lips across his. 'I'm glad you came.'

'As am I.' But even as his penis responded once again to her lovely nakedness, the magical clock in his head was relentless in its counting. He pushed away from her enough that he could see her, that he could lift her chin and look upon her lovely face, but not allow his manhood to dictate his behaviour. 'My dear Cassandra, though I would journey far for such pleasure as you have given me, and though you now occupy a considerably larger part of my thoughts than I would willingly allocate, I have come to you for more than the pleasure of sexual congress.'

She raised one lovely eyebrow and held him with her exquisite dark eyes, full of question.

'There is a demon who raises a dire threat to those I hold dear. There have been fatalities at the hand of this demon, a demon that, until recent events, we thought securely bound and unable to cause further harm.'

'Why are you telling me this?' she asked.

'My darling Cassandra, this demon, this monstrosity, appears to have found a gateway into the Ether, even perhaps a passage between the void and the Dream World, and through it he is causing harm. I do not know how. But when I returned to flesh after our last encounter, I saw flashes of him as I fell back into the world of the living. And since you seem to journey freely between the world of dreams and the void as no one I have ever known has done, I have come to wonder if perhaps you have knowledge of this passage he takes, if perhaps this is a part of your magic.'

The colour had once again gone from her face, and her hand that rested on his bosom was suddenly cold. The smallest sheen of perspiration dewed her forehead. 'My

41

darling? Are you unwell?'

'I don't know of any such passage, Anderson. My magic doesn't work that way. But this demon, is he called Deacon?' There was a slight tremor in her voice.

'Yes, my darling. Dear Goddess that he has not harmed you.' He felt as though his chest would burst at the very thought; he felt as though all that he was would break apart if harm came to this woman. Before he could contemplate the strangeness that he should feel so strongly for her, she spoke.

'No. No, I've never seen him but there's a ghost, newly dead, who comes to me. She has. And she's warned me about him.'

'Cassandra, my darling.' He took her hands, pressed them to his lips. 'You must heed the warning this ghost offers you. It is advice well given. I implore you, return to your body and stay away from this place. I am, as you know, capable of coming to you wherever you are. In truth, I think I could not possibly stay away from you now. But please believe me, you must not come back to this place.'

She pulled her hands away from him. 'Anderson, you're scaring me.'

'Believe me, my dear, I would not do so if it were not completely warranted. Please, promise me you will leave this place and not return until it is once again safe. Promise me.'

She nodded slowly, holding his gaze. 'All right, I promise you.'

He pulled her to him in such an embrace as though she were the long-lost and dearest to his heart returned to him at last. 'Then only tell me where I may find you and we shall not be lost to each other. This I promise you.'

She kissed him and pulled away. 'Don't worry about finding me, Anderson. I'll find you. And you know that I can. Now go. You must. Your friends are worried, and we've both been away long enough.'

Even as she kissed him, he felt himself falling back into his body, back into the waking world, but as he reached to stroke her face, the mirrors around her shattered in a great explosion, reflecting in their shards a wall of fire. There was the loud crack of a whip, and Cassandra called his name. It was the last thing Anderson heard before the Ether disappeared into blackness.

Chapter Five

CASSANDRA THOUGHT SHE WOULD have felt heat, thought her very flesh would burn off her as the flames erupted around her. But she wore no flesh, not real flesh, and her real flesh she could not get to at the moment. What she felt was warm breath blown across her naked breasts, raising gooseflesh, tensing already erect nipples to the point of pain. What she felt was the tightening of her clitoris and an unexplained flood of lust between her legs. What she felt was an embrace that was not welcoming like Anderson's, and yet even as terror flooded her with the desire to flee, her whole being longed for the embrace, longed to return it in full.

'The ghost does not know what you are, Cassandra Larkin, but I do.' The body that materialised to accompany the embrace was hard, masculine and enormous. And though physically heated to the temperature of flesh, the touch of it made her feel as though she would never be warm again.

'You must be Deacon,' she said, trying not to shudder.

'Ah, you know me, do you, my lovely?' He brushed a kiss across her lips and she both ached with lust and trembled with fear. 'I see my reputation has preceded me. And the ghost, he thinks you should fear me – he warned you of me, did he not?'

'He might have mentioned you in passing,' she replied, feeling the cold rising from her centre that was from more than just the presence of the demon. It was from being out of her body too long. She held very still, desperate to conserve her strength. If she were too weak, she would be unable to make the trip back from the Ether.

The demon chuckled softly, a sensation that felt like fur against her bare skin, a feeling that belied the danger she knew full well she was in. He would kill her. The chances of that were good, she was certain of it, but it didn't matter quite so much as long as she knew Anderson was safe. The demon's voice felt as though it came from inside her very chest, her chest that only her mind and her magic gave shape to. 'I do not want to harm you, my beauty. I want nothing so much as to return you safely to your flesh, the flesh to which I know you so desperately need to return.

'I want to return you to the comfort of your mattress in that foetid little bothy you now inhabit so that you may continue to feed surreptitiously off the pleasure of others like some beggar. That is what you do, is it not, my darling?'

The embrace tightened until she feared she would suffocate, and his voice filled her whole being. 'It saddens me deeply that one with such magnificent power as is yours should be too cowardly to use it to its full potential. I shudder at the thought of what you are capable, Cassandra Larkin, if you would only allow yourself to embrace that which you are. Oh, such a delight you would be.'

She forced herself to focus, which was no easy feat when it was a struggle just to hold her ethereal body together. 'I'm fine with that, then. Just let me return to my body and my foetid little bothy and my cowardly ways, and we can pretend this never happened.'

There was a sudden crunch of bone and, ethereal or not, it hurt like hell. She caught her breath, refusing to cry out, but she couldn't keep the tears of pain from the corners of her eyes.

'Most think that pain does not exist without the body.' This time it felt as though he had knotted her insides and set them on fire. She cried out, she cursed loudly, she doubled over and shivered. 'But those of us who know of the realms beyond flesh and bone know that flesh and bone are only the beginnings of pain, do we not, my darling? Flesh and bone only limit pain. Pain of the flesh is barely worthy of notice in the grand scheme of the universe, is it not, Cassandra Larkin?'

'What do you want from me?' she breathed when she could speak again.

'I told you, my beauty. I want to send you home, back to your temple of flesh and bone.' Once again the pleasure of the embrace was almost as exquisite as the pain she had just endured. 'I want to send you home, my darling, and I want to come along with you for the ride.' The pleasure intensified until it was all she could do not to fly apart to nothingness with the distraction of it.

'Consider me as simply a hitchhiker; I believe that is the term used these days. The ride would be short and painless, and then you would be back in your precious flesh, and I would leave you unmolested.' The embrace was once again so tight that Cassandra wasn't entirely sure he wasn't holding her together, keeping her from flying apart so that there was nothing to return to her dying flesh. 'You would return to the captivity of your puny, finite flesh, and I, in turn, would be set free. I think it's a fair trade, don't you?'

'And if I refuse?'

Even before the words were clear of her throat, the embrace tightened once again to nearly unbearable.

'If you refuse me, my darling, I shall hold you captive here while your body slowly dies in the world of the living. Pain can be prolonged and enhanced in so many exquisite ways in the Ether if one only has the skill. And I assure you, I do.'

She braced herself, figuring he was about to demonstrate. Instead, the embrace became tender, almost loving. 'And there are other methods with which one may cause suffering, methods far more exquisite than physical pain, methods with far more finesse. Tara Stone could tell you all about suffering with finesse. You do know Tara Stone, do you not? Of course you do. I am well aware of how flawlessly you have researched her coven of misfits in order to learn more about her lapdog ghost.' His voice vibrated inside her head with such intensity that she feared her brain would explode.

'He will come for you, Tara Stone's ghost. You know this.

And when he does, and when I bring him before you, captive and defeated, then you shall see just how exquisitely one without flesh can suffer.' The voice in her head became a whisper. 'And I promise, you will see every minute fraction of a second of his agony as though it were a thousand years.'

In his mind, Anderson struggled mightily against all the powers of all the gods. In his mind, he exerted every ounce of strength with which he had been gifted, called upon every bit of magic at his disposal, and yet he fell away, farther and farther from her voice, farther and farther from her warmth.

He came to himself with a bone-crunching jerk. The heavy weight on his body was Tim Meriwether, clothed from the waist down, straddling him, his face pale, his lips tightly drawn. At his left shoulder knelt Marie, hand nearly crushed in his own. To his right, and somehow no surprise, knelt Tara, both hands pressing his chest, her lips moving rapidly, weaving what he thought to be a healing spell. But as the world of the living burst into harsh focus around him, as his wit became less fractured, he realised it was a binding spell, and it was him that she was binding, and the look on her face was truly frightening.

'I must go back. I must go to her!' The words burst from his throat even before he was fully in his body. 'I must go back, he has taken her. Dear Goddess, he has taken her!' In what felt like the shudder of a titan, with strength that frightened even him, he shrugged them off. Tim's elbow cracked against the coffee table and he cursed. Marie's breath rushed from her lungs and she fell stunned against the sofa. But Tara held him tight, and her spell met his strength like two walls of fire swallowing each other, and he came back to himself wrapped in her arms. Somewhere in his fevered mind, he could hear Tara saying over and over again, 'I told you not to go, I told you not to go.' The magical clock that he had set in the Ether still ticked mockingly in his head.

'She's trapped,' he breathed. 'I must go back to her.'

Tara tightened her embrace. 'You can't, Anderson. You

47

know you can't. Not weakened as you are. You'd never make it past the threshold.'

'He is with her. Deacon. He has taken her. He forced me out and trapped her there, and she did not tell me where I may find her. Dear Goddess, she did not tell me.'

The sandwich Tara cajoled him to eat could have been cardboard for all that it mattered to him. It was simpler to devour it than to remind her that he did not need it. He ate it mechanically.

'She approached you through the Dream World,' Tim Meriwether said, nursing the bruise on his elbow. 'Perhaps we can approach her that way too.'

Anderson shook his head. 'I knew nothing of Cassandra Larkin from any world other than the Ether. I have nothing with which to ground myself.'

'Her essence is all over you,' Marie said. 'It's almost a magical luminescence. Surely yours must also be on her?'

'We pleasured each other only in the Ether, and though I bring back her essence on my flesh, she is not now in her flesh.'

'Her fetch came to you the other night, Anderson.' Tara waved a hand. 'Yes, I know that. I was wide awake.'

'And yet I say again, she sent her fetch to me from the world of the living, not from the Ether.'

'My point is –' Tara moved to sit next to him, closer to the now blazing fire of which, in the flesh as he was, he was in desperate need. 'Your essence was so strong, even on the woman's fetch, that she could pass through all of our protection spells, pass through all our defences, defences even Deacon himself couldn't penetrate. It was almost as though she had covered herself with you. That kind of connection requires much more to wash away than a shower after a fuck. And when she sent her fetch to you, you were asleep, you were dreaming, and had you not been next to me, you would have followed her back to her body, wouldn't you?'

Anderson nodded, feeling the ache of what might have been. 'Would that I had done just such.'

48

Tara held his gaze. 'If it's any consolation, I did try to follow her, but whatever magic she used disguised her retreat. Still, the connection began in the dream, extended into the Ether, and was carried home in the flesh. Anderson, she wears you like her own skin, like you do her. You were pulled into the Ether in the dream,' Tara reminded him. 'If you try dream magic and that happens again, you know you're not strong enough to pass through the threshold.'

He set down his plate. 'Then I am left with only one choice. I will send out my fetch.' It was rude of him, and he would make certain his heartfelt apologies were expressed upon his return to the flesh. The clock that still ticked torturously in his head was a constant reminder of how little time was left to Cassandra, and of how that little bit of time could become an eternity in the hands of one as twisted as Deacon. He vanished from Tim Meriwether's lounge as though he had never been, loosening the bonds of his flesh as though he had simply removed a garment or, more accurately, as though he had simply willed the garment to exist no longer. At the end of life, what remained, if the ghost lingered among the living, was little more than fetch, and in truth, it was as Marie had said – Cassandra's essence enveloped him even when he was without flesh.

The room was cold. Way colder than it should be for the comfort of the living. Serina knew that Cassandra was frugal with the wood she burned, but this wasn't right. There was something wrong with the whole situation. Cassandra Larkin's breath rose in thin wisps of vapour from between lips that were unnaturally translucent, lips that were ever so slightly tinged blue. And if Serina had been in the flesh, her heart would have raced with terror. She knew exactly what would produce such symptoms. Without flesh of her own, she could not take the woman's pulse, but she knew she would find it thin and thready.

She knew the woman would appear to be in a coma. But it was no coma that afflicted Cassandra Larkin. Cassandra

Larkin was in the Ether. That in itself, for one who was adept at riding the Ether, was no concern but the symptoms were all there. The same symptoms Serina had seen with Maybell. Cassandra Larkin had stayed there too long. Dear Goddess, please let it be only in a pleasurable romp with that Anderson ghost. She couldn't imagine anyone wasting their energy fucking in such a dangerous and horrible place. But even as the thought crossed her mind, she knew the pleasure would have passed by now into problems of simple survival in that inhospitable place, and if Cassandra had not yet returned to her flesh, it was almost certain that something prevented her from doing so.

Even without flesh Serina felt a chill. There was only one thing capable of holding such a powerful witch in the Ether against her will. She would go to the Elementals. That was all. She'd have to go to them now. But what could they do? The only one who could return Cassandra Larkin to her flesh was Cassandra Larkin. Serina paced and wrung her hands, desperately thinking what to do.

It felt as though the entire Ether had just exhaled, then the feeling of soft fur swept up her spine once more, and Cassandra roused from her semiconscious state with a start, reminding herself she dare not lose consciousness.

He sensed it. Of course he sensed it. 'I thought perhaps you could use a little rest, my darling, before our journey.' Deacon spoke next to her ear. 'Unless, of course, you would prefer to stay here. In which case I am quite sure you will need the tiny bit of respite I have given you and more.'

She forced open her eyes, or the equivalent thereof, and found herself on a four-poster bed draped in red velvet – but beyond lay the empty void of the Ether.

He sat next to her, his large hand stroking her cheek. 'Can you feel him?' he breathed. 'Your ghost is seeking you, anxiously seeking you.'

Panic rose in her like bile. Dear Goddess, please don't let him come here.

'Oh do relax, my darling Cassandra. He has not the strength to come for you in the Ether. Yet. He seeks you in spirit, can you not feel him?' Deacon chuckled softly. 'Oh, he is indeed desperate to find you.' He bent and kissed her, and as much as she longed to be disgusted by it, she wanted to linger in it.

'Feel. Feel the brush of him, wearing your essence like a fine robe, seeking you.' He kissed her again, this time with parted lips. 'But you did not tell him where you were, and he shall not find you, shall he? No. He shall not.' He ran a thick finger down along her breastbone, and what began as a feather touch ended at her navel like a lead weight. She squirmed and tried desperately to focus. She could endure what she had to, but she could not bear the thought of Anderson suffering because of her. She had been so certain that he could give her what she needed, and that she could, with him, for the first time, give back, and this was what she had led him to.

'He'll rest, this ghost who wears your essence. When he cannot find a way to you in the spirit world, he'll rest. Then he will return for you, no matter what Tara Stone commands of him, and even you, who are so besotted by him, even you know that he is no match for me.' Once again he kissed her, and his breath was sweet, so sweet. 'Take me home, Cassandra Larkin. Take us both home, and I will leave you in peace. You and your ghost.'

She closed her eyes so tightly that they would have hurt if she had been in the flesh, closed her eyes and struggled hard to focus. Could it be so bad? Would it not be easier if they fought him in the flesh? And clearly they would have to fight him.

It all happened so fast that if she had been in her flesh, in her own bed, she would have doubted that it had happened at all, would have thought it only the tiniest snippet of a dream from her deep unconscious, but in the Ether, it was there behind her eyes like a 3D film.

A frail woman in a hospital gown, bare feet bleeding from

51

the sharp cut of the icy snow. She didn't have the strength to lift herself from her pillow and yet she ran like a marionette on twitching strings, ran into the street in front of the bus. The impact felt like a bruise below Cassandra's heart. And the body was instantly empty, the spirit wending its way to freedom while the unwelcome visitor of the remaining flesh cursed and struggled and lost control of the now battered, empty vessel of flesh and bone. Then the image flashed bright and burned away and, for the tiniest of moments, she felt the brush of Anderson somewhere far away looking for her, longing for her, wearing her essence proudly.

It seemed he had been gone only a second when he returned to the flesh. Tara, Marie and Tim Meriwether all sat exactly as they had before, and all erupted into action at his return. Marie folded a blanket around his shoulders and kissed him. Tim thrust a hot cup of tea into his hand. Tara only watched him, reading already the look on his face.

'I could not find her,' he said. 'Dear Goddess, I could not find her. I felt the very brush of her essence, but I cannot tell but what it was still only her crying out from the Ether. I must go back into the Ether. I must. Tara, my love, I would tear out my own heart before I would act against your wishes, but I must beg this of you. I cannot leave her there with him. And you would not either.'

She held his gaze in a hard stare, and he noticed that her hands, clasped around each other, were pale, the knuckles white and tense. She released a breath that was so near a sob, he thought his heart would break.

'You've already gone against my wishes, Anderson, and you know it.' The ice in her voice was more disturbing than anything he had ever felt, but then, almost as quickly as it was there, it was gone, and she blinked, and for a second he thought he saw mist in her eyes. She pulled a deep breath and spoke. 'All right.' Suddenly, there was fire in her eyes, and he felt the power of the full essence of the woman whom he had companioned and loved all these many years. 'But you're not going alone.'

'My dear, there is so much more ritual we must prepare if one who walks among the living travels with me. I fear we have not the luxury of that much time.'

'Fiori and Sky know the ritual that must take place. They can prepare me while you rest. You don't have to be there with me for the preparation, and you can't go until you're rested. Even you know that.'

For a brief moment he considered leaving his flesh because his chest felt as though it would burst from the helplessness raging through him, from the anger, from feelings for the strange woman in the Ether whom he hardly knew, and yet he would do whatever he must to return her safely to her flesh, to his arms. 'Very well,' he said. 'Then I shall rest quickly.'

'I have ways of keeping you just strong enough to survive, my dear Cassandra,' Deacon said. 'Of course, after so long I cannot guarantee what condition your body will be in when you return to it, or how old it will be. And certainly that is of no concern to me. I can, however, tell you that it is astonishing the lengths to which modern medicine can go to keep the flesh alive and viable.' He tut-tutted. 'It would be a pity, though, after an endless eternity of watching me torture your ghost here in the Ether, that I should return you to your flesh old and wizened, rather than young and nubile and much to your ghost's liking.'

She made no attempt to fight back the tears. How many of them were anger and frustration, he need not know. If he saw her weakness, what did it matter? She had never doubted her weakness, not from the days in the home before her grandmother had come for her. She had never doubted her own brokenness. It had taken up residence at the very core of her from her earliest memories, like a scar that healthy flesh had grown around but could not hide, deep and hard and always, always there. So she wept openly for what she was about to do, and he stroked her as though he were comforting

53

a child with a skinned knee.

'There, there, my darling. You have decided, then? Have you not?'

She nodded, unable to speak, as she allowed the core of her anguish to grow.

'That's a good girl now, do not weep. You'll be back in the flesh in no time, back in the arms of your ghost, and you will hardly notice my presence on the journey. And then I shall leave you in peace, and all shall be well, my lovely. All shall be well.'

'What do I have to do?' she whispered, folding her arms around herself, trying to stave off the shakes that racked her weakened body.

'First, I shall give you the strength you need to get back to your body, my darling, just as I have promised. Then you will feel a fullness as I enter you through your breath – barely noticeable, only a slight fullness as though you have eaten a satisfying meal, nothing more. All you need do is go home. I shall not prevent your reunion with your flesh.'

She nodded her consent in between sobs.

'That's it, my darling, let me make it better for you.' He tut-tutted again and stroked her hair. 'I sense your thoughts, my lovely. Of course you are not weak. You want only to protect the man you love. Of course this is not weakness, my sweet.'

Instantly, she felt a surge of strength. Far away, as in a dream, she could see her body, her home. She could see a frightened Serina pacing next to her, and she closed her eyes and let Deacon's strength flow into her, his voice becoming like background noise as she fought to focus. And when she was ready, when she was certain the time was right, she opened to him. She wasn't sure how she knew to, but she did, and she felt him move inside her with her breath and settle near the pounding of her heart.

'Now, my love.' She felt his voice. 'Shall we then go home?'

She released a long, even breath, folded her arms around

herself again and began casting the spell.

Almost immediately, she felt the harsh pull of flesh retrieving its own from an unnatural and prolonged absence. In her mind's eye, she held the image of a yo-yo returning along its string with the flick of the fleshly wrist that held it in place. And just when the string was at its most taut, just when the return journey was all but inevitable, she pulled the image of Deacon's beautifully formed four-poster bed into her mind, then just one post at the headboard, that closest to where her head rested on the satin pillow he had created for her. The pillow. She focused on the pillow, the place of dreams, and stretched and twisted the image until the string, controlled by the momentum of the yo-yo, came in contact with the post. The yo-yo ricocheted from its path and wrapped around the bedpost. For a second, Deacon noticed nothing. It was only when the void thickened and darkened that he roused.

'What are you doing, girl?' His voice held a tight edge.

'Only a slight detour,' she said.

'This is not what we agreed upon, Cassandra.'

Before he could speak further, she let the dream space erupt into an image, dark and hideous and hungry. Hungry enough to devour the whole world, hungry enough to feed on the sex of men, to ride them until all that remained were empty shells, and with each feasting, with each gorging of lust, the strength grew, and with growing strength, there was always, always growing hunger, growing lust.

'Cassandra, this was not our agreement. What are you doing?'

'This is my worst nightmare, Deacon.' She spoke, trying to keep her voice from trembling in this place where she least wanted to be. 'That's me. Do you like what you see? This is the power you so admire. I am that monster, and you are in the very gut of the monster, Deacon.'

With the strength he had given her, she concentrated on sexual pleasure, felt her desire bloom, felt her lust flare like a flame in a dry forest. All that she had was the strength he had given her but it was a taste of him – a taste of what drove him, a taste of his lust. It would have to be enough. She felt him pressing out from the inside, trying to escape, but this was her dream, her nightmare. He had no power here. She tightened her grip. She couldn't destroy him, but she could send him back. He wouldn't have the stomach for the thing that devoured the very power he thrived upon.

His laugh was tight, close below the surface of her skin as though he would burst from her, and yet she held. 'Very well, Cassandra Larkin. Go home to your flesh. But I promise you, the next time I take up residence within you, death will be the escape you beg for, the escape you will be denied, and you will long for the safety of your nightmares.'

Just like that, he was gone. The bedstead in the Ether vanished, and the yo-yo regained then doubled its momentum, and Cassandra sank like lead in a pond, into the painful, aching depth that was her own precious flesh. And before all consciousness faded, she felt a sense of certainty that she wouldn't have to wait for death nearly as long as Deacon promised. The smile on her cracked lips took monumental effort, but if she had to rob the bastard of his release through her death, well so be it. Anderson was dead, after all. Maybe she'd join him for real. That was the thought she embraced as the world faded to black.

Chapter Six

MARIE WARREN FELT A chill crawl up her spine as she stood over the sink doing the washing-up, and she knew she wasn't alone. But the ghost was upon her before she could fully register her presence. Thinking it was Lisette, one of the ghosts around Lacewing Farm, she was about to chide her for sneaking up on her when she turned to find Serina Ravenmoor standing almost on top of her.

Marie jumped back, hitting her hip against the edge of the counter. 'What the hell are you doing here?'

'Sorry.' The ghost stepped back. 'I'm not a very good judge of distances any more, but I need you to come with me. Where's Mr Anderson? He has to come too.'

'Now why would I want to go with you? And who do you think you are, waltzing right into my kitchen like you own the place and –'

'I know where Cassandra Larkin is, and if you don't come quickly, she'll die.'

The ghost barely got the words out before Anderson materialised out of nowhere. He ignored Marie and focused on Serina. 'I felt her leave the Ether just as we were preparing to enter. Do you know where she is?'

Serina nodded. 'Please hurry.' Her eyes welled up. 'I don't know what happened but I'm afraid she'll die.'

'Then take me to her at once.'

He turned his attention to Marie. 'I shall send Miss Ravenmoor back with directions to where we are as soon as I am with Cassandra.' He didn't wait for a reply, but vanished and rematerialised next to Serina Ravenmoor in a small, dark

57

space, curtained off, only just big enough for the mattress on the floor. Books stacked against the wall overflowed into what little space remained. And there beneath a tangled duvet, looking so much like the dead that it twisted his heart, was Cassandra Larkin.

'This is not how I would have wished our first meeting in the flesh, my darling.' He spoke softly, sinking onto the mattress next to her. Serina watched him as he took her pulse, which was barely there. 'Has she spoken at all since her return?'

'Only that she lost Deacon in her nightmare.'

'My clever darling.' He brushed the hair away from her pale cheek. 'Clever and ever so reckless.'

Even without flesh, Serina Ravenmoor trembled with impatience. 'She's dying, and you're the only one who can save her now.'

He would have offered a sharp retort, but the look in the woman's eyes stopped him.

'You still don't know what she is, do you, Mr Anderson? Or what she needs?'

Irritation at Serina Ravenmoor rose like fire in his chest. 'Tell me if you know what she needs, madame, and do not waste precious time.'

She took a step closer, still holding his gaze. 'She's been kind to me. She doesn't deserve this.'

'I can tolerate little more, Miss Ravenmoor. I beg of you, speak plainly!'

'She's a succubus. And if you want to save her, then she'll need your energy.' She nodded to the front of his trousers and the seat of his manhood.

'A succubus?' He would have laughed at the utter absurdity of such an idea had the circumstances been different, had Miss Ravenmoor's countenance not been deadly serious. He felt as though the woman had kicked him in the vitals, had ridiculed him in some cruel way by so slandering his beautiful Cassandra. 'Surely I have not understood your meaning, madame.'

'You understand me. Perfectly,' the little ghost reassured him. 'And if I weren't dead, she'd kill me for telling you.'

'But I had not thought such beings to be more than legend,' he whispered, feeling his heart race at the thought of the magnificent woman who had bedded him, a creature whose power was even more sexual than his own and far more dangerous. She was a being completely unlike that which the legends and myths had spawned in his imagination.

'She doesn't exactly advertise,' Serina said. 'I've never seen anyone so full of self-loathing.'

Anderson's heart twisted still further at the very thought that one so exquisite should loathe herself. 'Now that you have said it, I certainly do see how she could be such. When we were together, I would have happily stayed with her, derelict in all other pressing duties, stayed with her and let her take me until I was completely empty of myself.'

'She would never have let you do that.' Serina Ravenmoor seemed horrified at the very thought.

Anderson shook his head. 'No. She would not.' He laid a hand on the clammy cool of her forehead. 'Then it is my … It is my seed that she needs to be healed.' He spoke softly to the Ravenmoor woman.

The ghost shook her head. 'It's more than that. Much more. It's your lust she needs. Your essence. She won't take from anyone but you, and she may not even take from you now that you're not in the Ether. It was only there that she felt she could safely control her lust and not do you harm.'

'She told you this?'

She looked into his eyes, and shook her head. 'She doesn't know how much I know, but I often stayed with her when she didn't realise I was here, watched what she studied, read over her shoulder.' Serina shivered and chafed her arms. 'You know, to pass the time. I doubt you can persuade her to take from you all she'll need.'

'Do not worry, Miss Ravenmoor. I shall persuade her.' He turned his attention back to the woman lying helplessly on the mattress, and the pull in his heart was nearly unbearable. 'Go

59

and tell the others where I am. It may be that I have need of them, for I have every intention of giving Cassandra Larkin all that she needs to heal.'

Serina did as he asked, and then he was alone with the exquisite woman who, in spite of their intimacy, had hidden far more from him that he would have imagined possible. He removed his clothing and slid under the duvet next to her cool flesh, pulling her to him gently, offering her his warmth. And even in her weakened state, the touch of her flesh vibrated over his body so deliciously that the power of his own lust surprised him under the circumstances.

As he gathered her to him, in spite of being reassured by Miss Ravenmoor of what she needed, he feared that even the first brush of a kiss against her lips would be more than she could bear. And yet even in that briefest moment of contact, the cool of her lips warmed to his touch, and her chest rose with a shudder. For the tiniest of seconds he feared that he had injured her still further, and it was he who could not breathe for the weight of such fear. And then she spoke, and he thought his heart would burst with the relief of it.

'I'm not dead?' There was surprise in her voice. And pain.

'You are most definitely not dead, my darling, nor shall I allow you to pass when I have not yet known the pleasure of your exquisite flesh.'

Her lids fluttered and with what seemed a tremendous effort, her dark eyes opened to gaze upon him, and she forced the slightest of smiles on to her parched lips. 'Anderson, if I'm dreaming, don't wake me.'

'It is no dream, my darling. I promise you it is not.'

'I'm home?' She forced the words up through the tight muscles of her throat, words that sounded abraded and raw.

He nodded. 'In the flesh.'

'And you're here.'

'Also in the flesh.'

Her eyes widened and her pulse raced, and in spite of her weakened condition, she tried to rise from the bed. 'Deacon is –'

Anderson covered her mouth with his hand, stopping her words, and settled her back on the bed. Then he spoke. 'Deacon is not here in the flesh, thanks to you, my darling.'

She could not hold back the tears of relief, but there was no strength to wipe them away. Anderson did that for her. 'Sh, my darling, Shshsh. He is not here, and you are safe with me now.' Perhaps it was the press of his ill-mannered member against her thigh that suddenly brought to her attention the fact that he lay next to her naked and fully aroused. And, as he feared, it was not a thing that pleased her.

She thrashed weakly. 'Anderson, you have to go. You can't be with me here like this. You have to go. Please! You can't stay. You mustn't.'

'No, my darling. I will not allow you to send me away.' He held her until she stopped struggling, then he kissed her again, more insistently.

'I know who you are, Cassandra,' he whispered when he pulled away. 'Why did you not tell me? You insult me to believe I would have thought less of you because of your gift.' Fearing that her struggles would weaken her further, he wasted no time, but slid his hand down over her mound to ease open her womanhood, sliding a finger carefully down between the folds of her, and she gasped, pulling oxygen into her lungs as though she had only just remembered how to draw breath. She was surprisingly warm and wet to his touch, and she responded by shifting her hips upward to his probing. Only a little, only just, weakened as she was, but the response was there, and it was the response of arousal.

Ever so gently, he pushed back the duvet until her lovely breasts, nearly translucent in the pale light, were exposed, then he nursed at each of her bosoms until her nipples rose to greet his tongue and lips in a delicious caress of their own. With each press of his mouth on her flesh, with each probing of his finger into her wetness, she strengthened, and the feel of her against his body became more and more exquisite, kindling his arousal to a heightening flame, filling him with a sense of well-being and ecstasy that he had only ever felt in high magic. And yet even that paled in comparison to the feel of Cassandra Larkin, naked and needy in his arms.

It was only when he carefully pushed her legs apart and eased himself on top of her that she panicked. 'You know what I am! Dear Goddess, Anderson,' she croaked, shoving at him with all the strength she could muster in her still-weakened state. 'If you know what I am, then you know why we can't do this here. We're not in the Ether. It's the only place you're safe from me. Please.' Her words became nearly incoherent in her tears, in her weakness. 'Please don't do this. I can't live with the thought of hurting you. You don't know what I'm capable of. You don't know what a monster I am.' She struggled beneath him, but she was too weak, and he held her, cradled her, careful that his weight was not on her.

'I will hear no more such talk, my darling. You are by no means a monster, and you can take nothing from me that I do not freely give.' This time he kissed her hard and spoke between the thrustings of his tongue and the suckling of her lips. 'I have already told you, Cassandra, you cannot harm me, and we will hear no more of this. I will not be denied. You will take what you need from me, all that you need from me until you are sated, until you are healed. I shall hear no argument.'

'You're not my boss.' She tried to shove him with the flat of her hand against his chest. 'You can't tell me what to do.'

He held her hand to his chest and gripped it tightly. 'Then when you are healed and once more yourself, you may punish me as you see fit for my transgressions – a thought which I relish.'

She wept against his neck, and though she yielded willingly to him, she was still weeping when he entered her with the slightest shifting of his hips. It disturbed him deeply that his arousal was such when she was in anguish, but he knew how close she walked to the gateway of death, as only one who has already passed through it could know. And he would not allow her to make that journey, no matter how she protested. And she was, indeed, ready for his penetration, slick and dilated with need, need that he understood was now far beyond the simple drive for sexual satisfaction. The satisfaction of such need would make the difference as to whether Cassandra Larkin crossed through that dreaded gateway or woke healthy and strong to breathe the blessed air of the living.

With the first thrust, her back arched, she gasped for air and her whole body stiffened. For a terrifying second he feared he had hastened the very thing he sought to prevent. By the second thrust, however, Cassandra had the strength to wrap her legs around him. He pulled her to him with a sigh that was almost a sob. 'Dear woman, do not ever, ever do such a thing to me again. I was desolate without you,' he whispered against her throat. 'It cannot be thus again. I could not bear it. Take from me what you need, my love, all that you need. It is the desire of my heart that you do so.'

'I don't want to hurt you.' But even as she spoke, she curled her fingers in his hair and pulled him closer to her. 'You don't know me. You don't know what it's like when I need. When I'm empty, my emptiness is bigger than the void. Oh Goddess, Anderson, please don't let me hurt you.'

'You shall not harm me, my darling.' He spoke around the rise of euphoria in his head and the feel that his manhood could never get enough, but this was only his desire for her, he told himself. And even if it were otherwise, even if all that he was she took from him, then it was an exquisite ending to a very long existence. But he would not let it be so for he could not bear the thought of her anguish at such an ending for himself.

It was desperate and deep, her need, like that for oxygen, like that for food when meals have been missed, like the filling up of an empty ocean. And she wept even in her passion, wept that she was reduced to such raw need, wept that it was offered to her so freely, wept that if felt so good.

For his part, Anderson was surprised by it all when he had the wit to consider beyond the pleasure of her powerful lust. All the while she took from him he held his seed, feeling the

63

intense pleasure that one does when the weight of lust rests heavy and tight in one's loins, when every second longer that one may hold off one's release sees that pleasure become more exquisite. And it was long in the process of their pleasuring before he became aware that his strength was indeed waning.

She sat atop him, head thrown back, pale hair falling wild and tangled around her face. Her lovely bosoms danced with her thrustings. Her dark eyes had grown pale in the rise of her magic, the colour of the sky over Blencathra when it thins to the palest blue before it darkens. The room was awash with the sound of racing water and wind in summer trees, and he could feel himself being pulled into the emptiness of her need, filling it with his very essence, with something far beyond the life force which he had given up long ago.

Her orgasms began as tiny ripples from a place of weakness and grew to ocean waves washing over both of them, cleansing away Deacon's touch, imprinting upon her flesh Anderson's lust. And it was at that moment Anderson feared that Cassandra could no longer release him, no matter how badly she desired it; that she was beyond herself, and with each thrust that weakened him, she grew stronger. With a shudder of fear that he barely felt in the ecstasy of their sex, he knew that if he could not of his own accord pull back from her at the right moment, then he would, indeed be lost.

But the thought had barely entered the bleariness of his mind before his manhood convulsed mightily and he emptied himself into her, then she fell forward against him, gasping for breath and pressing her lips to his.

'There now, you see, my darling. All is well,' he whispered, easing her off him and once again down into the white fluff of bedding, when to his great relief, he realised he still had consciousness and essence and being, and though he was struggling to hold it together, he still had flesh. 'You have pleasured me deeply and healed from my pleasuring. Am I not twice blessed?'

The words came from his throat, feeling raw and tight with

emotions he could not, in his present condition, contemplate as he desired, not the least of which was relief. 'Rest now, my love. Rest and heal, and when you are able, we shall take you back to Elemental Cottage where you shall be safe.'

She was already asleep before he had finished his sentence. And it was just as well. He did not want her to see him in his weakened condition. It would only distress her, and for no good reason.

He slipped from the bed and pulled the duvet snugly around Cassandra's shoulders. Then, with trembling hands, he wrapped himself in an afghan and stumbled from behind the heavy curtain that separated the sleeping area from the rest of the bothy – where he was surprised to find the entire coven and Serina Ravenmoor squeezed into the tiny space amid the avalanches of books and notebooks. Everyone was present except Tara. Sky caught him before he fell to his knees and helped him on to the makeshift bench next to the small table.

With some effort, he cleared the growing fog from his head, then spoke. 'I am indebted to all of you for your help. Indeed, do not look so concerned. All is well.'

Sky laid an unnecessary hand on his forehead, as if he were still numbered among the living, and, though superfluous, it felt soothing, indeed. 'We didn't do anything, Anderson. She released you of her own volition.' She shook her head. 'I wouldn't have thought it possible in her condition, knowing what she is. But then, until today, who knew that her kind even existed?'

Anderson looked around the room again, and it was Marie who spoke, as though she had read his thoughts. 'Tara was here. She left when she knew you were all right. She's pretty upset still, about what you did. About what we did.' She squeezed Tim's hand.

'Don't worry, she'll get over it,' Fiori said. Then she nodded toward the makeshift bedchamber. 'Is Cassandra all right?'

Anderson forced a smile past the pain in his heart that he had so wounded Tara, but it was more than he was capable of considering at the moment. 'My dear Fiori,' he said. 'I believe Cassandra Larkin will not be journeying through the gates of death today. She is now resting peacefully. However,' he breathed, 'I am undone. Please do not make my condition known to her, as it will only trouble her unnecessarily, and I shall be well, only I shall be unable to manifest flesh for a brief time. But I am, indeed very well. Very well indeed.' It was only as the last words passed from his throat that Anderson realised he was no longer in the flesh and that Sky sat on the bench holding only the afghan he had been wearing.

Chapter Seven

'I'M OFF IN 20 minutes,' he'd said, his hand touching hers as he took the money for her drink.

Alice knew that. She knew that as surely as she'd known to come to this place, a place in Penrith, a place she'd never been to before, a place she hadn't even known existed.

'I'll wait,' she'd said, tossing back the whisky she'd ordered. He was young, maybe in his mid-twenties, not particularly handsome nor particularly well-built, but he smelled ready, hot and sweaty. The scent of the fag he'd smoked on his last break lingered on his shirt, the mint he'd recently sucked had faded and she could just make out the faint aroma of beer on his breath. But the smell that most interested her came from where his cock rested in his jeans – just a little too tight for comfort, just a little too anxious for him not to be distracted by it.

He had masturbated only a few hours ago, probably on his last break in the toilet, locked in the cubicle – tugging at himself nervously, glancing at his watch while he squirmed and shifted, imagining he was shoving his cock between the barmaid's huge tits, or even up her arse as he bent her over the snooker table in the back room. Alice could smell that on him too, the lust every time he looked at the woman's heavy breasts.

He wasn't really attracted to her, just her tits, and the way her jeans rode her arse crack too tightly, delineating the space in between, suggesting what was just beneath the surface. The wank in the loo hadn't been enough. It wasn't what he needed. Alice was what he needed.

There were other women in the pub, younger and prettier than she, but that didn't matter. She knew, as he did, that they wouldn't give him another look any more than the barmaid would, because they weren't looking for the same thing Alice was looking for. They were looking for someone who would sweep them off their feet, move them into the big house, give them children and status and happy ever after. Why they were looking here Alice couldn't imagine, but then people weren't very bright when it came to methods for choosing a partner. She knew that only too well. For a second, she was overwhelmed with sadness for what she knew they would probably never find.

She turned her attention back to the barman, who was chewing on his bottom lip as he mixed a gin and tonic for a young woman who was talking to her friends about the gorgeous arse of the bloke who'd fixed her tyre at the garage the other day, as though the barman wasn't even there. It didn't matter, though. Alice knew he was thinking about what he hoped she'd do to him in only a few more minutes. Her pussy slickened in her panties, and she shifted forward on the stool, feeling the pressure against her clit.

She vaguely remembered having another drink, then he was at her side. 'I've only got 20 minutes,' he said.

'Is there someplace we can go? It's colder than hell outside,' she said, leaning forward to give him a view down the front of her blouse. She wasn't wearing a bra. He'd noticed, and so had his cock.

He gave a quick glance around, then he nodded down the hall toward the loos. 'Come on,' he said.

It was a storage room, only just big enough to turn around in, but it would do. She wasn't looking for flowers and chocolates. Almost before he'd got the door shut behind them, he attacked her lips with wet, open-mouthed kisses and spasmodic dartings of his tongue. He squeezed her tits like they were uncooperative bread dough. His lack of skill didn't bother her. No particular technique was necessary for what she needed from him. She practically ripped his T-shirt off over his head. She spread her legs and positioned herself until his thigh rubbed between hers, rucking up her skirt until her wet knickers raked his jeans.

'You're a dirty girl, aren't you?' He breathed into her mouth. 'You want me to fuck your hot little pussy, don't you?'

He let out a little gasp of surprise when she twisted out of his embrace, grabbed his hand and shoved his arm up behind his back. 'What's going on?' He forced a nervous laugh.

'Just what you need, cunt,' she breathed against his ear. 'What we both need. That's what's going on.' With the belt from her coat, she tied his hands to the upright of the metal utility shelf – one, two, three times, she wrapped it around his wrists. That seemed important. She didn't know why. *Thrice bound and once released, thrice bound and once released, thrice bound and once released.*

The strange words passed through her brain, over and over like a mantra, as she tied the barman. And he let her do it. It was just as well. He had no idea how badly she could hurt him if he didn't. But she hadn't misjudged. By the time she had him secured, half-bent over with his back to her, his jeans could barely contain his cock. Her clit felt complete empathy for his cramped penis. She wriggled out of her knickers and stuffed them into her coat pocket.

'What are you doing?' he grunted. 'I want to see.'

'You don't need to see,' she said, lifting her shirt and rubbing her naked tits against his back while she reached around him to undo his fly and free his erection with a speed and precision that would have amazed her had the circumstances been other than they were. His hips rocked and shifted, and he humped air as she shoved at his jeans until they were down around his thighs, baring his arse.

The room felt tight and hot and everything seemed to be tinged in a red haze. Her cunt felt heavy and swollen. He was going on about what a filthy, dirty bitch she was, how she was gagging for it and … *fuck*, he was irritating.

'Shut up,' she said. Then, as an afterthought, she pulled

her knickers out of her pocket and stuffed them into his mouth. He moaned and shook his head, and she had to slap him to make him hold still. His cock surged and oozed pre-come. Jesus, she'd judged the little bastard right.

Her gaze fell to his belt, hanging loose from his jeans. She jerked it free, none too gently, doubled it and gave it a sharp snap. His eyes were large and round and watery, and his cock jutted so hard she was afraid he'd come before she was done with him. She reached around and squeezed him just below the head of it, then she whispered very close to his ear. 'You don't come until I say you can come, or I'll hurt you. Are we clear?' For emphasis, she brought the doubled belt down hard against the swell of one arse cheek. His eyelids fluttered, and he moaned and nodded. She smacked him again.

'You shouldn't lead women astray like this, you know,' she said, giving both of his now pink cheeks a hard squeeze. 'The man is supposed to be an example to the woman.'

She forced his knees apart a little more to get a good view of his hole, which quivered nervously, then she spat on her hand and slipped two fingers into the tight grip of his anus. He let out a strangled cry that could have been pleasure, could have been pain. She really didn't give a shit. Whichever it was, it made her pussy wetter and her clit harder. 'A man's the head of the woman,' she said, probing in knuckle deep, then bringing the belt down in quick succession on each of his buttocks in turn. 'He is to be her example.' Smack. 'Her strong protector.' Smack. 'Her lord and master.' Smack, smack, smack. Her first orgasm flooded her, and she laughed with the euphoria of it. The barman's cock looked like it would burst.

She spoke close to his ear again, making sure he felt her nipples on his back. 'You need something more than my two fingers up your arse, don't you, boy?' His eyes were wild, bulging, tinged with fear, maybe a little pain, but mostly lust, mostly the need to come. She smelled it all over him, all over the room, she saw it in shades of red beneath the dim bulb that shone over their head.

Then she noticed his glances at a case of some sort of alcopop, and she laughed out loud. She pulled her wet fingers free from his arsehole and wiped them on his bum cheeks. 'You are such a degenerate, aren't you, my lad?' She pulled one bottle out, opened it and took a long drag from it, then grimaced. 'Vile stuff. Not fit for human consumption. But consumption is not what either of us has in mind, is it?'

With one hand, she held his arse cheeks apart. With the other, she drizzled the pungent pink liquid over the dilated pout of his anus, and he squirmed and whimpered at the back of his throat – but all the while he thrust his anus closer to her efforts. 'You filthy, filthy boy,' she breathed. Still drizzling the river of pink down the valley between his buttocks, she bent to pick up the belt. She looped it around his neck and tightened it just enough to remind him that she was in control. The very act of which, combined with the smell of his arousal now tinged with the adrenaline of nerves and the sickly sweet smell of the alcopop, made her feel even heavier between her legs. She moved in close, gathering her makeshift leash so that the barman held his neck stiff and pressed his marred bottom out toward the last dribbles of the alcopop. She touched the rim of the bottle to his anus, which clenched tight in anticipation. But before she could thrust home, the little prick made a pained gurgling sound at the back of his throat and, fuck if he didn't shoot his wad in spite of her command not to. He came so hard she was taken by surprise and lost her grip on the bottle, which hit the floor and exploded into jagged shards reflecting the mean glow of the naked bulb into fractured pools of light. He was like a fountain, erupting against the canned goods stacked on the shelf and the bare brick wall behind. In her rage at his disobedience, at his coming without her permission, she would have punished him, punished him hard, but then she came too, with no more stimulation than watching him. *Thrice bound and once released. Thrice bound and once released.* Her rage dissipated with her orgasm, and she was left trembling and sickened and desperate to get out of that place.

'Bloody hell, that was amazing!' he gasped when she pulled her knickers from his mouth and stuffed them in his shirt pocket. She certainly didn't want them any more. She barely heard him over the strange ringing in her ears and the chant now repeating itself in her head over and over like a damaged CD. *Thrice bound and once released, thrice bound and once released.* As she jerked the sash from her coat free of his hands, she feared for a second she might pass out. She turned quickly and grabbed at the door handle.

'Wait,' he called. 'Can I see you again?'

'No,' she breathed, desperate for some fresh air. 'No, you can't.' Then she fled the pub.

When she came back to herself she was driving along the A66 toward Keswick, and the sliver of the moon hung cold and distant above Bleaberry Fell. With every fibre of her being, she prayed that it had only been a dream. But she knew that it wasn't. The feel of *his* presence was all around her, like the smell of something unpleasant that remained even after it was gone. She drove home feeling raw and desolate with the strange chant still ringing in her head. *Thrice bound and once released, thrice bound and once released, thrice bound and once released.*

Chapter Eight

SHE COULDN'T ACTUALLY REMEMBER how she had got to Elemental Cottage. There were vague recollections of being bundled into a blue Land Rover and buckled in by the farmer and the American whose company Anderson spoke so highly of. But Cassandra wasn't entirely sure she hadn't dreamed all of that. The woman, Marie, and one of the ghosts, Sky, maybe it was, they had helped her upstairs and into a bed that was almost as big as her entire bothy and tucked her in.

She wasn't sure how long she had slept but now she was showered and dressed in her best ratty jeans and a T-shirt that had been thoughtfully packed up for her, along with her few toiletries. She sat on the edge of the big bed feeling like she was about to face her trial. It was Sky who came for her and, sure enough, they were all waiting in the bright Victorian sitting room. All except Anderson. Her stomach, which was already in knots, knotted still tighter. She hadn't seen him since he had made love to her, since he had given her his energy, the thought of which made her pulse race with an insane mix of delight and horror. She had never taken so much from anyone, and had certainly never taken it on purpose. And she had never known the ecstasy of being brought back from the brink by such a powerful lover.

To her surprise, Tara Stone herself took her by the hand and guided her to sit on the sofa next to her, pouring her tea and offering her fresh gingerbread still warm from the oven. She remembered someone always bringing her food, usually the redhead, Fiori. And she had eaten like a starving woman each time, then returned to dreamless sleep. This time, however, no matter how good the cake smelled, she knew she'd never get it past the clench in her stomach.

'Welcome to Elemental Cottage, Cassandra,' Tara said. 'It's good to see you on the mend.' Her voice was friendly but distant, somehow. Cassandra figured the woman probably hated her, and could hardly blame her.

'Thank you, all of you, for all you've done for me,' she said, forcing a smile she didn't feel. In spite of herself, she couldn't keep back the blush when she recalled just what that had entailed. And now she was in their debt, something she had spent most of her life avoiding, but there was no help for it.

'I think we owe you a bit of gratitude as well, if I'm not mistaken, and a good bit, at that,' Fiori said.

That only made her blush harder. She sure as hell wasn't a hero. All she had done, she had done for Anderson, and even that was tainted by the fact that if she hadn't interfered with their dream magic and brought him to the Ether in the first place, none of this would have happened. She took a sip of tea and nearly dropped the cup, surprised that she was still so shaky. She usually had nerves of steel. Perhaps she was still weaker than she thought. And when Tara reached to steady her, she could hold it back no longer.

'Where's Anderson? Why is he not here? Is he …' The knot in her stomach migrated to her throat then settled tightly around her heart, and she couldn't speak, afraid that she would cry in front of them, and she had embarrassed herself enough already.

'Anderson's all right. He's fine, Cassandra,' Tara said. But Cassandra didn't miss the way the strong lines of the woman's jaw shifted and tightened at the mention of Anderson's name.

'Then why isn't he here? I need to see him.' Christ, she was making such a fool of herself, but she couldn't help it. 'I need to *know* that he's all right. Tara reached for her hand but she pulled it away. 'Tell me.'

The coven leader took a deep breath and her back stiffened

slightly. 'Anderson can't manifest in the flesh at the moment because –'

'Because of me.' She didn't have to ask, she knew. 'Because of what I did to him. Why didn't you stop him? Why didn't you stop me? You know what I am, what I can do.' She forced a laugh that felt like bile up the back of her throat. 'No doubt everyone knows after Serina got finished blabbing.' She suddenly felt like the room was closing in on her, like all the emotions she had tamped down after everything that had happened, so she could calmly sit and have tea in proper company, were more than she could bear. She stood and was halfway to the door before Tim Meriwether caught her by the arm in a grip that was gentle but firm.

'Serina saved your life, and if you think any of us could have stopped Anderson then you –'

'Then you do not know me, my darling.' Anderson appeared next to Tim, but his image wavered and shimmered like a wisp of mist rising off the fells. His voice, however, remained strong. 'Cassandra, my love, please do not trouble yourself. I am unharmed. I have not made myself known to you because I feared the sight of me as I am now would upset you. Forgive me, my darling. I see now that was a mistake. But I promise you, I am well.' He looked around the room and smiled at the others present. 'I heartily doubt that there is one among those of us in this room who has not spent the night in the grip of passion so powerful that an inordinate amount of rest was required to recover oneself. And I would also wager that none regret that passion, as I do not regret ours.'

Relief at the sight of him, even if it were only in spirit form, washed over her with such force that her knees gave, and if Tim hadn't held her, she wasn't sure she could have remained standing. There were a million things she wanted to say to Anderson, her whole being felt like it would burst from all that was in need of being said, and yet she remained dumb.

'Now please, my darling,' Anderson was saying. 'Sit.' He

75

nodded back to the sofa. 'Finish your tea, take some nourishment, and have no fear for me. I shall stay by your side, which is no hardship for me, and soon enough I shall be able to wear the flesh. You shall see.' He nodded once again to where Tara sat, and there was a visible darkening in his essence. 'There are very serious matters which must be attended to, and you play a vital role in those matters, my darling, as I am sure you must now certainly be aware.'

She didn't want to play a vital role in serious matters. She had nearly caused the destruction of the one man she cared about because of her lust. She was a fool to think there was a way she could safely channel it. In the end, everyone would be better off if she extricated herself as quickly as possible from the situation and disappeared again. Deacon was trapped back where he could do no harm; everything was as it was before, she tried to tell herself. She settled uncomfortably onto the sofa, while Anderson hovered next to her. She would be polite, do what was expected of her for the moment, but the sooner she was away, the better for everyone. Two cups of tea and, at Fiori and Anderson's insistence, three pieces of gingerbread later, she had told them what had happened. 'I'm sorry,' she said, staring into her now tepid tea. 'I try to keep a low profile. I've never bothered anyone before. It wasn't my intention to cause trouble.'

'But you have caused trouble,' Tara said, and the whole room bristled at her response. None more than Anderson who was practically a black cloud. 'More than you can imagine, Cassandra. We may have needed Serina Ravenmoor to tell us what you are, but Deacon will have figured it out a long time ago. And your little game with Anderson in the Ether was exactly what he was waiting for, a chance to see what you were capable of, and – the icing on the cake – a chance to get to us.'

She raised a hand before Anderson could respond, silencing him, and for the first time, Cassandra felt the very edges of the woman's power. 'You've told us what happened, something we could have pretty much figured out on our own, and only a fool wouldn't be able to see why Deacon is interested in you.'

'Look, this is not my battle. I was in the wrong place at the wrong time. That's all.' Cassandra felt her own power pressing up against Tara's, and she felt the bruise of it.

Tara leaned closer to her, and rested a hand that felt like fire against Cassandra's thigh. 'It's your battle now, Cassandra, now that Deacon knows what you can do. You're his ticket back to the World of Flesh and back to us. You can't really believe he'll leave you alone now that he's seen your power. Now tell us the truth, and maybe we can help each other.'

The knot in her stomach returned with a vengeance. Deacon had said he'd come back for her. That he could possibly use her to get to Anderson, to get to anyone, that he could use her at all made her feel ill all over. Her effort at a laugh came out sounding pathetic and weak, just like she felt at the moment. 'You really think you can help me?' she said.

'If anyone can, we can,' Tara said, without batting an eye. 'And it may well be that we can help each other.'

Still afraid to hope, and even more afraid to trust, Cassandra drained the dregs of her tea, weighing as quickly as she could what was safe to tell, as she'd done her whole life.

'I can't help you much. I don't know that much, not really.' She looked down at her hands clasped around each other, white-knuckled, in her lap and avoided the gaze of those around her. 'As Serina has already told you, I'm a succubus.' She forced the words through barely parted lips, and it was difficult. She couldn't recall ever claiming the title for herself before, and it fitted her like a garment of strange cut. She took a deep breath and continued. 'I don't know how I ended up being this … thing. That's what all the books are for. I've spent my whole life trying to figure out what I am, how to control what I am, and if there are others like me. So far I've found nothing.'

'And your parents? Tara asked. 'What about your parents?'

'I was raised by foster parents. I was in institutions off and on.' She shrugged. 'You know, for being loony. You can understand how people would think that under the circumstances.' It took her a second to realise that she was holding her breath, holding everything tight, like she did in the Ether to keep from flying apart in the void.

For a second she held very still, seeking out that place at the centre of herself, the space her grandmother had taught her would always be true, the compass that would always point her in the right direction. She felt Anderson settle around her almost like a cloak. Tara held her hand, bearing her suicide grip as though it were a gentle show of affection. She closed her eyes and continued.

'I've ridden the Ether since before I knew what I was doing. I always knew when to come back. I don't know how. I walked the Dream World with no spells, with no rituals.' She forced a smile. 'If you know the lore, then you know that a part of a succubus's power is based in dream magic, convincing people that they're dreaming such lovely dreams, putting them at their ease.' She suddenly realised she was trembling. 'But the power taken from the sleeper is much more satisfying, much more fulfilling the more the dream is filled with adrenaline. Sexual dreams are the best, but that's why my kind are also associated with nightmares.'

'And that's the magic you used on Deacon,' Tara said.

Cassandra nodded. 'I'd never attempted it before, but in the end I had no choice, did I?'

She folded her arms across around herself to fight off the sudden chill. 'I know it sounds insane. I never really believed any of it was all that strange until I tried to make love the first time. No one died, fortunately. But I learned my lesson.'

For a long moment, no one spoke. Tara pulled a throw off the end of the sofa and arranged it around Cassandra's shoulders.

'You've been abstinent all this time, then?' Sky asked.

'Until Anderson. Yes.' She was certain she could feel his protective warmth close to her, and she could use all the

78

warmth she could get at the moment.

'How?' Tim asked.

She bristled. 'What do you mean, how? I didn't have sex. People do that sometimes, you know.'

'But you're a … well. Don't you feed on sex?'

Marie elbowed him hard, and he flinched. The American seemed to be blushing almost as much as Cassandra was. Anderson was hovering over her like a cloud now.

'That's why you live where you live, isn't it?' Tara said. 'That's why you're squatting in a shepherd's bothy, because it's so close to Elemental Cottage.'

'That's right.'

'Wait a minute.' Tim spoke again. 'I don't understand. She hasn't fed on any of us, and there's no place more magically protected than Elemental Cottage.'

'No. I haven't fed on any of you, nor would I, Mr Meriwether. I'm not a vampire, though I understand how the similarities might confuse you.' Cassandra tore a corner off an uneaten bit of gingerbread on her plate and crumbled it onto the coffee table around the plate. 'I feed on crumbs,' she said. 'On the residual energy around places where libido runs high and there's lots of sex, or the potential for lots of sex.' She ran a finger along the sticky crumbs, collected them, and popped them onto her tongue. 'I've lived close to brothels, flats that house university students, and houses shared by lots of sexually active singles whenever possible. I've only lived near Elemental Cottage for a couple of months.'

She popped the remaining gingerbread into her mouth and swallowed, as though she needed the strength. Then she continued. 'There's a boundary, like a no-man's land, just at the edge of the Ether. It's the place where residual sexual energy collects, sort of half-in, half-out. I hang out there a lot.' She nodded to Tim. 'But I've learned to go a long time between feedings, as you call them.'

'Why Anderson?' Fiori asked. 'Why not just any ghost? I mean, we're not alive. And Serina tells us you know how to use the enfleshment spell.'

'I'm not sure about ghosts,' Cassandra said. 'The boundaries are so blurred with riders, and even though I can give flesh, I don't know what kind of damage I might cause, and I definitely feel energy, a sexual force when I'm with a ghost in the flesh. My research hasn't been conclusive where ghosts are concerned. But Anderson's different. Anderson rides the Ether, a place that has nothing to do with the living or the dead, a place where the only energy that registers is what we can manifest magically while we're there. And Anderson is the only man who has ever ridden the Ether, and therefore I could make love to him without doing harm.'

'You were that careful?' Tim said.

'Shut up, Tim,' Marie hissed.

But Cassandra had had enough of his interrogation. She snapped, 'I saw you there in the cave dreaming next to Anderson, Mr Meriwether. I could have taken you in a heartbeat. I could have filled your dreams with things that terrify you and leave you whimpering helplessly, with things that make you lust like you can't even imagine, and then I could have drained you dry before anyone even realised what was happening, so yes. I am that careful.'

The farmer folded his arms across his chest. 'So careful that you didn't even think twice about opening Pandora's box and letting Deacon back into the world.'

'Tim, shut up,' Marie repeated.

Tim jerked his arm away from her. 'Don't tell me to shut up when this woman waltzes into our lives, putting people I care about, people I love at risk just so she can get laid.'

Cassandra straightened on the sofa and squared her shoulders, forcing her feet down hard onto the floor so no one would see her knees shaking. She spoke into the charged air. 'I released nothing into the world, farm boy. Serina told me what was going on long before I came into the picture, and you couldn't have been so stupid as to believe the dream magic you were attempting could actually solve a problem in the Ether.'

'Guess we'll never know now, will we, since you barged

in and ruined the spell just so you could spread your legs.'

'Quiet, both of you,' Tara said. 'Accusations aren't going to help us, and we're only kidding ourselves if we think Deacon wouldn't have figured out sooner rather than later how valuable someone one would be to him who could ride the Ether and manipulate the Dream World.' She turned her attention to the farmer. 'Tim, I need you to drop it. I need you to cool down. I don't want you hot-headed for the magic we're about to perform. Are we clear?'

The man took a deep breath, set his jaw hard and nodded agreement, but Cassandra could still feel his fixed glare, which she returned in spades.

Now Tara addressed Cassandra. 'You released Anderson of your own accord, Cassandra, when you took from him, and you did it at a point when your control should have been the weakest. You took only what you needed to survive. Did you know that?'

Cassandra's heart did an anxious twist, and she felt like a flock of very large birds was suddenly taking flight in her chest.

'It is true,' Anderson said.

'We were all there to help if help were needed, but it wasn't,' Tara said. 'So if you can control your lust even in such extenuating circumstances, I think we can safely assume that, as with most gifts, you just need to develop the skills that will let you use yours to its full potential, and those skills can be learned in a controlled environment. We can offer that controlled environment to you. And in a place like the Elemental Coven where sex magic is the order of the day, your gift would be welcomed.'

Cassandra's heart nearly jumped out of her throat. Was Tara Stone really inviting her into the Elemental Coven? Out of the corner of her eye, she noticed even Tim Meriwether was nodding agreement. But before she could speak, Tara continued.

'I'll tolerate no more of your dangerous bullshit, though. You have no idea what you're up against, what we're all up

81

against. And believe me, now that Deacon knows who you are and what you're capable of, he'll give you no peace. Do you believe that?'

Cassandra swallowed hard, and for a second the room swam and she wasn't sure if she were going to cry or pass out. She only nodded, for the preservation of what little dignity she had left.

Tara leaned forward and wiped the single escaped tear from her cheek. 'Then you'll trust me and the rest of the coven to prepare you, to prepare all of us for what's to come?'

Cassandra nodded, feeling once again like she would explode if she didn't hold herself together. A simple yes was the best she could manage without losing the control she'd fought too hard for too long to get.

Chapter Nine

THERE WAS A STRANGE feeling of *déjà vu* for Cassandra when Sky led her into the Room of Reflection, with its circle of mirrors so similar to the space she had created for her meeting with Anderson in the Ether. For a desperate moment she wished he were there with her, in the flesh. She cursed herself for not being able to pull back from him sooner. The circle was already cast and the space within was heavy with magic – not just any magic, but sex magic. She felt it very low between her hip bones in a blaze of warm tingles, and it made her hungry.

The floor was piled with cushions and thick rugs. Immediately she knew what was about to happen but before she could turn to flee, Sky placed an arm around her shoulders and spoke softly. 'It's all right. We're prepared for you, and you need to do this. You know you do.'

To Cassandra's surprise, it was Tim Meriwether who came forward and took her hand. This time he was not glaring at her. This time it was lust she saw in his eyes, and she pulled away. 'You don't want to do this. You really don't want to do this.' She turned her attention to the coven leader. 'Please. Tara, this is not a good idea.'

'It is a good idea,' Tim said, taking her hand again. 'A very good idea.' Before she could protest further, he planted a parted-lipped kiss against her mouth with a tiny flick of his tongue. The slight gasp, the slight catch of his breath let her know that, even prepared as he had been, contact with a succubus was stunning.

'It's all right,' Tara said, from where she sat, cross-legged, at one end of the pile of cushions. 'What you're both feeling is exactly what you're supposed to feel. Cassandra, you've felt it before. Tim, you haven't.'

'The last time I felt it,' Cassandra managed, 'the man ended up in the hospital.'

Tim offered her a crooked smile. 'We're going to have to work on your talking-dirty skills.' To her total surprise, he kissed her again. In a series of nips, kisses and caresses and, almost without her knowing it, he eased her toward the cushions. As he settled her onto them and guided her to lie down, with her heart hammering at an explosive pace, she laid a hand against his chest and stopped his progress. 'You trust me?' she asked.

His chest heaved with obvious arousal, and his libido was now visible to her as clearly as the stubble on his jaw. His face was suddenly tender 'Anderson trusts you and Tara trusts you,' he said. 'If they trust you, then I trust you.' He undid the clasp to the silver-blue ceremonial robe she had been given and lowered his mouth to the swell of her breasts as she arched up to meet him.

In her peripheral vision, she noticed that the other two ghosts and Marie were in the beginnings of a threesome opposite her and Tim. They were fondling and kissing and cupping. Tara, who did not join in, spoke. 'You're in a safe place to test your control, Cassandra, control you'll no doubt need very soon.'

Tim had shoved his way out of his robe and pushed hers off her shoulders. She could feel the raw, human energy of his need in the way she always did. But this time it was more up close and personal, something she hadn't allowed herself to feel in a very long time. She could tell he felt it too. In the more feral part of her magic, she could see the heat radiating off him in waves. It was her heat, her magic influencing and coaxing his need. And when he opened her legs with one knee to push into her, she caught hold of him by his hair and forced him to look into her eyes. 'Don't,' she gasped. 'Not yet. It'll be too much, too soon.'

'What, then?' he breathed. 'What should I do?'

She was pleasantly surprised to realise he still had enough focus and awareness to be cautious. Caution was usually the first thing to go when she'd tried to have sex in the past.

'Go slowly,' she said. 'No matter how hard it is, make the foreplay last. Kiss my breasts, play with my clit, go down on me, I don't care, but think about pleasuring me the way you would Marie or Sky or Fiori, because if you think about how I make you feel, when you enter me, when I start to take, then you'll have no control, and I may not either.' She wasn't sure how she knew to articulate these things when there had never been a need to before, but she knew with a sharpness of instinct that was surprising. While it was true that she'd been researching for years to try and understand what she was, up until now it had all been only theory.

She was prepared for Tim's argument, but there wasn't one. Instead, he fearlessly held her gaze for a split second, took a deep breath in an effort to slow his accelerating arousal, then kissed her and began to lick his way down her body with a finesse she would have loved the pleasure of getting lost in, had she not known better. She still couldn't risk the loss of control.

He tongued and nibbled at her navel, then he planted kisses on the soft curls of her mound and allowed just the tip of his tongue to slip down and flick over her erect clit. He fingered her open with little tugs and tweaks of her labia, rubbing her wetness over the hard nub of her arousal. Then he stroked and thumbed and explored down to her perineum, pulling and stretching and probing until she was open and slick and begging. And when she least expected it, he gathered her moisture onto his middle finger and pressed it up into her anus.

She arched her back hard, sucked in a deep breath and felt herself take in the power of the people around her – not their vital forces, but the residual energy that hung in the domed bubble of the circle they had cast, far more powerful than what she was used to surviving on. The creature in her woke and clamoured like a leopard caged, and as it pressed hard against the boundaries she had created for it, pressing closer and closer to Tim, she felt another presence and knew it was Tara's.

'Our desires, our needs, our secret self cannot be caged forever, Cassandra,' Tara's voice whispered inside her head. 'That wild part of us will break free and the havoc it can wreak doesn't bear thinking about. Set her free, Cassandra. She is you. Let her feast, then call her back to you. She'll come willingly, and you won't need a cage.'

Tim had tongued his way down to lap at the valley between her swollen labia, in deep hungry lavings, and she felt him in her head as well as between her legs. She felt his sex, his energy, his very essence. If she tried, she could map every secret space in him, every cell, every rush of blood. His cock was stiff and anxious and the weight of his balls, the depth of his lust, rubbed against her own lust and the creature pressed hungrily against the cage.

'Unlock the door, Cassandra.' It was Tim now, speaking against her pussy, but it was also Tara whispering in her head. And suddenly she could hear the three other women chanting something softly in the middle of their groping.

Tim rose on his hands and looked up at her, his face wet with her pleasure. His gaze locked on hers as he positioned himself, one hand easing open her labia, the other supporting himself.

'Are you sure?' she breathed.

'I'm sure,' he replied. His eyes were fevered. His voice was shaky. She could tell by the feel of him that he was in the grip of her power, and yet in the horrendous need she knew he felt, she could still sense the fullness of all that was Tim Meriwether. It was dream magic he practised, she reminded herself. He was no stranger to the creatures that prowl in the Dream World.

As he pressed up into her, the creature lunged, the cage shattered, and her hunger expanded to fill the world, then came rushing back to the place where she and Tim were joined as one.

'Oh Goddess!' She heard Tim gasp from somewhere that now seemed both far away and at the same time just below the pounding of her heart. He pushed into her deep and hard, forcing her knees up against her breasts, forcing her bottom up off the floor. And she clenched down tight on his cock and rode him, and just when his essence was all there, open and laid bare before the gaping mouth of her hunger, she did something she had never done before, something she had not known herself capable of – she tasted his essence, nibbled at it, licked deliciously at it like he was a gourmet feast to be savoured.

It was awkward at first, especially when the smell of him, the feel of him, the very essence of him threatened to overwhelm her in his own hunger. But carefully, amid the physical rough-and-tumble in which she was completely engaged, she fine-tuned her own hunger to partake of him, to delight in him, to make it last. And when her first orgasm rolled over her, she tightened her grip on him still further, knowing in her mind's eye that it was enough. And he came, raging and growling and pounding into her deep and hard. It was only when she felt his wetness that she realised this was the first time any man still in the flesh had ever come inside her.

He rolled off her and on to his back with his forearm flung across his face. She had barely managed to catch her breath before she realised he wasn't moving. 'Tim? Tim!' She shook him gently, but he didn't move. Tara was instantly at his side, her fingers resting on his pulse. The others gathered around and Cassandra felt the world stretch and elongate, and she heard their voices from a long way off. 'I told you I'm not safe,' she heard herself saying. 'I begged you not to make me do this.' But everyone was focused on Tim. She stumbled to her feet, felt the magical boundary of the circle abrade her fetch – as though it would skin her alive as she forced her way through its unyielding protective shield of magic – and ran naked down the hall to her room.

She dressed quickly, threw the battered rucksack over her shoulder and was out the front door before anyone could follow.

It was cold and windy, but she had walked in worse. Besides, she owned no car. Twenty minutes later, she pushed her way into the bothy and shoved the door shut behind her. She could see her breath inside, rising on the cold air. With numb fingers, she built a fire in the little stove and lit the lantern by her bedside. There was nothing to eat but a box of stale Jaffa Cakes. Even though she could feel Tim's energy coursing through her body, she ate them. Food after magic was the rule, and she had a long night ahead of her. She pulled her mobile phone from her rucksack and called the only number she had in her directory.

'It's me. I'm ready. Yes. I know it's sudden.' She fought back tears. 'No, I'm all right. Just come, OK?' She hung up, went to the small cupboard and dragged out the packing boxes. They smelled musty and felt slightly damp to the touch, but she was used to that. She boiled the kettle, made tea and set about the work of packing up her precious books. It was like a meditation, packing books, and it was a good thing because whenever she packed books, she was usually in need of something to take her mind off stuff.

She knew Tim wasn't dead. She had seen the rise and fall of his chest before she'd fled. She was sure he would recover. She had been so careful. Still, how could she have been stupid enough to believe she could actually ever make love to an ordinary man, even a powerful witch, and have that same post-coital bliss other women enjoyed? She wasn't other women. How many people would have to suffer before she stopped with the fantasies of what might be and just got on with it – whatever *it* was. She was on her second pot of tea when she felt Serina Ravenmoor's presence. She said nothing, but kept packing. There was nothing to say, really.

At last the ghost spoke. 'He's all right. Tim is.'

'Good. That's good,' she said, but since it was just Serina, she made no effort to stop the tears of relief.

'It wasn't you.'

'Excuse me?' She wiped her nose on the back of her hand and looked up at the ghost.

'I said it wasn't you. I mean, it *was* you, but it wasn't because you lost control, and you didn't take too much.' The little ghost settled herself on the bench by the table and watched Cassandra pack. 'Tim Meriwether practises dream magic, you know, and what happened to him wasn't you. You were his first threshold, his first attempt at dream magic with a fellow dreamer.'

'But we weren't doing dream magic.'

Serina shrugged. 'Your magic is more dream magic than anything else, and if anything it was heightened by your taking from him. If you'd stayed around and not run off like a scared lamb, you'd have known that.'

'I don't need you to lecture me, Serina.' Cassandra continued to pack. 'Now go away. I'm busy.'

She was actually a bit surprised when the ghost did as she was told. Serina wasn't, generally speaking, all that well-mannered. And strangely enough, just this once, Cassandra wished she hadn't been so obliging. The loneliness in the room felt like a leaden fog closing in on her. She tried to force it back. She had been alone before. Hell, when was she not alone? And in the end, it didn't matter if what had happened to Tim wasn't her fault. She had put everyone at terrible risk, caused irreparable damage just because she'd wanted to know what it felt like to actually have real sex. Best she just disappeared. This time maybe she'd go abroad again. That might be the best thing to do. The farther away, the better. She liked Tara Stone. She liked the Elementals, all of them, and she didn't want to torment herself with what could have been, how she might have been a part of them. It was more important that she protected them. They had enough trouble to deal with without her.

Tim had eaten a fry-up and a half and was still shoving toast and home-made raspberry jam into his mouth. His hands had stopped shaking and his brain no longer felt quite so scrambled. 'We should go after her,' he said around a mouthful of toast.

'Anderson is with her,' Tara said, sipping at her tea. 'I told him to stay invisible. I'm also pretty sure Serina Ravenmoor is with her too. She seems to have a fondness for Cassandra Larkin. We all knew up front that Cassandra was lying, or at the very least keeping secrets, but until we find some answers, we have to play with what she gives us. We can't risk losing her, but neither can we risk drawing unwanted attention to her after what happened with Deacon.'

Tim rubbed his still-throbbing temple. 'I think we've already done that. I don't know how he managed it, but Deacon saw me in the Dream World. I was well and truly into her nightmare and then I caught a flash of him – just his backside really, he was fleeing. But I most definitely heard him say he would be back for her.' He shivered.

Tara cursed under her breath. 'This is my fault. I should have realised that the magic for you to have sex with a succubus was way too similar to the basic ritual for dream magic, and she even told us that she's as adept in dream magic as she is in the Ether.'

'Still,' Fiori said, ladling more scrambled eggs onto Tim's plate. 'Within the confines of the circle, in the Room of Reflection, and with the intent clear, this shouldn't have happened.'

'Lots of things shouldn't have happened, Fiori,' Tara said. 'But they still did. And who the hell knew that there really was such a being as a succubus? We're all way out of our depth.'

'Except her,' Sky added, from where she sat at the breakfast bar, arms folded across her chest. 'Except for Cassandra. Didn't she say she'd spent her whole life studying and searching for what she was and for ways to control her power, and we all knew she was holding out. We've got to convince her to spill the beans.'

'And how are we going to do that when she runs like a

rabbit at the drop of a hat?' Tim asked.

'She has reason to be gun-shy,' Marie said. 'I reckon we'll have to earn her trust, though I have no idea how we go about that. But I bet if anyone can do it, Anderson can.'

Cassandra had just taped the last box shut when the black SUV arrived in front of the bothy, looking a bit the worse for wear after negotiating a road that was little more than a rutted, muddy sheep path.

Neither Cassandra nor the pale, thin man dressed completely in black spoke as they exchanged a tight hug. And though she couldn't really see the expression on his face in the dark, Cassandra was pretty sure it was one of total displeasure. Ferris never approved of her housing choices. She reckoned those things mattered more to him than they did to her. Still, he never argued with her, never tried to persuade her to do other than she did.

When he pulled away, he held her gaze in the darkness, his eyes reminding her of cat-eyes, and she half expected to see a *tapetum lucidum* glow gold in the reflected light from the bothy. 'This isn't a fitting task for you,' he said. 'I shall make you some tea, then *I'll* pack the vehicle.'

She did as she was told. Ferris was small and frail-looking but she knew, had always known, that in his case, looks were most definitely deceptive. Not for the first time, she was glad he was her ally.

Once the tea was made, the man put his hands on his hips and looked around at the jumble of boxes. 'I'll have to fill the passenger seat, or make two trips. You didn't arrive with this many volumes.'

'I picked up a few at car boot sales and estate sales,' she said. 'Don't worry. I'll take the train in the morning, and I'll be back at Storm Croft tomorrow afternoon.'

Again, she knew this wouldn't please Ferris, but he said nothing. When everything was secured in the vehicle, he gave her another hug, tight enough to make joints pop, then got into the SUV and headed back down the rutted road.

Cassandra returned to the empty bothy, banked the fire and crawled, fully clothed, under the duvet on the mattress. They were all that remained in the bothy other than her rucksack. She just needed a little rest. Just maybe an hour or two, and she'd be off for the bus from Keswick to Penrith before first light.

Chapter Ten

JUST A LITTLE DOZE, that was all she needed, she reassured herself. Just a bit of rest. She hadn't intended to sleep, but she did. And she dreamed.

And she wasn't alone. Someone else was dreaming. It was the middle of the night. Of course someone was dreaming. Someone was always dreaming, but once Cassandra realised why she could sense other people dreaming, and how her gift allowed her to focus in on just the right dreamers for the taking, she had taught herself to block out the other dreamers, forced herself to ignore their temptation until they filled her head now, like so much white noise. But this dreamer was different. This dreamer wasn't alone in her dream, and though she was not one of the Elementals, she was not that far away. Perhaps it was someone in the next village, someone who moaned and thrashed in her dreams but couldn't escape them no matter how hard she tried.

And no matter how hard Cassandra tried, she couldn't block out the woman's moans and cries. In spite of her efforts to stay snuggled in the warmth of her bed, she found her fetch drawn out into the heavy, freezing mist of the night, moving along the gossamer threads of the Dream World, out along Derwentwater, along the River Derwent, past Grange and into Rosthwaite. The bungalow was painted white, well kept, and around its borders was an amateur and useless attempt at a protection spell. But what was happening inside drew her with the irresistible urge of metal to a lodestone. Inside, beneath a pale duvet, the dreamer, a small woman with short brown hair, tossed and moaned. 'Go away,' she breathed. 'I didn't invite you here. Stop tormenting me.'

For the tiniest of moments, Cassandra thought the woman spoke to her. Then, in a sudden wave of horror, she realised the truth. Even in the Dream World, Cassandra felt her insides turn to ice. There, hovering over the sleeping woman like a noxious cloud, was Deacon. It took her a second to realise he was, at least at the moment, completely unaware of her fetch's presence.

'I have no wish to torment you, my darling.' He spoke to the sleeping woman, who writhed as though she were in the grip of the very worst of nightmares, and the power of that nightmare drew Cassandra closer, as the smell of food draws the starving. Deacon continued. 'I only wish to offer you the power that every fledgling witch dreams of, the power of the lust that even now gnaws at your insides with hunger you cannot understand. But *I* do, my darling. I understand it perfectly.'

Cassandra had never felt such a powerful pull. Whatever was happening inside the woman's mind was sexual and horrific and magical. Cassandra longed to turn and follow the gossamer thread back to the bed in the bothy where she lay dreaming, but then the adrenaline in the woman's brain spiked with such fierceness, and the nightmare flashed both bright and dark, more terrible than anything Cassandra had ever experienced, more delectable in its temptation, and she could not pull back.

Deacon appeared to be little more than a wisp of smoke, his mouth pressed to that of the sleeping woman as though he kissed her, as though he gave her breath. But Cassandra knew with a chilling certainty that the opposite was true, and the beast within her ached for such a feast, even as everything human and ordinary in her cried out to run away and hide. But her fetch pushed forward, closer to the bed, closer to the writhing, sweat- drenched woman and her delicious aroma of fear and lust, close enough that she could have reached out and touched her. And it took all of the control within her not to push her way in, in spite of the demon, and take the woman for herself. And still, miraculously, Deacon didn't sense her presence. Still, she had the power to turn and run away to safety, but every second she lingered that power became more tenuous, and yet to leave could very well mean the woman's death.

'Oh, my dear Alice,' Deacon was saying, 'when I look at you, I can understand why your husband had no desire toward your flesh. You're hardly the kind of woman who would stiffen a man's cock, are you, love? But never mind that. That is all in the past now, is it not? I am here, and I can help you. You know that I can help you, don't you, Alice? I can make you most desired among women, just as I did the other night in Penrith. Do you not remember, my love, how powerful the man's lust was for you? I can make certain that your empty cunt is filled as often as you wish it. Would you like that, my darling? Of course you would.' The writhing woman threw off the duvet and shoved her nightshirt off over her head, all the while whimpering and crying like a distressed kitten.

The decision was made almost before Cassandra realised it. In an instant that happened so quickly it was barely even thinkable, she thought of Anderson. Then she reached out and placed a hand on the woman's fevered forehead, and there would be no turning back.

'Fucking hell!' With a jerk that nearly broke bones, Tim tumbled out of bed, almost banging his nose on the hard wood floor. He rolled then crab-walked backward until he bumped the back of his head against the bedside table, almost spilling the glass of water. Then he sprang to his feet, cursing and gasping, every muscle tense, his heart racing like a drum roll. 'What the fuck? Jesus Christ!' The world spun in a flash of infernal heat, the air went out of the room and everything slid out of focus, then back in again, like a spyglass being toyed with. And he found himself sitting naked on the edge of the bed, fighting for breath, with Marie and Tara on either side of him, steadying him. 'Cassandra's in trouble,' he gasped.

Sky and Fiori rushed in just as Serina Ravenmoor

appeared out of nowhere. 'He has her. He's taken her. Oh dear Goddess,' she keened. 'Deacon has her.'

'Quiet,' Tara called over her shoulder, then turned her attention to Tim. 'Tell me what you see.'

'Serina's right. She's right!' Then he grabbed Marie's hand as she tried to smooth the hair out of his face. 'The Rosthwaite witch. Remember? The Rosthwaite witch, Alice … Christ, I can't remember.'

'Oh God,' Marie gasped. 'Alice Hartley. He promised he'd hurt her. Deacon did.'

'You have to do something,' Serina cried.

'Can you remember her address?' Tara said.

Marie was saying she thought she could find it, but then Tim was no longer sure what anyone was saying. The sounds became like those of a radio caught between channels and, almost in slow motion, as though a heavy weight forced him back, he fell against the pillow.

For a brief moment, he could still see Marie and the other Elementals standing around him, talking to him, but he could no longer hear them. He heard other voices, voices not that far away, voices that were familiar. He made one last reach for Marie and Tara before they faded completely from view, and he watched. He watched helplessly, standing on the cold tile floor in a bungalow in Rosthwaite. He watched Cassandra Larkin's growing hunger beneath Deacon's roiling power.

'I had not expected you quite so soon, Cassandra Larkin.' Deacon didn't look at her, though he did pull away from the sleeping woman, who seemed to calm under Cassandra's touch. But that wasn't necessarily a sign of the woman's ease – certainly not a sign that she was now safe from harm. Cassandra knew that only too well. He chuckled softly. 'Ah, of course, the ambrosial scent of her lust and her terror would have drawn you. Have you come to fight me for your dinner, succubus?'

Even as he spoke, the hunger raged inside her down low, down deep way beyond any hunger that food could satisfy.

Whoever it was that spoke, surely it could not have been her. And yet the voice was her own. 'Her dreams, her lust are my realm, demon. Not yours.' Even as she said it, a part of her mentally kicked herself for not keeping her stupid mouth shut.

'You have already fed and fed well, I see,' Deacon said. 'Such a greedy little succubus you are.' He heaved a sigh. 'But I am not without manners, my darling. Of course I will share this one with you. Although she is hardly worth our efforts, I fear.'

'Then why bother with her? Leave her alone.' Even as she spoke, she could see the deep wounds not visible in the World of Flesh, wounds that had been recently inflicted upon the woman, no doubt by Deacon.

'She means nothing to me,' Deacon said. 'She's not strong enough to give me what I need, any more than the stupid witch Maybell was. You know about Maybell, I'm sure.' Suddenly the room pulsated with his power, and Cassandra was certain that if she had been in the flesh, her knees would have given beneath her.

'However,' he continued, the use of such incidental beings will get the attention of those who can give me what I want. Sooner even than I had hoped, it would appear.' His laugh felt like the edge of a serrated knife. 'I must admit, though, I had not expected you to be such a bleeding heart, Cassandra. Certainly your father was not such. But then he shared none of your human frailties.'

The weight of his power was crushing, and the information he offered felt like a physical blow. He didn't wait for her response.

'Yes, my darling. I knew your father.' And suddenly his presence felt physical, sexual, erotic, as he wrapped himself around her. 'I will tell you all you long to know and so much more. All you need do –' his words felt like a caress, hardening her nipples, making her wet, even beyond what the scent of the woman's dream had done to her. 'All you need do is bring me back into the world of the living. It's a simple trip to the Ether and back. You can go there and return, and no time will have passed at all. You're already away from your precious flesh. It would be such a simple task.'

Deacon pressed tight against her body, tight enough that she could feel his erection – no more physical than her own raging lust yet every bit as powerful. Then he spoke against her ear, his breath warm and sweet. 'I have so much to tell you, Cassandra, so very much, knowledge you have need of. Was it not your dear grandmother who told you that knowledge is power? Such a wise woman, your grandmother.' He pulled away so quickly that the sense of her own self felt suddenly distorted and stretched and, as quickly as he had embraced her, he wound around the body of the dreaming woman like a serpent, and she screamed a raw, feral scream, and her body arched until Cassandra feared her spine would snap.

If the situation weren't bad enough, if the woman weren't in enough danger, all that was in Cassandra pressed tightly outward in eager anticipation of the adrenaline cocktail of horror and arousal, a feast beyond imagining, a feast there for the taking. Cassandra held herself tight, fearing that she would explode and destroy the whole world if she lost control.

'Oh, I will not kill her, Cassandra, not just yet, but you know only too well how I can make her suffer and beg for release.' He looked terribly sad, even a little embarrassed to be the bearer of such information, information of which he knew she was well aware. 'I have no wish to harm her. I, like any captive, long only for my freedom. Give me but that, dear woman, and this one I will release completely. Give me but that and I shall tell you all that you have spent your whole lifetime struggling in vain to discover.' He moved against her and his lips brushed hers. 'I will tell you who you are, and you will be astounded and amazed. Choose now, Cassandra Larkin. This woman's fate is in your hands.'

The hunger in her rose like a fire raging through dry reeds, and her control crumbled. In her mind's eye, Tim Meriwether dreamed, Anderson's spirit lingered nearby, and Serina

Ravenmoor raged. Beyond that, somewhere just outside her peripheral vision, the Elementals reached out to her. And she could no longer remember why any of that mattered.

'She's not yours to take,' Cassandra heard herself saying. And her fetch flashed bright, filled the room, then settled into a tight embrace around the woman, settled in to gorge on the adrenaline of fear and lust that filled the narrow space and no doubt spilled out into the village. The woman writhed beneath her, this time all fear swallowed up in lust, lust for which Cassandra knew she was wholly responsible.

She heard Deacon laugh a hideous laugh, and his voice roared in her ear like a heavy wind. 'Go ahead, succubus. Take her. I've made her ready for you, even invited you to the feast. Go ahead, gorge, revel in your nature, and I shall revel with you, knowing how Tara Stone shall suffer for what you will do, how she will suffer that she was unable to tame you, unable to make you into one of her lapdogs.'

Cassandra felt her fetch swell with the surge of energy as she pressed in close to the sleeping woman, who now convulsed in her arms with growing lust. There was a sudden sense of pressure, as though the room could not contain all that was within its walls. It was as though a rubber band had been stretched to its breaking point and then snapped, and Deacon vanished.

It was Anderson's fetch that eased her away from the dreaming woman, who lapsed back into dreamless sleep just as Fiori and Sky appeared next to the bed. There was a brief discussion about staying with the woman, which Cassandra barely heard over the ringing in her ears from her gorging of energy. Then Anderson wrapped an arm around her shoulder and guided her back to the bothy, back to where her body slept.

Chapter Eleven

CASSANDRA WOKE WITH A start to find Anderson kneeling over her and, to her surprise, his hand resting on her forehead. 'You're in the flesh.' She spoke groggily, but her body responded to his touch with a much sharper sense of focus than her mind did.

'I am indeed, my darling, as are you. And we must go now, quickly.' It was then that she noticed Tara standing in the open door of the bothy and the outline of her Land Rover outside, and everything came back to her like a landslide. 'It was real, then.' This was not a question.

She got to her feet and grabbed her rucksack, all that was left in the bothy other than the bedding. 'Is the woman all right?'

'She's fine,' Tara said. 'A bit shaken. Marie and Sky are bringing her back to Elemental Cottage where she'll be safe.'

'And Tim?' Cassandra asked as she pushed past Tara and settled into the back seat of the Land Rover.

'Tim's fine. Lucky you bonded with him in the Dream World, so we knew what was happening.' Tara got into the driver's seat, then looked over her shoulder at Cassandra. 'We know everything,' she said, holding her gaze until Cassandra blushed hard and looked away, feeling suddenly exposed and desolate. Anderson sat in the back seat next to her and slipped a protective arm around her, and she was nearly overwhelmed by the feel of him, so solid and reassuring against her.

Tara and Anderson hurried Cassandra into the enormous kitchen of Elemental Cottage where Fiori shoved a steaming bowl of porridge into her hand and draped a red crocheted shawl around her shoulders. Then Tara vanished into the bowels of the house. Tim sat across from Cassandra, hunched over his own bowl of porridge, looking definitely the worse for wear.

'I'm sorry,' she said softly, struggling to meet his gaze.

He offered her a smile that belied the dark circles under his eyes. 'Why should you be sorry? The bastard trapped you – and, fortunately for Alice, underestimated you, big time.'

Anderson sat down on the stool next to Cassandra's and took the porridge Fiori offered. And Cassandra found her pulse racing and her stomach somersaulting at his closeness. But before she could dwell on the feel of the man in the flesh, Tara returned with Marie and Sky close behind, and once everyone had been served, Tara spoke without preamble.

'Alice is sleeping soundly, and she won't dream. We've made sure of that. The woman is clearly exhausted. What Deacon's been doing to her I have no idea, but it was pretty evident he meant to get to me by making her the sacrifice for our resident succubus.' Before anyone could protest, she continued. 'Get used to it, Cassandra, because that's what you are, and right now, Deacon knows more about your kind than you do. And you know more than you've told us – a lot more, don't you?'

'Cassandra, my love.' Anderson spoke softly. 'You have need of us, as we do of you. Deacon will find you wherever you run. Surely you must know this by now.'

'Marie and Sky have been doing a little research,' Tara said. 'You covered your tracks well, Cassandra, but not well enough. Your grandmother was Elizabeth Dalton, wasn't she?' Before Cassandra could do more than nod, Tara continued. 'She was one of the finest riders of the Ether I've ever known, so it's not surprising that her granddaughter should be as well. She raised you, didn't she?'

Cassandra nodded, looking down at her hands curled tightly around her teacup.

'Why did you lie to us?'

'What I told you was true. I didn't know my parents. My mother died not long after I was born, and I was in homes and institutions until I was almost seven. That's when my grandmother finally found me.'

'Did she know about your father?' Anderson asked.

'She suspected. She suspected that was why my mother gave me up. But she chose not to say anything until …'

'Until your first attempt to have sex.' Tara finished her sentence for her, and Cassandra felt a flash of shame she was sure would burn clear through her chest, but she nodded and held the witch's gaze.

'I'm sorry,' Tara said softly. 'That was a mistake on your grandmother's part, not yours. But what happens to you from now on, Cassandra Larkin, whatever mistakes you make will be yours and yours alone. Do you understand?'

Cassandra nodded.

Tara studied her for a long moment, then she spoke. 'Why didn't you tell us?'

'I've never told anyone anything. Ever,' Cassandra said. 'It's safer that way. For everyone.'

Tara settled back in her chair. 'I think we can all agree that's no longer the case.' Before Cassandra could respond, she said, 'Tell us about Storm Croft. It's in Surrey, isn't it? Prime property, worth a fortune. That's a huge inheritance. I knew your grandmother, and while she did OK for herself, she wasn't rich. It didn't belong to her.'

Cassandra played with the spoon in her empty bowl. 'I don't know how I got it. I inherited it when I was 21. Up until that time it was held in trust for me, though I didn't know anything about it until then. The stipulations were that once I inherited, I was to know nothing of my benefactor.'

'And Mr Ferris?' Anderson asked. He offered her a slight shrug and a half-smile. 'Of course I was watching over you, my dear. Surely you do not think that I would leave you alone in these trying times.'

The butterfly dance in her stomach at the thought of Anderson watching over her was something Cassandra promised herself she would revisit later when there was more time and she wasn't under the microscope. 'He's the caretaker of Storm Croft. I inherited him with the property.'

'Is he a rider?' Tara asked. 'He certainly couldn't have come to you so quickly from Surrey.'

Cassandra shook her head. 'He has some sort of magic. I don't ask and he doesn't volunteer information. Anyway, he wasn't in Surrey. He was looking for me. Somehow he knows if something's wrong then comes looking for me. And when I call him, he's never far.'

Tara leaned over the breakfast bar toward her and looked into her eyes. 'Is it possible that he may be your father's familiar?'

The sound from around the table was a mix of laughter and disbelief, as though Tara had just said she believed in Father Christmas. But then again, until recently, none of them had believed in succubi either so she ignored their incredulous reaction and continued.

'You said it yourself, you don't know anything about your father. And out of the blue, you were given a very generous mystery inheritance when you turned 21, complete with a strange caretaker. You've never lived at Storm Croft, and yet you've never attempted to sell it either. Is that because you think it might be from your father? What about the books?'

'They were my grandmother's, most of them. The rest I've found on my own. Oh, there's a library at Storm Croft, a good one, but not the kind of books I need.'

'You still haven't answered my question,' Tara said. 'Are you afraid that Storm Croft belonged to your father?'

'I don't know. Maybe. I suppose.'

Tara moved to stand by her side and lifted her chin so she couldn't look away. 'Deacon believed wholeheartedly that you would kill Alice Hartley or he would have never left so easily. You know that, don't you?'

Cassandra held her gaze. 'Anderson pulled me away from her. That's all, or Deacon might have got what he wanted.'

'I did nothing,' Anderson said. 'That you were taking from

103

her was clear, but you were by no means out of control. Had you been so, I fear it would have taken much more than any power I possess to intervene.'

Cassandra shivered. 'Then what?'

'These are all questions we have no answers for, Cassandra,' Tara said. 'But if it's true, if Deacon does know about your father, then he has more answers than we do at the moment. He made you an offer, a rather generous one for him. He offered to tell you about your father, and you weren't even tempted. Why?'

Cassandra pulled away and nearly upset her stool in the process. 'You know why. How can you even ask?'

Tara took her face between both hands and held her there, held her with such pressure that it almost hurt. Anderson stiffened, everyone else shifted uncomfortably. 'You're not your father, Cassandra. You've proven that to everyone else. What will it take to prove it to yourself?' She released her grip, and smoothed Cassandra's hair with a gentle touch. 'On this one thing, Deacon is right. Knowledge is power, and you need that knowledge now. We all do, because Deacon won't stop. He'll never stop until he's destroyed this coven, every single person I hold dear, every friend, every relative, every confidant, every ally. All.' She shot a glance around the room, and Cassandra felt the place vibrate with the woman's power and her passion. 'We, all of us here, we're all that stand between Deacon and the end. And, like it or not, you're now numbered among us.'

Cassandra squared her shoulders as she struggled to process everything that had happened in the past few days. 'I don't know my father. I know nothing about him. I know relatively little about Ferris. I swear to you. If I'm keeping anything else from you, I don't know what it is. If you think there's anything at Storm Croft that can help in any way, then I'll take you there.'

'Were you planning to go back there?' Tara asked.

'I was planning to stay there till I could go somewhere else. But now I don't know.'

'Call Mr Ferris and have him bring your books here,' Tara said. 'Though I can't force you to stay, this is the best place for you to be, Cassandra. And if two heads are better than one, then seven should be even better yet. I told you before, you're welcome. That hasn't changed.'

Cassandra only nodded, the tightness in her throat making it impossible to speak.

Tara held her gaze. 'Sky can lend you some clothes until you can go shopping. Stop living like a pauper, Cassandra. You're an heiress in more ways than you know, and you're going to have to embrace all of yourself if we're to battle Deacon and win.' She looked down at her watch. 'I would imagine it'll be a while before Alice can tell us anything. The poor woman was beyond exhaustion. And from the looks of you lot, I'd say we all could use some rest. It's been a rough night.'

Tim offered a smile. 'No rest for the wicked, I have a farm to run.' He pushed away from the table and patted the pocket where the bulge of his mobile was. 'I'm only a phone call away.'

'I'll help you,' Marie said. 'That way we can both get some rest. Besides, I left my laptop back at Lacewing, and I'm almost finished with last quarter's VAT for the shop.' Cassandra knew from her research of the Elemental Coven that Marie Warren did the accounts for the herbal shop the witches ran in Keswick. It was a far cry from the high finance she had left behind in the States, but she didn't seem to mind.

Anderson found Tara in the greenhouse, tenderly ministering to seedlings which he could not identify, having never had the passion she did for horticulture. She stiffened at the feel of his presence, and that saddened him deeply.

'You should be with Cassandra,' she said, without looking up at him. 'All of this is very difficult for her, and she needs to be with someone she trusts. Someone she cares about.'

He moved into the warmth and shut the door behind him. 'I shall not go to Cassandra while there is unfinished business between us, my darling.'

She said nothing, only continued to thin the tray of seedlings, but the slight trembling of her hands, usually so steady, told him that she was not at her ease. It was a thing he should not have been so bold as to do, but he was unable to stop himself. He moved close to her, took her hands in his and turned her to face him.

And she slapped him. Hard. He stepped back, face stinging, eyes tearing.

'You disobeyed me. When I was acting as our high priestess, you disobeyed me. You went completely against everything I asked.' She waved a chlorophyll-stained hand. 'Oh, please don't get nit-picky with me, Anderson. Don't drag out the letter-of-the-law bullshit. Using dream magic to get to the Ether doesn't change the destination. The end result of what you did was the same. You knew it would be, and you did it anyway.' She slapped him again, and he stood rooted to the spot.

'Tara, my love, I would cut out my own heart before I would disobey the orders of my high priestess, and more so before I would displease my dear friend. But I could not leave Cassandra in such danger, and you would not have either.'

'Don't tell me what I would do!' She stomped her foot. 'You don't know.'

'But I do, my love, I do know what you would do, and you would never have left anyone to suffer at the hands of the demon. Never.'

He moved to take her into his arms, and she hammered at his chest with closed fists. 'I could have lost you, goddamn it! I could have lost you!'

He caught both of her hands in his, raised her knuckles to his lips and settled a kiss on each fist. 'But you did not lose me, my darling. And you shall not lose me, and in the end I have done what I must. I could do nothing else.'

She looked up into his eyes. 'You could have trusted me. Do you really think I couldn't see how you felt about her, how she mattered to you? Do you really think I couldn't understand your heart after all these years?' She opened her fist and laid her hand against his chest. 'You could have trusted me. That I wouldn't have left Cassandra Larkin in the hands of Deacon, that I would have done all that was in my power to free her from that monster. If you truly believed that about me, if you truly know me so well, then you could have trusted me.'

She pushed past him. 'I can't talk about this now, Anderson. Not right now.' At the door, she turned to face him. 'Go to Cassandra. She needs you, and you need her.' She held his gaze. 'We'll talk later, when I'm … We'll talk later.' She fled to the house, leaving him to feel the ache of her pain as if it were his own, nay more so because he had been the cause of it.

Back in the kitchen, Sky looked up from chopping herbs of some sort. While Tara was the expert in horticulture, it was Sky whose expertise was in herbal apothecary magic. No doubt she was preparing some tincture for the Elementals' shop in Keswick. Next to her were a dozen delicate bottles of tinted glass, all with the shop label in artfully done calligraphy. Being a ghost herself, she had no more need of sleep than Anderson or Fiori and seemed less inclined toward the luxury of it than they. Sky seldom partook, and was not fond of dream magic. She smiled up at him, then nodded to where Tara had just disappeared up the stairs. 'Give her time, Anderson. She just needs a little time.' She wiped her hands on the kitchen towel and came to his side. 'She was doing the ritual to go into the Ether herself when she felt you leave through your dream magic.'

Anderson felt his heart clench and twist in his chest. 'She did not mention her reckless plan to me. I would have discouraged her heartily. She is no ethereal mage.'

'She tries to protect her people. You know her. Besides, she figures Deacon's not interested in killing her when he has so many worse ways to make her suffer. She believed her entrance was safest and least expected.' Sky smiled at him again. 'She's just hurt, that's all. Hurt that you'd think she'd

107

leave anyone to Deacon's tender mercies.' She reached out a hand to stroke his cheek. 'But in the end, she knows you share a powerful connection with Cassandra Larkin, and you could have done nothing else. She'll come around. Just give her space.'

After Sky had made sure she was, once again, comfortable in her suite, Cassandra called Ferris, who had only just arrived at Storm Croft, and had errands to see to for the running of the property. He had offered to return immediately, but Cassandra insisted that he rest, though she never really knew if he needed rest or not. Clearly he felt she was safe in the hands of the Elementals, or he would still have been hanging out in Cumbria, SUV full of books or not. She thought she could almost hear his relief over her mobile. But then she was probably just imagining it. Hugs aside, Ferris wasn't known for his show of emotions, a thing for which she was very grateful.

Once she was as settled as she was ever likely to get, she did something she hadn't done in a long time. She stripped and drew a hot bath. She seldom thought of such luxuries, and no doubt she would chide herself later for such a waste of her time. But not right now. Right now it felt like she never wanted to do anything ever again but linger in the warm, fragrant water. She reheated the bath several times, unable to bring herself to move from its steamy caress. It was comfort, and there hadn't been a lot of comfort in a long while.

She lay back, languid, half-asleep, feeling the heat work away the aches and pains – at least the physical ones. There were others that would take more than warm water to be rid of, and most of those she had just learned to live with. In truth, it was comfort that made her aware of those deeper aches and pains. No wonder she avoided its vivid contrast to the sharp edges of her world.

Her eyes fluttered open at the soft knock on the bathroom door, and Anderson stood before her, his whole body haloed in the winter sunlight streaming through the lace curtains of her room. He wore the black suit that seemed to be his wardrobe of choice. She had only discovered this since seeing him in the flesh for the first time. He stepped fully into the room, his eyes locked on hers. 'Please forgive my intrusion, Cassandra, but I can stay away from you no longer, my darling. I beg you do not make me wait beyond my endurance.'

'I wasn't making you wait, Anderson. I just … I wasn't sure you'd want to be with me after everything.'

'Woman, do not be daft. I have wanted nothing so much as to be with you.' He took the large towel from the rack next to the tub and held it open for her.

Trembling with a lifetime's worth of nervous anticipation, she pushed to her feet, slipped and nearly fell back into the tub, causing a wave of water to wash over the edge and onto the blue-tiled floor. Then Anderson pulled her to him, gently wrapped the towel around her and brushed her lips with his. 'I am in such need as you can scarcely imagine, my love.' He guided her wet hand to rest on the strain of his erection beneath his trousers. 'Please do not deny me the pleasure of your flesh, now that we are both able to revel in it together.'

He helped her from the tub and began to dry her, lingering to cup and caress the hollow of her throat, the small of her back, the curve of her buttocks with the thick soft towel, while he kissed and suckled the droplets of water from the tightening pucker of her nipples.

'Are you sure?' she whispered against his throat, her hips already shifting with the ache between her thighs. 'Oh Goddess, Anderson, are you sure?'

'In all of my long existence, Cassandra Larkin, I have never been more sure. You must trust me, as you have trusted me from the beginning, as I have trusted you. You are now well and strong, and what you take from me will not, cannot be too much.' Then he lifted her into his arms and carried her to the big four-poster bed.

'Wait.' As he started to ease her back onto it, she wriggled free, then the towel fell away as she slipped from his arms to stand in front of him. 'Sit,' she commanded.

He chuckled softly as he perched on the edge of the bed. 'I have never known such a demanding woman,' he said. Then he laughed again as she knelt on her haunches to remove his shoes and socks, her body positioned suggestively between his open thighs. His eyes seemed suddenly sad, but only for a moment, then he ran a large hand through her damp hair. 'That is not entirely true. I have never known other than demanding women. That is more the truth of it. And it would appear that it is in the company of demanding women I am most at my ease.' She rose to her knees and rested a hand on his fly, and he caught his breath and his eyelids fluttered. 'Oh dear Goddess. Woman, how I am at your mercy.'

She opened his trousers and his cock jostled against her cheek. She took it in her mouth and he cried out, curling his fingers tightly in her hair. Then she pulled away. 'Let me touch you,' she whispered. 'I need to touch you, to know what you feel like. Just let me touch you.' She practically ripped his shirt open, shoving her hands inside to caress the swell of his pectoral muscles, the rise of his nipples, the solid bridge of his sternum. She ran her hand over the tensing of his abdomen and the soft down of dark hair below his navel that led to his anxious erection.

'I can hold back but a little longer,' he breathed.

She stood and kissed him, letting her tongue explore the delicious cavern of his mouth, then she pulled away, breathless. 'I won't keep you waiting, Anderson. I promise.' She turned her back to him, bent slightly with her legs open enough for him to see her own need, then she moved back onto his lap, holding herself open just long enough to feel the head of his cock press against her, and then she sank down on the length of him, impaling herself to the very core.

He kissed and nibbled at the back of her neck and shoulders, causing great shivers of pleasure to rise up her spine. His hands came to rest first on her hips, then moved splayed up over her ribs and around to cup and caress the undulations of her breasts as she found a rhythm, his rhythm, their rhythm. She slid a hand down to stroke her clit, but he pushed it away. 'Do not deny me the caress of your swollen pearl, my love. It is yours whenever you wish it, but mine only with your kind permission.'

She leaned back and kissed his throat. 'Then you have my kind permission.' She took his hand and guided it down to her clit, and he gave it a gentle rub with his thumb, then a pinch, then he chuckled softly.

'My dear, I think we shall have great need of that towel, as it appears we shall both wet each other with our pleasure.' He gave her one more teasing pinch and she came, gripping his cock until he shuddered against her with his orgasm. And there was no turning back. She felt his lust, his greed for life, his intense longing for fullness and beauty and wisdom and pleasure and all the things that mattered. They were all open and laid bare for the taking. She pulled away with a little gasp, feeling the warmth of his semen trickle down her thigh. But he grabbed her hand and coaxed her onto the bed, and nestled her down next to him.

'I know that you are frightened, my love, but you need not be. I can feel your hunger and your need. Take but a little from me at first, if you are fearful, and we will learn together how we may pleasure each other in the flesh and do no harm. Only trust me, my darling.'

For a long moment, they kissed, nothing more, and it felt like the calming of a wild beast, the reassuring of a spirited horse. They kissed until they could breathe again, until her fear had calmed a little, then he eased a hand down to open her legs. 'Your womanhood is heavy with the weight of my release, my love. My need was great, indeed, and I have filled you so.' He lowered himself to kiss her just above the apex of her cunt, then whispered against the swell of her clit. 'Shall you taste our pleasure, my love? Shall you drink it from my lips?'

She nearly came from his words. The man was so filthily delicious, but his follow-up was even more so. He lowered his mouth and suckled hard against the pout of her pussy, nearly sending her through the roof with the intense pleasure of it. Then he rose, teased open her lips and offered, with the press of his tongue, the blending of their sex.

And she went wild. The room flared like it had burst into flame, colours danced behind her retinae, and she ate his mouth, trembling all over as though every cell in her body were orgasming at once. It only lasted a short time, and yet it seemed a lifetime that he fed her with his mouth, and when he pulled away with a soft grunt that tightened the muscles low in his belly, she felt the wetness of his second climax against her thigh. Quickly, she caught it on her palm and wiped it up over her belly and breasts and onto her neck, still warm from his body.

And he spoke breathlessly against her throat. 'You see, my love, there are many ways you can take from me, and not only shall you not harm me by so doing, but you shall offer me pleasure beyond any I could imagine. And in this body I now wear, I may give of my loins as often as you have need.

'And now, when you are ready, my love, it would please me greatly if you would take my manhood inside you and let me make love to you thus so that I might see the beauty of your face while you are pleasured –' he held her gaze '– while you take from me. Only do not be afraid, Cassandra. All shall be well. You shall see.'

She was already open and ready, and he made no effort at stealth, only pushed into her with a low groan and drew her tightly into his arms, lifting her so that her hips were off the bed and her legs were wrapped around his waist. She felt when it happened. She felt the pull of his essence into the vortex of her hunger. The halo of his lust was indigo and bright and deep, and she took hungrily, without so much as a waver until they both came again, and tumbled back into the middle of the big bed wrapped tightly around each other. And this time something happened that had never happened to Cassandra before. Her lover slept in her arms. Anderson, still fully in the flesh, with his cock still sheathed inside her, slept in her arms.

112

Chapter Twelve

ALICE SAT IN THE dappled sunlight of the conservatory nursing her second cup of tea, not thinking, not doing more than just breathing, and even that felt like it bruised just a little. With the gentle coaxing of the redhead, Fiori, she had managed a little breakfast. Food didn't interest her a lot at the moment. It was too much of an effort. But at least she felt a little stronger.

She was pretty sure the interrogation would begin soon, and though she dreaded it, she owed these people her life. How they had managed to keep Deacon away from her this long, she couldn't imagine. It was both a relief and a distress. How could she possibly feel such emptiness without him when he had done such horrendous things to her, had made her do such horrendous things?

She focused on the antics of a robin and the flit and flutter of blue tits and sparrows on the bird feeder outside the conservatory, anything to keep her thoughts from him. Anything. She was still watching the birds when the group that called themselves the Elementals joined her. She had known nothing of them before they had whisked her away from her bungalow, too weak and too frightened to ask questions, and brought her to the safety of Elemental Cottage.

But the last two to enter the room, the pale blonde with dark eyes – eyes much too old for her years – and the bearded man in the black suit, they had been with her before. And the woman … the woman had fought Deacon for her. Alice's stomach flittered below her ribcage. The woman had fought Deacon and something more, something she couldn't quite

113

remember, something that made her tingle down low in her belly.

She didn't know how it could be, but the woman made her feel sexy, beautiful, alive, different from the way Deacon made her feel, like all that drove her sexual hunger had been taken into the sunlight, up high into the brisk fell air and made wholesome again. A stupid thought, and yet it made her almost want to smile, almost want to primp and preen in front of this strange woman. But while the others studied her with interest, not rudely, but surreptitiously, as one does in polite company, the woman gripped the arm of the settee as though she were afraid it would toss her out. She wouldn't meet Alice's gaze.

Tara Stone introduced everyone to her but Alice, usually good with names, found that the only one she remembered was Cassandra, who seemed far more uncomfortable than she was, though she couldn't imagine why. She forced her attention to what Tara was saying.

'I suppose there's not too much that shocks you after what you've been through, Alice, so if you answer our questions, we'll do our best to be honest with you as well, even though some of the answers may surprise you. But first we need to know all you know about Deacon. Hold nothing back because I promise if you do, he'll use it against you, and it may be the very thing that will help us to make sure he can't hurt you again.'

'Hold nothing back,' Alice repeated. It was supposed to be a laugh, but it came out a weak little sob, and she frantically wiped at her eyes. She'd never get through this if she started blubbering.

'It wasn't that long ago, maybe a month and a half.' Strange, it seemed so much longer than that. She could hardly remember her life before. She raised her eyes and took in the interested gazes of everyone in the room, everyone but Cassandra, who kept her eyes lowered. 'I wasn't doing anything I hadn't done a hundred times before. It was just sitting mediation. I'd been making some progress and I was pleased. I felt calmer, and I'd had some amazing experiences, almost out of body but not quite.' She shook her head. 'Not that I was trying for that sort of thing. I wasn't trying for anything actually, just to be a little more at peace with myself.'

She folded her hands in her lap, hoping no one would see how badly she was shaking, but then they had seen her at her worst already, hadn't they? 'I found myself in this empty space. It was terrifying at first. It was like there was no beginning or end to it, and I had no way of knowing where I was or how to get back home.' She paused for breath, which suddenly seemed very difficult to get. 'And then, just when I was ready to panic, he was there. All he did the first time was wrap his arms around me and guide me back to myself. And just before he left, he whispered in my ear.'

'What did he say?' Tara asked.

She bit her lip. The back of her eyes stung, and her heart felt like it was too big to stay in her chest. 'He said, "I've been waiting for you." That's all. Then he left. And I …' She shifted in her chair. 'I masturbated, and it was good, really good.' She pressed on, not wanting to hear the sniggers she felt sure such a confession would bring, but there wasn't even a twitch of a smile. She continued. 'I hadn't done that for a very long time.'

'I don't understand how she got there, to the Ether, I mean,' the other man in the room said. Tim was his name, Alice thought.

'If Alice has a latent gift as an Ether rider,' Tara said, 'then even untrained, it would have been very easy for Deacon to pull her in and make it appear she had done it herself, especially if he was waiting for her, if he had planned it all along. If he did the same to someone who doesn't have the gift, it would have been much more unpleasant, I fear.'

Alice didn't want to think about how it might have been more unpleasant. But before she could ask about the Ether, the redhead changed the subject.

'Have you … had sex with him?' she asked. She looked

pale and unwell all of a sudden.

'No. I've had sex with … well, several other people … sort of. Because of him. But not with him. He's never been physical. I've never actually been able to reach out and touch him, nor he me, but he just … I don't know … He just constantly eggs me on. Only it's more than that. It's not like a dare from kids in a school playground. It's like I can't resist. I really can't resist, no matter how hard I try. And I've pretty much stayed aroused since that first encounter. I masturbate. A lot. But it seems to help less and less. That's why I started … looking for partners, people I didn't care about, people I'd never see again. Oh, it was never deliberate. It just happened. I'd find myself in the car, dressed for it, knowing exactly where I was going and what I would do when I got there. And when it's happening, when I'm in the midst of it, I'm like a stranger to myself, and yet at the same time I feel like I've never in my whole life been more myself.' She looked around the room desperately. 'Does that make any sense?'

To her surprise, everyone nodded. No one seemed shocked. The man in the black suit now had his arm around Cassandra, and she looked as though she wanted to run away. Alice knew how she felt.

'I stopped meditating. I even got a therapist who I practically sexually assaulted.' She blew her nose on the crumpled tissue from the pocket of her cardi. 'She didn't press charges. She didn't even give me a referral to someone who could prescribe meds. She just said she couldn't help me. I reckon that was his doing as well. And anyway, by that time, it didn't matter if I meditated or not. He came and went as he pleased.' She ran a hand through her hair. 'I thought I was going crazy. I even contemplated killing myself because I was afraid I might hurt someone, or worse.'

'And the people you had sex with? Tara asked.

'They were always willing. More than willing. And even when I hurt them, they were willing, and that made me want to hurt them more. Then the last time, I was at a pub in Penrith, and I'd tied up the barman before we, before I …

116

And this chant kept going through my head and getting louder and louder, and I remembered it from when I was with my therapist, the last time, when I hurt her. I don't know what it means. I only know that it made me feel all cold inside, then it made me feel like I had the power to control the whole world, like I was more than myself, like no one could touch me. And then like I wasn't even there. Just gone forever.' She shivered. 'Like I'd never existed.'

Tara scooted closer and laid a hand on hers. 'Alice, this is very important. Do you remember the chant?'

She nodded, suddenly no longer able to control the trembling. '"Thrice bound and once released." That was it, over and over again, like some sort of spell or curse.'

This time Cassandra uttered a little gasp and stood up so quickly that she rattled the cups on the table beside the settee, slopping tea into their saucers. She fled as though the room were on fire. They all heard her footsteps up the stairs, and the suited man went after her.

Almost before the room had settled again, they returned – her carrying a scruffy rucksack. She dropped back onto the settee and dug through the bag. It was full of books, mostly. Alice was amazed that the woman didn't have a hunched back from the weight of so many books. She pulled out a battered leather portfolio, laid it in her lap and unzipped it. Carefully, she took out a book that was wrapped in what looked like black silk that slid from the binding onto the floor. There was a collective gasp in the room and a strange shift in the air.

The book looked even more worn than the portfolio. The cover was cracked black leather, the pages were brittle and yellowed.

Tara stiffened and all the colour left her face. 'Where did you get that?'

'It was in my gran's things, in a trunk locked away. It's not my grandmother's, though. I don't know who it belonged to or why she had it, but it's not her writing, and it's far too old to be hers. I found it after she died, when I went through the house looking for answers. This didn't have any. But it

117

might help us.'

'It's a book of shadows?' Alice really didn't have to ask. She knew what it was, and for some reason this particular book of shadows made the knot that now resided permanently in her stomach tighten even further.

Very carefully, Cassandra opened the book on her lap. She turned the fragile pages gently, almost lovingly, until she came to what she was looking for. Then she read the passage in a voice that sounded far away, in a voice that sounded ancient and detached. She read words that made Alice feel like her skin was about to crawl off her body.

Thrice bound and once released. The spell shall reverse what was not meant to be, so shall it be done.
Thrice bound and once released. Banish the demon, the smoke and the flame, as above so below.
Thrice bound and once released. The reflection of reflection. His seed passed to dust as though he'd never been. So completes the circle, so begins again.

It was only when Cassandra's gaze met hers for the first time that Alice realised she had been chanting the words with her, words she should not have known, but words that felt weighted and faceted with power that made her spine tingle and her heart race. She stood, half- stumbling on unsteady legs, and moved to Cassandra, who responded as though there were something frightening about Alice, scooting back in her seat and squirming until the book slid off her lap and onto the floor with a heavy thud. Everyone else looked on in alarm. Alice paid no attention.

'You were with me. You came to me. You knew I was in distress, and you came to me. How?'

What colour there was in the woman's fair cheeks faded, and she forced herself up from her seat, eyes darting toward the stairs. But Alice grabbed her hand, and then pulled back with the shock of it. Everything inside her shifted and roiled and pressed forward toward the woman with her dark eyes and pale skin, the woman who was suddenly the most beautiful, most terrifying person she'd ever seen. Alice would have fallen if Tim hadn't caught her from behind. And Cassandra trembled like a leaf in the arms of the man in the black suit, as he eased her back onto the settee in spite of her protests.

Before the room could settle, Tara Stone's voice broke into the charged atmosphere. 'Cassandra's a succubus, Alice. Do you know what that is?'

'Fuck,' Cassandra uttered a strangled whisper and Alice could see the dark man straining to keep her from fleeing. Alice nodded dumbly as Tim helped her back into her chair.

'Tell her, Cassandra. Tell her what happened.'

'Tara, I do not see that this is a helpful –'

'Shut up, Anderson. We don't have time to play polite parlour games.' Tara addressed the man in the suit and the look he returned to her was nothing short of fire, not that she saw it. Her gaze was still locked on Cassandra, whose own look was little short of rage. But she sat up straight in her seat, set her feet firmly on the ground and faced Alice.

'I was drawn to you by your arousal and your distress.'

Alice suddenly felt her own desire to run. 'Were you … going to hurt me?'

'No! No. Your energy drew me. I … succubi feed on sexual energy and the adrenaline that drives nightmares.'

Alice released a long, slow breath. 'And I must have been off the scale on both.'

Cassandra nodded, holding her gaze.

'He brought her there.' It was Tim who spoke this time. 'Deacon did. He tricked her. It was a trap.'

Tara shot him an acid glance, and he glared back.

Alice found it suddenly difficult to breathe. 'So you were … aroused by what I was feeling, by what he was doing?'

Cassandra only just held her gaze, looking pale and a little bit ill.

'You were … taking advantage of what he did to me?'

'She saved your life,' Tim said, glaring at Tara, breathing

119

like his chest might explode.

Tara stood and helped Alice to her feet. Then she motioned for Anderson to do the same with Cassandra, but she balked.

'No, don't make me do this. Don't make me a part of this.' Her words were breathless, tight, struggling to escape her lips.

'Cassandra, my darling, please,' Anderson said. Both of his arms were now wrapped around Cassandra. 'I believe I understand what it is Tara wishes of you, and I believe it is a thing that you must do.'

When both women stood at the centre of the room, Tara spoke softly. 'Cassandra, take her.'

'No.' Cassandra was trembling so hard now that Alice was amazed she could even stand. 'You don't know what you're asking of me. You don't know.'

'I do know,' Tara said. 'I know better than you do. Now take her in your arms.' She held Alice's hand in a grip that threatened to break bone if Alice tried to escape.

Cassandra was taller than Alice, bigger, and her embrace was as Alice remembered it to be in her bed. Had it only been two nights ago? It was encompassing, all-encompassing, and when the strong arms closed around her, Alice heard herself sigh, felt her insides tighten and tremble as a liquid warmth and a sense of well-being flooded her. 'Oh Goddess,' she whispered. Then – and it seemed like the most natural thing in the world – she lifted her mouth to Cassandra's and kissed her, and the warmth of it was like nothing she'd ever felt before. 'Oh Goddess,' she whispered again. She wanted to melt into the woman, to be absorbed by her, to be taken completely by her in every way. But just when Alice could have stayed there forever in the embrace, Anderson eased Cassandra away from her, and a shudder ran up through the woman's spine. She turned and glared at Tara.

'Are you happy now? Is this what you wanted?' She fled the room and disappeared up the stairs.

Anderson moved to follow her, but Tara grabbed his arm. 'Leave her. She'll be OK.' She nodded to Tim, who guided

Alice back to her chair. And when she was settled and Fiori had given her more tea and practically forced her to eat a biscuit, Tara spoke again.

'It was Cassandra's lust that saved you, Alice, and you can't even imagine how tenuous the edge of that lust is. But in her arms your death would have been clean, blissful. I promise that won't be the case with Deacon.'

Anderson said something under his breath in a language Alice didn't recognise, but she figured whatever it was probably wasn't very nice.

Alice looked around the room and nodded to the farmer and this Anderson bloke, who spoke so strangely. 'They don't believe she would have hurt me. Do you?'

'I didn't say she would have. I'm saying she could have,' Tara replied. She moved to where the book of shadows still lay open on the floor. Very carefully she picked it up and wrapped it once again in the square of black silk. 'This same quote is in my mother's book of shadows. I always knew it was there, I even thought it might have something to do with Deacon, but I didn't know what.'

'We still do not know,' Anderson said.

'But now we have more to go on than we did an hour ago.' Tara stroked the book gently, then turned her attention to the people standing around her. You all have work to do. Fiori, feed Alice. Then feed her again.' Then she looked at Alice. 'You'll need all your strength for what's ahead.'

When Anderson turned to go, Tara grabbed him by the arm. 'Leave her alone. We don't have the luxury of playing games or being coy, and we certainly don't have the luxury of being squeamish. She's got to learn, and you know that as well as I do.'

Cassandra expected a lecture from Tara, so she was surprised when it was Sky who knocked softly on her door and stepped inside. Her arms were full of clothing. 'I took the liberty of raiding the closets.' She laid her burden across the foot of Cassandra's bed. 'You can wear these until you can shop for yourself. I wasn't quite sure what would fit you best or what you would like, so there's a variety.'

Cassandra reached out her hand and stroked the pile of soft, brightly coloured fabrics. 'It's been a long time since I've thought much about clothes. Not sure I ever have, actually.'

Sky surprised her by taking her hand, with little more than a flutter of her eyelids to acknowledge what it felt like to touch a succubus. 'You're young, and you've not had it easy, Cassandra – and believe me, everyone in this house knows that and knows what it feels like. But it's too hard if you don't take a little pleasure now and then, if you don't allow yourself to feel and embrace all of the things that are worth fighting for.' She nodded toward the door. 'And Tara, well, no one has lost more than she has. If she seems hard, it's because she wants to make damn sure no one loses anyone else dear to them.' She lifted Cassandra's chin with a curled finger and forced her to meet her gaze. 'Do you understand?'

Cassandra nodded, and the vision of the blonde was refracted through the misting of her eyes.

'Good.' Sky kissed her on the cheek, then pawed through the pile of clothing. 'Now let's see what we can find here that will make Anderson's cock stiff –' she giggled '– though you don't seem to be having much trouble with that as far as I can see.'

Cassandra raised an eyebrow. 'I'm a succubus.'

Sky offered her a wicked smile. 'So you are. I nearly forgot.'

'It's not a good idea to forget such things.'

Chapter Thirteen

CASSANDRA FOUND HERSELF DOING something she'd never done before – trying on girlie clothes in front of a full-length mirror. Sky was seated on the edge of the big bed, watching and giving her fashion advice. She was about to slip a turquoise cashmere sweater with a deep plunge neck over her head when Sky stopped her.

'Oh hon, don't wear a bra with that, especially not *that* bra. What did you do, go for the ugliest one you could find?'

'I went for the cheapest, actually.' Before Cassandra could say anything else, Sky came to her feet, unhooked the offending garment and shoved it off Cassandra's shoulders, causing her to offer up a soft yelp.

'Number one rule,' Sky said, standing behind Cassandra with her hands resting on her shoulders. 'Better no underwear at all than ugly underwear.' Then she hooked a finger in the elastic of Cassandra's equally plain knickers and tugged them down, her gaze never leaving the reflection of the woman in the mirror. And when Cassandra made an effort to fold her arms across her breasts, Sky slapped them away. 'Oh for Goddess' sake! If you've got it – and you most definitely do – flaunt it, especially in a house where everyone practises sex magic.'

'Yes, but –'

'I know, I know, I got the memo. You're a succubus. But I still want to see those great tits and that very nice muff. Oh, for fuck's sake, are you actually blushing?'

Before Cassandra could respond, Sky grabbed her by the shoulders, spun her around and kissed her, hard and deep, and

Cassandra stiffened.

Sky pinched her right nipple and giggled when she gasped and moaned. 'Don't hold your breath when I kiss you, 'cause I promise, I can hold mine longer. I saw what you did with Tim. I know you can control yourself, even if you aren't so sure. Now give us a proper kiss, or I'll pinch harder next time, and then I'll spank you.'

'You'll spank me? Oh really? I'd like to see you try.'

'Maybe next time.' Sky flicked her tongue over Cassandra's bottom lip. 'For now, I'm all about a little exploration.'

She left Cassandra with little choice, really. And the small moan of surprise she gave when Cassandra took her first nip of Sky's energy encouraged Cassandra to the next taste.

The ghost knew her way around a tongue-kiss, and Cassandra was carefully nipping and tasting her energy when Sky slipped a hand down over her belly to caress the tight curls of her mound. 'Serina tells me you eat good pussy,' she said, sliding a finger down and dipping into Cassandra's soft, wet pout, making her breath hitch.

'Serina has a big mouth for such a little ghost,' Cassandra breathed.

Sky took her hand and pulled her down onto the bed. 'She certainly does. She also tells me that you never let her return the favour. I, on the other hand –' Sky shoved her back on the mattress and pushed her naked thighs wide apart '– won't take no for an answer.' She tugged Cassandra until her butt was nearly off the side of the bed, then she knelt on the floor between her legs, positioned Cassandra's feet onto her shoulders and buried her face in between the slippery folds of her pussy. And the room slid out of focus as the delicious friction of Sky's tongue swirling around Cassandra's clit became the centre of attention.

'Mmm,' the ghost sighed when she came up for air that she didn't really need, sliding two fingers deep into Cassandra's cunt. 'Poor Serina. She really missed out.'

'Poor Serina stayed safe,' Cassandra said, struggling to

124

breathe against the growing pleasure Sky offered.

Sky extended a finger up to stroke her G-spot, and Cassandra nearly went through the roof. 'You're not taking from me now, are you?'

Cassandra shook her head when she could manage to breathe again.

Sky bent and suckled her heavy clit, then gave it a little nip, and Cassandra drenched the ghost's face with her orgasm. When the tremors had calmed to ripples, Sky slid up onto the bed next to her, face shining with Cassandra's pussy juices, and kissed her gently with only the slightest flick of her tongue. 'There, you see? You can receive without taking.' She cupped Cassandra's breasts, settling a kiss lightly on each nipple in turn. 'It may be just ordinary pleasure, no fireworks, no magic, but it's good. Sometimes it's the best. Believe it or not, Cassandra, all of us at Elemental Cottage are pretty safe with you. Your strength only enhances what's already here. And what's already here will help you gain control. Then –' she kissed her and pulled her into a tight embrace '– then we'll all be better.'

Cassandra hoped that was true. She desperately wanted it to be.

After lingering way longer in a shared shower than was actually necessary to get clean, Cassandra dressed in the turquoise sweater, worn over a flounce skirt awash in abstract splashes of colour. She and Sky were admiring the swell of her braless breasts beneath the cashmere when there was a hard knock on the door. Marie Warren stuck her head in. Her face was pale and urgent. 'You need to come now. Both of you.'

Tara met them at the front door and handed a heavy wool coat to Cassandra. 'Stay with Alice,' she called over her shoulder to Sky, 'and don't let her out of your sight.' Then she tugged Cassandra, still struggling into the coat, out of the door with her.

The second they pushed it open, the icy wind shoved their

breath back down their throats. Even from the front garden, they could see the flames and the dark roil of smoke against the iron-grey sky. From a distance, Cassandra recognised the figure hunched on a boulder.

'Ferris!' The knot in her chest, with the help of the wind, felt like it would suffocate her. As she broke into a run with Tara right at her side, she could just make out the lights of the fire engine coming up the road, followed by an ambulance. Ferris was bleeding and bruised, and Tim was examining him for further injuries. It took Cassandra's brain a second to register that the dance of flames and smoke was coming from Ferris's SUV, upturned in the ditch, nearly unrecognisable in the pall.

It was then that she realised what was happening. 'My books!' Cassandra shouted, and her insides felt as though they were burning right along with the vehicle. Tara grabbed her arm and pulled her back as she lunged toward it. She tried to pull away. 'That's my life there. Everything I have that matters, everything that I am. All gone. Destroyed.'

'Don't you say that! Don't ever say that in this place.' Tara grabbed her by the shoulders and gave her a jaw-rattling shake. 'It's not all you are, Cassandra. It's not your life, and it sure as hell isn't all that matters.' Her gaze was fierce and wild, and it made Cassandra feel things, things she had no name for, things that both ached and leapt with excitement at the same time, as though somehow sorrow and joy could be blended together, as though everything she knew to be true, or thought to be true was turning itself inside out. 'They're just things.' Tara said. 'Do you understand? Just things. They can be replaced. In the end they don't matter. What matters is that you and Ferris are here and you are safe.'

She pulled away and stumbled to Ferris, barely able to see through the mist of tears. He pushed up from the boulder and took her in his arms. 'I'm sorry, Cassandra,' he said in a voice closer to emotion than she had ever heard coming from him before. 'There was nothing I could do. There was nothing I could do.'

She tightened her embrace. 'It was Deacon.' It wasn't a question. She knew.

Ferris nodded as the paramedics pulled him away from her in a barrage of questions and began to dress the cuts on his face, while Tim talked medicalese with them. She had nearly forgotten that Tim volunteered with the Keswick Mountain Rescue. The fire engine was now disgorging the firefighters, and everything seemed suddenly slow motion, magnifying her loss, magnifying and stretching the end of how her life had been.

'I don't know how he did it,' Ferris said. 'It was as though I suddenly had no control over the vehicle. And he wanted me to know it was him. He wanted there to be no doubt.'

'It's a boundary,' Tara said. She stood with her arms folded across her chest against the cold.

Anderson was suddenly standing next to Cassandra. He slipped a protective arm around her and pulled her close.

Tara continued. 'What Deacon did, he had to do here, in this place. It's also a crossroads, a liminal place, a place where magic can break through.' She gestured to Elemental Cottage. 'Our protection spells extend to here. Our property extends to here. Here there's a crossroads and the meeting of property belonging to four different owners. A place divided is a place vulnerable.'

Ferris had suffered only minor cuts and bruises, and once the police and firemen had left, he returned to Elemental Cottage with everyone else.

Sky had a fire roaring in the fireplace in the lounge. Fiori served tea to warm everyone up and Ferris sat dwarfed in a huge wing-back chair with his pale hands folded in his lap. It took him a second to realise everyone's attention was on him. He cleared his throat softly, raised his pale eyes and spoke. 'You want to know, first of all, what I know about this demon, Deacon, who destroyed Ms Larkin's books.'

There was an affirmative rustle and murmur around the room.

'Until today I knew nothing.' He turned his attention to

Cassandra. 'It would have, perhaps, been helpful if you'd told me what you were up against, who you had angered.' Before she could reply, he addressed the rest of the company again. 'But, as I said earlier, even though you did not, the demon made certain I was informed. When he attacked my vehicle, he wanted to be sure I knew who he was and why he was doing it. It was only a thought, one he placed in my head.'

'I suspected as much,' Tara said.

Before she could speak further, he continued. 'While I can't fully express my relief at seeing Ms Larkin safely in your care, Ms Stone, I'm saddened to say I can be of no more help with your next question than I was with your last. You wish to know about Ms Larkin's inheritance.'

Again there was a general nod of affirmation.

For a second he sat still, so uncanny in his lack of emotion and his lack of movement that Cassandra thought anyone watching from the outside at that moment might have thought him a pale, thin mannequin displayed on the chair. Even when he spoke, the illusion was only barely dispelled. 'Ms Larkin's inheritance was given into my care by the same solicitors who informed her that Storm Croft was now hers. It was given into my hands, and I was told to change nothing unless Ms Larkin requested it, and she hasn't. Therefore it's as it has always been, as I first found it.'

'Then it seems even more likely to me that this inheritance was set up by her father,' Tara said.

Cassandra shivered and felt as though something cold was crawling in her stomach.

'I know nothing of her father, only what she's seen fit to tell me, which has been very little.'

'And you've never tried to find out, never tried to use magic to understand?' Tara asked, her gaze moving from the caretaker to Cassandra and back again.

He made no attempt to deny that he could have used magic, and Cassandra realised she had never doubted that he was way more powerful than he appeared. 'She's never asked it of me,' he said.

Cassandra leaned forward in her chair, shivering with cold that had nothing to do with the temperature in the warm, cheery room nor the chill she had felt outside. 'I'm asking it of you now, Ferris. Please help us, if there's any way you can. I know that it's something I never wanted to know, but he knows, Deacon knows, and we can't afford to let him use it against us.'

He held her for a long moment in a gaze that seemed faraway and cool, then he blinked, opened his pale hands and rested them on the arms of the chair, seeming suddenly larger somehow. 'I'm not sure there's anything I can do. In truth, I have no memory of my life before Storm Croft, and though I never thought about it until now, it has never seemed strange to me.'

There was a murmur in the room and Cassandra shivered again. Ferris offered the best effort at a genuine smile she had ever seen on his thin face. 'However, I am aware of magic that comes to me as I need it, and there are certain spells and rituals that may help me recover the memories I no longer possess. I shall do what I can.'

Fiori had a meal waiting in the dining room when they were finished. Even with Anderson sitting on one side of her and Sky on the other, both trying to coax her to eat, Cassandra could manage little more than a few bites. All she could think about was the loss of her books and, worse yet, the chill in her gut at how close she had come to losing Ferris. Ferris, who had been her only ally all these years. She did, however, notice that he had no trouble shovelling in Fiori's beef Wellington. For that she was grateful. She reckoned he'd had very little pleasure in his life of babysitting the succubus. Neither did she miss the spark between him and Sky. She was pretty sure the man wouldn't be sleeping alone tonight.

That pleased her even more. It came as no surprise, really, that the man she had known so little about should desire the same pleasures of the flesh as any other person desired. She had thought very little about Ferris, actually. He was a part of the package. And he was there when she needed him. Keeping a distance had always seemed the safest thing to do. Now, she was sorry she didn't know the man a little better.

When the meal was finished, Tara pushed back from her chair and beckoned for Cassandra to follow her. Cassandra reckoned this was when she'd get the lecture for bringing such danger into Tara's home. And she certainly deserved it, didn't she? Anderson squeezed her hand as she stood, then she followed Tara silently, just wanting to get it over with.

Tara led her down the long parquet hallway to a huge room that she had only noticed in her peripheral vision when she had sent her fetch out to visit Anderson. Had that really been just a few nights ago? As Tara led her into the room, her knees went weak and her pulse went into overdrive. The huge space was furnished generously with several grey-blue armchairs, a love seat and a large sofa. The carpet in front of the fireplace was richly coloured and thick, but it was the books that took Cassandra's breath away by their sheer number.

Tara offered a knowing smile. 'You're not the only one among us who loves books.' She brushed the hair away from Cassandra's cheek and whispered against her ear, 'Special, hard to find volumes are a favourite here at Elemental Cottage.'

She led her into the middle of the space and gestured at the floor-to-ceiling bookshelves, a good number of which were in glass-covered cases. 'I'm guessing you keep your most treasured volumes with you in that ratty rucksack you're always lugging around. Fair enough. But I'll wager that between Fiori, Sky, Anderson and myself, and several others of our beloved family who have passed on, Elemental Cottage has a far more extensive library than what you're used to. The books, they're not here just because they make the room look good, though they do. This is the most popular room in the whole cottage. No witch can have too much knowledge, Cassandra. You've known that all your life. And you, maybe more than any witch I've ever known, appreciate what that means.'

As she turned to leave, Cassandra grabbed her hand. 'I'm sorry.'

Tara raised a dark eyebrow. 'For what? For bringing another gifted witch into our midst? I'm not sorry. Not in the least. And neither is anyone else here.'

Cassandra held her hand until their touch began to feel more than a little uncomfortable, but the coven leader didn't pull away, nor did she drop her gaze. 'I'm sorry for the pain I've caused between you and Anderson. I know how much he loves you, how much you love him.'

Tara's shoulders stiffened only slightly and she held Cassandra's gaze. 'My relationship with Anderson is not your problem, Cassandra.'

'And I don't want it to be your problem either,' Cassandra said.

Tara surprised her by leaning in and kissing her on the mouth, offering only the tiniest gasp at the feel of her power. 'Make good use of the library, Cassandra. I doubt anyone will appreciate it more than you do. The fire's always laid in the fireplace to take the chill off, and Fiori's special instant hot chocolate mix is always available in the kitchen next to the kettle, for those long, cold nights when you just can't drag yourself away.' She kissed her again, then she turned and left Cassandra standing weak-kneed and misty-eyed, heart racing in the middle of the incredible room.

Alice threw the suitcase onto the bed and began randomly tossing clothes into it as quickly as she could. How was she meant to focus on a task that was as simple as the need for clean clothing and toiletries in the midst of the insanity that had become her life? Since Deacon's arrival, it had been so far removed from the simple things, the normal things, the routine things of just living and getting on with it.

Marie Warren stood at the foot of the bed doing the adult equivalent of holding a child's hand after a nightmare. But this nightmare had been real, and Alice didn't want to be by herself. In fact, she wasn't sure she'd ever want to be by herself again.

'Is there anything I can do?' the American asked.

Alice shook her head. 'No. No, I have it under control. It won't take a minute.' She could hear Tim Meriwether pacing in the lounge, and she knew he was as anxious to be away from the place as she was, and that made her really sad. She had loved the little bungalow from the first moment she'd seen it. It had been her home. It had been the first place she had celebrated her independence away from her ex and all his control and his lies. She felt a great emptiness descend over her. It had been an independence all too brief, she thought, and now Deacon had turned everything upside down for her. She wondered if the place would ever feel like home again.

She shivered, wishing they could have come in the daylight. Even with every light in the bedroom switched full on, she saw reflections where there were none, shadows, movement, heard sounds that made her jump, made her pulse race, especially after what had happened this afternoon at Elemental Cottage. The wreck of the SUV with Cassandra's books was the reason why she was here at this hour rather than earlier. Tara had suggested she let someone else pack a few things for her, but she wanted to do it herself. She wanted to be in her space. Perhaps it was her insane adult version of peeking in the closet to see if the monsters were real.

Even the thought of what had happened in the unmade bed where her open case now sat made a chill run up her spine. It felt as though he stood right behind her, mocking her, waiting for her to wake up and find there was no Marie Warren, no Tim Meriwether, and she was once again alone with him – him filling her mind with horrors while at the same time making her ache inside like she had never ached before. She shuddered so hard that Marie stepped forward, a look of concern darkening her pretty face.

'I'm all right,' Alice said, forcing a smile she didn't feel. 'I'll just get a few things out of the bathroom then I'll be ready.' She took her make-up bag and went into the en suite

132

bathroom to pack toiletries. With trembling hands, she shoved the lot of it into the little cloth bag. She'd sort it in the safety of Elemental Cottage. She had just packed her toothpaste and toothbrush when the bathroom door slammed shut behind her, and she yelped and grabbed for the doorknob.

'Marie? Marie, is that you?' she called out. But she knew it wasn't Marie. Just as she always knew when it happened, when he happened. Terror clawed at her throat, just as the lights surged bright then went completely out. But even before she could utter a scream she heard him, and she knew, even if she screamed her throat raw, it would do her no good. She heard him breathing. That's all. Breathing in the dark, like he was standing right next to her, close enough to raise the hairs on the back of her neck. He was just breathing the breath which she knew so well he didn't need, which she knew so well he only teased her with – teased her that one day he'd join her in the real world and then … Dear Goddess, she couldn't even bear to think about what would happen then. But at this moment, his breathing filled the whole universe, and as the lights shivered back on, she looked up to see him looking back at her through the bathroom mirror, and her blood turned to ice in her veins.

She had never seen him before, but she was sure it was him. He had a way of making her feel him, feel who he was, feel him so that she didn't need to see him. It was as though little tendrils of himself had crawled up inside her and spread some strange mix of pleasure and pain and pure, unadulterated terror, and, oh yes, this was him, and he was lovely with his dark hair and deep broad chest, more lovely than she could have imagined back when she'd fantasised about him, back when he had made her feel better than anything, back when he'd made her happy. Yes, he was lovely with his wide smile and his bright eyes that filled her with both terror and lust.

'Are you enjoying your stay at Elemental Cottage, my love?' His voice was warm and honey-sweet, flooding the inside of her head. 'I was surprised the succubus didn't finish you off. Apparently she has more control than I would have believed. But then you wouldn't have minded, would you, my dear? You liked the way she made you feel, didn't you?'

His gaze slid over her as though he would eat her with his lust, and her nipples were suddenly hard and she felt wet between her legs. How could she possibly feel this way when she was paralysed with terror? He chuckled. 'I suppose I should be jealous, and in truth I am.' He tisk-tisked. 'Not of you, of course, but that she would choose you over me.' He pouted his lips. 'I could offer her so much more than she could imagine.'

Then he nodded toward the closed bathroom door. 'They've told you that you're safe with them, haven't they, Tara Stone and her lot? That's why you're packing your bags and moving into their little commune.' He laughed, and it felt like something warm and soft climbed up her spine, ready to embrace her in sheer decadence. 'They lie, you know? You are not safe there with them. No one is. Why do you think Tara Stone is surrounded by ghosts?' He raised an eyebrow. 'I see no one has bothered to inform you that there are more ghosts occupying Elemental Cottage than there are living. Strange the things people overlook when it suits them, isn't it? But yes, my love, Tara Stone surrounds herself with ghosts, and do you know why that is, my dear Alice? It is because she could not protect them. And they died. It's the truth. Ask her.'

'She's weak, Tara Stone is. And so are her people.' She felt as though he had just scooped her into a tight embrace. She could feel the contours of flesh that wasn't there, the press of an erection that didn't exist, and the want of it surged through her like a tidal wave riding the crest of terror. 'As much as you want to run back to them, you miss me terribly, don't you, my darling? Yes, I can feel it on you, smell it all over you, the need for me, the need they can't meet. They can't do for you what I can, my lovely, and you know it. They can't make you feel what I do.'

Just when she was sure he would either suffocate her or

consume her, she thought of Cassandra. And she breathed, as though she hadn't drawn breath since the beginning of the world. And as her lungs filled with blessed oxygen, the lust shifted into something clean and hot that flashed in her mind, double-edged and deadly and exquisite in its purity. Alice forced the words up over the tight knot of fear. 'She can. Cassandra Larkin can make me feel what you can, and more.'

Just then the bathroom door burst open and both Marie and Tim shoved in, practically on top of her. Tim grabbed her and pulled her tight against his chest, then, from dark cords that hung around their necks, they both raised amulets that consumed the reflection in the mirror, just as the fluorescent bulbs around it popped and exploded in a rain of paper-thin glass.

Then she was trembling in Tim's arms. 'It was him,' she gasped. 'He was there.'

'I know,' Marie said, still clasping the amulet in her hand. 'We saw him.'

Chapter Fourteen

'ANDERSON, WHAT ARE YOU doing here?' Tara carefully laid down the book of shadows she'd been searching through in the pile of who could tell how many lifetimes of books of shadows, from how many other witches whose paths had been blest enough to cross Tara Stone's path. She rubbed tired eyes. 'Why aren't you with Cassandra?'

He moved into her study and closed the door quietly behind him. 'In truth, I think I have lost her heart to another, for she is at this moment ensconced in the library in such a state of bliss as I am sure, even if I possessed all the skills of the greatest masters of the art of pleasure, I could never visit upon her.'

He took much comfort from the slight chuckle that passed Tara's lips. 'I suppose I'm to blame for that. How could any man, even one as irresistible as you, compete with a library such as ours?' She shrugged. 'Mind you, a fair portion of those books are your contribution. There, you see. No one to blame but yourself.'

'Yes, I suppose that is the truth of it, sadly. But she has not been unkind to me, our Cassandra. In her wisdom, she has sent me to the place I most wish to be at this moment, to the company of my dearest friend.' The tension in her shoulders was visible even in the lamplight, and he knew that this time he had not been the cause of that tension, though in truth he sincerely wished that it had been only a squabble between friends and not the added burden of Ferris's encounter with Deacon and the destruction of Cassandra's treasured books.

When she said nothing, he continued. 'Though it is true

that I am desperate for your forgiveness, desperate to be restored to you once again, at this moment, knowing as I do the weight of your burden, I would ask you, nay, beg you, to let me help you shoulder it, let me give you respite in whatever way I may, my darling Tara.'

She scrubbed her hands over her face and sat silently for a long moment, lost in thoughts, the weight of which he was certain was unimaginable. Then she heaved a sigh that was so much like a sob that he thought it would break his heart.

'I hoped that I'd find something,' she said, nodding down to the stack of aging books. 'You know, after the conversation with Alice this morning and what was in the book of shadows Cassandra had. And maybe I have. How would I know? The fact that I may have missed the obvious haunts me, Anderson, haunts me every second I'm awake, and even sometimes in my dreams.' She hugged herself and shivered, and he could bear it no longer. He moved into the room, settled his hands on her shoulders then began to massage in an effort to release the deep tension.

'You have missed nothing, my love. You have done all that is yours to do and so much more, so very much more.'

She placed her hands on his and leaned back so that her head rested on his belly, and everything in him warmed with the feel of her. He ran a hand along the side of her face, and she nuzzled at it in the way he had seen felines do. Her breath caught as he stroked his thumb across the swell of her bottom lip and he felt the warmth of it, the moist caress of it, and, dear Goddess, he loved her. He loved her as he had always loved her, as they had loved each other longer than forever, it now seemed to him.

He loved her not in the way his heart swelled inside him when he thought of Cassandra, nor in the way he loved Sky or Fiori, nor even Marie and Tim, all of whom he loved deeply. But his covenant of love was different with Tara. He had held her heart for safe keeping through all of the anguish of her long battle with Deacon. He held it because she had pushed it away from herself, pushed it away so that she might face what

137

she must. And he would hold it safe next to his heart until she was free from Deacon, free to take it back to herself, free to share it with the living as she once had so willingly done.

Her breathing, the blessed sound of her breathing, had accelerated; her nipples pressed tight against the dark jumper she wore, and his manhood felt as though it would split his trousers in the effort to get to her. He ran a hand down to cup her bosom and she held it against her. 'Please forgive me, my darling, Tara,' he blurted. 'I can bear the rift between us no longer. I beg you, receive me back into your heart.'

She stood and came into his arms, burying her face against his neck. 'Anderson, you've never been anywhere else but my heart.' She brushed her lips against his and held his gaze. 'I know you. I know why you did what you did, that you could have done nothing else, but it was reckless, so reckless, and so like you. So very like you.'

He felt as though his heart would burst with the relief of it. He raised her hand to his lips and kissed her cool knuckles, still holding her gaze. 'I am told that your plan of action, had I not gone into the Ether for Cassandra, was certainly no less reckless.' When she raised an eyebrow in surprise, he kissed her lips. 'There are no secrets at Elemental Cottage, surely you of all people know that, my dear high priestess.' Then he kissed her again, and she returned his pleasure, letting his mouth explore familiar territory, pleasing territory, welcoming territory.

She moved deeper into his embrace, closer to the press of his erection, until it strained tight and low against her belly. Her breath quickened against his, as her tongue darted and probed into his mouth, until at last she pulled away with a gasp and looked up into his eyes. 'Anderson,' she whispered, 'make love to me. I need you to make love to me. Give me something wonderful to think about, for at least a little while.'

Everything inside him leapt with the joy of friendship and love restored as he lifted the jumper off over her head and plundered her exquisite breasts with hands and lips and teeth.

She was already opening his trousers with skilled hands.

Oh, how many times she had freed his aching manhood into the pleasure of her company, and each time was a treasure to him, each time he was the one, the only one to catch the tiniest glimpse of Tara Stone vulnerable and open and free from the cares that weighed upon her. Would that she could always be so.

She manoeuvred his member and his testicles free from his trousers, shoving and pushing until his backside was exposed, then she guided him to sit on the settee that he knew she, as often as not, slept on when the nights were long and she was in the middle of her research.

'I can't wait. Anderson, I can't wait. I need you inside me,' she breathed. She lifted her flounce skirt and, with anxious fingers tugged aside the dark lace that covered her womanhood, exposing the moist warm swell of her, smelling of the sea and the rich earth and the heady needs of a woman.

With one hand, he guided her to him and with the other, he splayed her, creamy and heavy, then shifted his hips just enough that she rested her knees on either side of his lap. Then she squatted onto him, sheathing his penis in the wet, trembling grip of her. Her eyelids fluttered, her nipples pearled even harder and her breasts rose and fell with the deep intake of breath as he thrust up into her depths, then ran his hands around beneath her to cup and knead her pillowed, round bottom.

With urgency, she tore at his shirt until it was open and off his shoulders, then she pressed her bosoms against him and he felt the tender raking of her stiffened flesh on his chest. Round, full, soft – all of what it was that a man found desirable in the flesh of a woman, Anderson found more than desirable in Tara Stone. She lowered her full lips to suckle and nibble each of his nipples in turn and ground onto his lap with such gusto that he knew he would not long be able to maintain control over his flesh. But she gave a guttural grunt, gripped him with such convulsions of pleasure that he was completely beside himself, and took his release, feeling his manhood pulse into her again and again, as her own release gripped him in waves.

'Tara, my love,' he whispered in her ear, as the last tremors of himself lessened and calmed. 'I have missed you so terribly. I rejoice in my restoration.'

'Me too,' she whispered. 'Me too, Anderson.'

The mood was shattered by a knock on the door and Tim Meriwether stepped inside. 'I'm sorry to interrupt,' he said, averting his eyes out of politeness. 'We need both of you. Deacon paid a visit to Alice while we were at her bungalow.'

They all settled in the library because, with the fire blazing in the hearth, it was the warmest room in Elemental Cottage. Even wrapped in a brightly coloured woollen blanket and sipping Fiori's hot chocolate as she was, Alice was still shivering. 'I've never seen his face before,' she said. 'He's only ever been in my mind.' She looked down into her cup and took a deep breath. 'He said that I'm not safe here. He said that you're all ghosts and you're dead because Tara couldn't protect you.' She looked up. 'Is that true?'

Sky bristled. 'Deacon's a liar. Some of us are ghosts, that's true, but did he tell you that our deaths were at his hand? I bet he didn't mention that, did he? It's not true that it's because Tara couldn't protect us.'

The woman uttered a little gasp and nearly dropped her cup. Tara steadied her, and shot Sky a quick glance. 'That's enough …'

Ignoring the coven leader's warning, Sky continued in a rush of words. 'There were circumstances, situations. He tricked us, he used us, he hurt …' Her voice trailed off. Then she took a deep breath and spoke again. 'Some of us are ghosts. Some of us aren't.' She nodded to Tim and Marie. 'Fiori and I died because of Deacon, it's true, and Anderson was already dead when we met him. But it was not because Tara couldn't protect us. It was never because Tara couldn't protect us'

'That's enough, Sky.'

'No, Tara! It's not enough,' Sky retorted. 'She needs to

140

understand. She needs to know. There were lots of people who died at Deacon's hand – your husband, your sister, my niece, Fiori's father, people we loved, people we cared about.' Her eyes locked on Tara. 'We've lost a lot. All of us. She needs to know that. She needs to know why we fight him, why we fight Deacon.

'And she needs to know how we fight.' She lifted her hand in front of her face. 'We, those of us who are ghosts, still wear flesh because of the type of magic we do. We're able to give ghosts flesh in order to offer them the pleasures of the living.'

'Oh Goddess,' the woman whispered, her hand resting against her throat.

'Alice, I told you we'd be as honest with you as we could,' Tara said, 'though some of what you hear will surprise you. And some might frighten you.' She gripped Alice's hand. 'Sometimes the truth *is* frightening, but as far as it's in our power, no matter how frightening it is, we'll tell you the truth. We'll always tell you the truth.'

Alice nodded, set her cup down on the coffee table and straightened in her seat. 'Is what he said true, then? Am I not safe here?'

'You are safer here than anywhere else in the world,' Anderson said. 'All the destruction Deacon has caused has been beyond the protection of this property.'

'I can't stay here forever,' Alice said. 'At some point I have to …' Her voice drifted off, her hands trembled, and she stared into the space above the table.

'That's true,' Tara said. 'And that's why we have to find a way to end this. We have to find a way to bind Deacon again so that he can do no more harm.'

'Forget binding the bastard.' Cassandra spoke up. 'We need to destroy him. That's all. We need to destroy him. No one will ever be safe until we do.' She surprised herself with her own fury, raw from her own loss and now like a salted open wound, from the sudden realisation of the destruction Deacon had brought upon the Elemental Coven. 'The book of shadows I found at Nan's says thrice bound, once released.

141

That's what Alice kept chanting too, and Tara, you said your mother's book of shadows said the same.'

'We bound him last spring,' Fiori said. 'He had escaped the first binding through a scrying mirror, so that was the second binding.'

'Then if what the books of shadows say is true, the third binding should be the release,' Marie said. 'Or at least that's the way I read it.'

'It was my scrying mirror,' Serina said. She was perched next to Cassandra on the arm of the chair, visible to everyone in the room except Alice. 'It was never found. I know where it is, though.'

'What? What do you mean you know where it is?' Marie said. 'You were dead. Deacon said he found it and destroyed it.'

'Well, he lied. There was something special about that mirror. I knew it when I first saw it.' Serina said.

'If there wasn't then, there certainly is now, Serina.' Tara said.

It was the confusion on Alice's face that prompted Cassandra to reach out her hand to Serina and enact the enfleshment spell. For a second she was sorry she had done it, when Alice cried out and nearly crawled up the back of the chair. And judging by the number of raised eyebrows and shocked looks from the others who could already see Serina, Cassandra deduced she had clearly committed a faux pas. But Tara only offered a tick of a smile and Anderson, sitting next to her, sniggered under his breath, something that sounded very strange coming from his erudite throat.

Serina offered the poor woman a sympathetic smile. 'I know. It's a shock to me too. I'm Serina, by the way. Serina Ravenmoor. I practise sex magic, or did when I was alive, anyway. I've only been dead for a few months.' She held Alice's gaze. 'He killed me, Deacon did.' Then she shrugged. 'Well, actually, I killed myself, but he left me no choice.'

Alice whimpered, and Tara placed an arm around her. 'Never mind that, Serina. What do you mean, you know

142

where the mirror is?'

Cassandra placed the throw from the back of their chair over Serina's shoulders, realising that the little ghost still wore only the nightie she had died in.

'I cast a spell on it so he wouldn't find it after I died. The last thing I saw in it before I died was his face.' Serina shivered and pulled the throw tight around her thin shoulders. 'His real face. It was then that I came to myself, then that I knew I had to jump.' She looked around the room, almost as though she were seeking a quick escape, then composed herself. 'I only had a few seconds, just a few seconds before he realised that I knew, that I'd come back to myself. I knew I could never overpower him, and I could never be free of him while I lived.' Her voice sounded empty and desolate. 'I wanted him too badly. Even after what he did to me, I still wanted him.'

Cassandra took the little ghost's hand and was surprised by the strength in her grip, the strength of suffering and fear and no small amount of anger.

Serina continued. 'It was important to him. I knew that from the beginning. He asked me to bring it with me that night. And no matter where we were or what we were doing together, his eyes were always drawn to it. He didn't realise I'd noticed, but I did. I did.' She forced a laugh. 'I stupidly thought he admired my skills with it. But it wasn't that. I think he feared it. He said that she released him through it the first time.' She nodded to Marie, who blushed heartily.

"The reflection of reflection", Cassandra said. 'That's what it says in the book of shadows. The reflection of reflection.'

Tara nodded and scooted forward in her chair. 'We know there's a connection. There's always been a connection. The question is, what? That he feared the scrying mirror, that he always wanted to know where it was, that he planned to destroy it, those are all valuable pieces of the puzzle.'

'When he came to me in the Ether, when he took me –' Cassandra couldn't hold back an involuntary shudder '– there were mirrors all around.' She waved a hand dismissively. 'I magicked the mirrors. He didn't. But in the end, he used them.'

'When I tried to force him to look into my amulet, he broke it, crushed it in my hand,' Marie said, rubbing her palm as though it still hurt. 'And he said that he destroyed Serina's mirror when she died.'

The little ghost shook her head so hard that her red hair flew around her face. 'That's a lie. He didn't break it. He never touched it. When I was alive, he never touched it. And after I died, he never found it. He looked for it, but he never found it.' She worried her bottom lip with her teeth. 'That I made sure of, if nothing else.'

'Was your amulet remade, then?' Alice asked Marie. 'You used it at my house when you saw him.'

'No.' Marie's hand automatically reached for the amulet that she had tucked down the front of her shirt. 'This is a new one. Mine was …' She swallowed hard and Tim took her other hand protectively. 'It was a mess by the time it was all over. But …'

'But we saved it,' Tara said. 'It carries Marie's magic and the blood of her sacrifice that bound him. It's more powerful now than probably any other power object we have in this house.' Tara moved forward in her seat and placed a hand on the ghost's arm. 'Serina, Can you find your scrying mirror?'

The little ghost looked up at Tara, eyes shining. 'Of course I can find it. I can take you there now.'

Tara shook her head. 'It's the middle of the night. We're all tired, and Raven Crag is not a safe place after dark,' she said softly.

Serina held her gaze. 'I'm already dead, and I don't need rest. I can go. I'd feel better if it were here, safe in this house.'

'Not by yourself,' Tara said.

'I have no need of rest,' Anderson said. 'And as I am also already deceased, it would seem an expedient use of time, if Miss Ravenmoor will allow me to accompany her.'

Serina took a deep, superfluous breath and nodded. 'If you

144

think it will help. Of course.'

'I'll go too,' Cassandra said. 'I don't need much sleep.'

'No,' both Tara and Anderson said at the same time.

'My darling Cassandra,' Anderson said, looking around the library. 'I think your energy would benefit us much more here in the office you are well suited to. It is indeed a daunting task we all face, and Tara will have need of your gifts here if we are to find the magic that will bind the demon. And really, my love, Miss Ravenmoor and I will be in no danger, and we shall not feel the cold Cumbrian night as you would, my darling.'

'I'll go with,' Fiori said. 'Someone needs to be able to drive if we're going to get the mirror back to Elemental Cottage. Besides, Raven Crag's a big place.'

'Not that big. Not where we'll be,' Serina said.

'I would like to volunteer my services.' Up until this point, Ferris had sat quietly and only listened to what was being said. He sat as unmoving as he had this morning, silently observing and listening until now, and in all honesty, Cassandra had forgotten he was there. The reaction of the rest of the coven suggested they might have also forgotten.

He continued. 'I have considerable skill at masking spells and magical signatures from prying eyes, and I have never been overly bothered by the cold. Under the circumstances, perhaps I might be useful.' He barely glanced at Cassandra, who stared at him as though he had suddenly grown two heads, but he offered her the tiniest hint of a smile. The man, it seemed, was full of surprises. And suddenly Cassandra wished desperately that she had taken the time to know him better.

Fiori and Ferris left together long before Serina and Anderson did, as their corporeal journey would take longer. When, at last, it came time for the two ghosts to join them, Anderson motioned Cassandra from the her pile of books in the library, pulled her into a quiet corner near the stairs and took her mouth hungrily, sighing at the feel of her. 'I shall return as quickly as I am able my love,' he said softly, running a large hand through her perpetually mussed hair. 'And do not you worry, I shall be safe. We all shall be safe.'

Cassandra threw her arms around his neck and held him tightly. 'You'd better be.'

He nipped her ear playfully and whispered, 'Shall you welcome me to your bed when I return, my darling?'

'I'll keep it warm for you.'

He kissed her again and held her gaze. 'Then I shall be well motivated to complete our task as quickly as possible, that I might return to your arms.'

He vanished without preamble, and Cassandra hurried back to the library, anxious to bury herself in her research, anxious to think about something other than the four people searching Raven Crag for the macabre artefact of a dead woman.

She knew a lot about scrying, though it was not her particular gift. She could do it if she had to. She understood that Marie Warren was very gifted, and it had been Serina's pride and joy before her death. The Room of Reflection, where high magic was performed at Elemental Cottage, had, with all its mirrors, an element of scrying, but its real purpose was to serve as a prompt and a reminder that flesh was only a reflection of what was beneath, and that there were always reflections of reflections.

Ultimately, the real gift of magic, whether it was scrying or dream magic or riding the Ether or enfleshing a ghost was in the seeing. Sometimes what appeared to be reality was not. That was one of the earliest lessons she'd had to learn in the Ether. It was all about seeing clearly and understanding the difference between what was magicked and what was real. And that was the problem now, seeing clearly, seeing what was missing.

She was sitting in the middle of a plush floral carpet in front of the fireplace surrounded by piles of open books when she looked up to see Alice standing at the door, wrapped in a pink terry robe.

'Are you all right?' Cassandra asked.

Alice nodded and stepped into the library, moving close to the fireplace. 'I just didn't want to be by myself.' She looked around the room. 'I'm guessing I'm probably not ever really by myself in this house, with the ghosts and all. I mean, everyone has been so protective of me. I'm still amazed by their kindness.'

'Yes, I'm amazed by that too,' Cassandra said. 'And at their penchant for taking in strays.'

Her comment made Alice smile. It was good to see her smile. Cassandra could see Sky in non-corporeal form at the woman's side, but she said nothing. It was unsettling enough having just discovered that she was surrounded by ghosts. Alice didn't need to know that one was shadowing her, even though she already suspected it.

'You can't sleep?' Cassandra said.

'I was asleep,' Alice replied, easing herself down onto the carpet next to Cassandra, as close as she could get amid the clutter of books. 'Then I woke up thinking about you.'

Cassandra forced a laugh. 'Me? Sounds more like a nightmare.'

'No! No, it wasn't a nightmare.' She held Cassandra's gaze. 'You were the relief from the nightmare. It was you. When you … took me and chased him away. It was you I thought about at my house tonight when Deacon had me trapped in the bathroom.'

Cassandra pushed aside the book she'd been perusing. 'I wasn't there, Alice. I didn't even know till afterwards.'

Alice scooted closer, shuffling books until her knee, now poking out from under the robe, touched Cassandra's thigh. 'He makes me crazy. I feel like I'm losing my mind when I think about him, when I want him even though I know what he is, how he is, how he frightens me, how he makes me do things I don't want to do …'

'He's a bastard,' Cassandra said.

'My point is –' Alice moved still closer till Cassandra could feel the woman's warm breath on her cheek. 'My point is that when you took me, I felt clear-headed.'

'You wouldn't have for very long if I'd kept taking.'

She shook her head. 'But you didn't keep taking, did you? And tonight when he came to me, when he made me feel all of those things, and I was trapped, when I thought of you, my head cleared. And when I thought of you, Marie and Tim were able to get to me.'

Cassandra tried to edge away, but the pile of books gouging her in the hip kept her from it. 'Don't make me sound like a hero, Alice. I'm not. He tempted me, and I succumbed. I could have killed you just as easily as he could have.'

'I know, I know! He expected you to. The truth is, I wouldn't have cared.' She pushed on before Cassandra had a chance to become irate. 'You were clean and pure and wholesome compared to him.'

'I would have murdered you in your bed. I would have –'

Before she could finish, Alice lunged at her and kissed her full on the mouth. It was an awkward kiss, and she fell back on her haunches with a little yelp, her hand resting against her mouth, her eyes wide.

Cassandra's posture was nearly a mirror image of Alice's, sitting with her fingers pressed to her lips, where the woman's energy burned warm against her like the first sip of Fiori's hot chocolate. 'Do you have any idea what you're doing?'

Alice held her gaze, hand still touching her mouth, and nodded slowly. 'I know exactly what I'm doing.' Her eyes were wide, pupils dilated. 'I don't want to think of him in the night. I don't want to … I don't want to *want* him. And when you took me, it was bliss. When you took me, I felt strong and clean and …' She rested a hand against her throat and a single tear dropped onto the carpet, leaving a dark spot in the middle of a pink rose. 'And I felt beautiful.'

'You are beautiful,' Cassandra said, reaching out and taking her hand, feeling the spark at her touch.

'Show me,' Alice whispered. 'Please. I really need to see me through someone else's eyes, and not through his wickedness.'

Still standing non-corporeally at Alice's left shoulder, Sky gave a nod of reassurance, reminding Cassandra that she wasn't alone.

'I could hurt you,' Cassandra said to Alice. 'Badly.'

Alice held her gaze. 'You couldn't possibly hurt me as badly as he has.'

'You have to understand, I'll be taking energy from you, not giving it. I'll be making you weaker, not stronger. And if I don't stop, you'll die.'

'I understand exactly what you're doing, Cassandra. I understood from the beginning. I felt it. And I want it. I need it. Please. I don't want his touch to be the touch that I go to sleep every night and wake up every morning remembering.'

Cassandra released a shaky breath. All of her was shaky, and with a little quiver of surprise, she realised some of that trembling was anticipation. She pushed aside the books and moved closer to Alice. She smoothed her sleep-tousled hair and brushed the lightest of kisses against her lips. 'I'll only take a little. I don't want to hurt you or frighten you. But a little will make you feel good, and Goddess knows you've not had much to feel good about lately.' She glanced up at Sky, hoping the ghost understood her implied request for help if it became necessary. Sky nodded slightly and offered a smile.

Then Cassandra took a deep breath. She could barely believe she was doing this deliberately, that she trusted herself enough to do what she had lived in fear of her whole life. And yet, it was the right thing to do. She was as sure of that as she was of her own name.

She eased Alice down onto the carpet with kisses that were barely more than feather touches against her mouth, flicks of her tongue, nips of her teeth. The she pushed open the woman's robe and ran a thumb over dark rosebud nipples atop small, high breasts. Alice caught her breath, whimpered and arched up to meet her touch. Cassandra pulled away long enough to slip out of the turquoise sweater she still wore and Alice reached out to cup and caress. 'I haven't done so good with men,' she whispered. 'Maybe I'll do better with a woman.'

'Maybe you'll do better with a succubus?' She kissed down the writhing woman's body, shoving the robe completely open to find her shaved, bare pussy wet and swollen. For a protracted second, she tweaked Alice's clit, dipping a finger in and out of her slippery hole to lubricate the swell of her, all the while watching her squirm and moan. Then, with her back almost turned to her, she lowered her head between her thighs and began to suckle and lick, holding Alice's distended labia open with one hand, while the other slid up her belly to cup and knead her breasts in turn.

Alice tried to grab Cassandra by the hips and rearrange her so she squatted over her face with her pussy splayed against her mouth, but Cassandra slapped her hands away. 'You don't want me to sit on your face, Alice. It's a position of power for me. If I mount you like that, I take, and I take a lot. You're not strong enough, and I'm not sure I can resist if I start to take you that way.' Once again, she had no idea how she knew this, but she did. She was dead certain of it.

She kissed the tip of Alice's swollen clit and scissored two fingers into her gripping cunt. 'I'm going to eat your pussy and lick you until you come, Alice. I can feel you're getting close. It won't be long now.' She ran her tongue up over her clit and the woman whimpered again. 'I'll make love to your pussy with my mouth, and I'll take from you that way. It'll feel good, better than anything, but I'll be able to pull away when you come, and you'll be able to let me. And I promise – ' she rose on her haunches and settled a wet kiss onto the woman's lips '– I promise you'll feel almost as beautiful as you really are.' She nipped her bottom lip, then smiled down at her. 'Almost.'

Then she buried her face in Alice's cunt and felt the flood of energy almost as though the fire had escaped the hearth and danced in high, bright colours all around them. She could feel every cell of her, every breath of the woman who convulsed beneath her mouth, every sinew, every drop of blood that coursed through her veins giving of itself, giving of its

150

sweetness, of its fullness, of its life force. She could feel every ebb and flow, every rise and fall, all open to her, all offering itself up wholly and completely for her taking, down to the very last heartbeat, down to the very last breath.

And then it was as though the ground gave way beneath her, and she found herself feeding on the meat, the very marrow of Alice's dreams, her fantasies, her hopes, and her darkest nightmares. Even above Alice's moans of pleasure, the coursing of adrenaline, the intense flood of pheromones, Cassandra saw the terrified therapist struggling while Alice raked nails across her soft, perfect face and tore at her hair, while Alice shoved a hand, far more powerful than it should have been, up under the woman's skirt. She saw the barman in a storage room, bound, gagged, and beaten, but it wasn't enough. She saw Alice's long ride back to Rosthwaite, full of fear and self-loathing, and even in that vortex of despair, lust unsatisfied burned like fire.

And in the depths of it all, Cassandra heard Deacon's voice whisper to Alice as she drove along Derwentwater. 'It will never be enough, Alice, never, until you have bound and beaten and cut and felt the life force drain away between your fingers. In the nightmare, the adrenaline spiked and Cassandra struggled to hold back as Deacon spoke in Alice's ear. 'Without my help, who would have you, Alice, unless they were bound and gagged at knifepoint? At knifepoint.' He made the word sound filthy and sexy.

The adrenaline spiked again, and this time Cassandra felt Alice writhe beneath with her approaching orgasm. 'Oh dear Goddess,' Alice gasped. 'Oh dear Goddess, don't stop. Please, don't ever stop.'

But she did. Cassandra pulled back when Alice's body convulsed so hard, she feared she had caused damage rather than pleasure. Alice came in waves, crying and trembling and curling her fingers in Cassandra's hair. When the tremors of pleasure eased, Cassandra pulled back and lay down on the carpet next to her, drawing her tightly into her arms, the horror of what she had felt in the woman's dreams still

151

coursing through her obscenely in the mix of arousal and pleasure.

'That was incredible,' Alice breathed. 'So incredible. I've never felt anything like it.'

For a long moment, Cassandra studied her face, which seemed the epitome of bliss. At last she spoke. 'I can't make it go away, Alice,' she whispered against the woman's ear. 'I wish that I could. I really do.' She could still make out the shape of Sky, settled into the wing-back chair at the far side of the room. Dear Goddess, had she seen? Had she somehow sensed what had just happened? If so, she didn't show it.

Alice had already fallen asleep. In a surge of guilt, Cassandra slid away from her and covered her with the throw from the wing-back chair. For a long moment, she sat watching her. Cassandra hoped the look of bliss on the woman's face meant that she had been unaware of her discoveries, of her taking from where she had never intended to take. As she picked up the book she had been studying before Alice had arrived, she knew that she had just lied to Alice. She knew that in the end she would make it go away, she would make Deacon go away. She would have to. She didn't know how she'd do it, but she'd created the situation with her lust, and now she had to find a way to make it right. She laid aside the book she had been reading, went upstairs and retrieved her ratty old rucksack.

When she returned to the library, Alice still slept soundly and the fire had been stoked. If Sky were still there, she was staying invisible. Cassandra settled on the floor and pulled out her grandmother's book of shadows and two dog-eared books on incubi and succubi. Deacon believed she was his vessel back into the world of the living. Perhaps she could be his vessel for other places as well, places she knew he would not go willingly.

Chapter Fifteen

THE NIGHT WAS BLESSEDLY clear and there was little wind, but the temperature had dropped and the bite of it, Anderson was certain, would have made the search very unpleasant for the living, though Mr Ferris seemed to suffer little from the inclement weather. And it was well that he did not, since someone would have to wear flesh in order to return the mirror once it was found.

Anderson hoped that Miss Ravenmoor was as sure of herself as she had sounded in the warmth and comfort of Elemental Cottage. In truth, he was more concerned at the moment for her emotional state, as it was clear the return to the place of her death had distressed her terribly.

'Miss Ravenmoor.' His voice sounded loud to him in the silence, though of course no one else would have heard it had there been anyone other than ghosts and the strange Mr Ferris, who seemed quite at home in the company of spirits, though clearly he walked among the living. He was far more agile and resilient than his appearance would have suggested, and not for the first time, Anderson wondered just what strange magic the man practised that he moved with such ease through all manner of circumstances, as though none affected him.

'Miss Ravenmoor, you must not agonise so,' Anderson said. 'What is done is done, and all of us who have passed beyond the gate into death have felt as you do, but there is no undoing what fate has dealt us. Now please, do lead us to the mirror, or others who now live may be joining us to our great sorrow.'

That others might suffer a similar fate seemed to calm the little ghost somewhat. She made a show of wiping tears that no longer needed to be wiped, caught her breath that no longer need to be caught, and took in her surroundings. She pointed. 'I fell from up there.'

'Are you sure?' Fiori asked.

'Of course I'm sure. I hung around close to my body for a long time.' She shivered. 'It was horrible seeing myself that way, but I couldn't bring myself to leave, so I hung around until Mountain Rescue came, until Tim came to take it away. It felt like I was here in this horrible place forever, surrounded by this dark wood, cold and wet, watching my own blood seep into the ground like rainwater.

'And the mirror. How he roared when he knew the mirror was lost to him. He could have hurt me.' Her countenance darkened and her fists clenched. 'He could have hurt me much more after I was dead. I didn't know that at the time. Of course, I thought once I died it would all be over. I thought my suffering would end. I was so stupid. So terribly stupid.'

'Miss Ravenmoor, please.' Anderson interrupted her reverie. 'However sympathetic my heart is toward your suffering, and I assure you it is and always has been, others will suffer far worse fates if we cannot find a way to end Deacon's reign of terror, and much of our solution may depend on you and the salvaging of your lost mirror. Now please, dear woman. I beg you.'

She blinked and looked around her again. There was another superfluous wiping of eyes and sniffing of nose. 'Yes, of course. I'm sorry. Bad memories of this place, you understand?'

'Having fallen to my own death, my dear Miss Ravenmoor, I do indeed understand,' Anderson said. 'It was long before I could go to that place without distress.'

She stepped slightly to one side of the trail where the water of a streamlet ran sluggishly and would no doubt be frozen by morning. And there in the flow, as though it had only just fallen, was her mirror, clearly protected by powerful magic, for Anderson would have no doubt seen it had it not been so. He was certain it was magic she had only possessed under the stress of her imminent death.

'It had to be hidden in the stream,' she said. 'A reflection of a reflection. Just like from the book of shadows.' She shivered despite having no flesh to feel the cold and wrapped her arms tightly around herself. 'A reflection of a reflection,' she repeated. 'Even then I knew that. Even then I understood but I don't know how.'

'May I have the honour, madame?' Mr Ferris asked.

Serina nodded and stepped back. It was as though, now that she beheld the mirror with her own eyes, lying there in its sheath of strong magic, it had become an object of disgust to her.

The man walked in a circle three times widdershins, three times counter to the clock, each time stepping over the stream, careful that his feet did not disturb the water. The magic the man performed now was magic of great importance at this moment, for he was about to touch an object of power, an object that did not belong to him, an object coveted by a very powerful demon.

It was not an enviable task, nor a task to be undertaken lightly. From his trousers Mr Ferris took a silver-handled knife, opened the blade and cut a quick, efficient gash across his left palm. Serina caught her breath and whimpered, then moved closer to Anderson.

As the cut in his palm ribboned crimson, he held it just above the surface of the water that barely covered the glass of the mirror and let the droplets fall into the flow.

Though Anderson had thought the night silent before, even death had not been so silent in its first moments upon him as when blood mixed with water over the surface of the long-submerged mirror. And then the sound of the water shivering over the rocks rose eerily, and a breeze blew through the high branches of the trees, then swirled down around the one living man, lifting his pale hair until it danced with a life of its own around the cap of his skull. The very trees themselves seemed

155

to hold back the thickest of the darkness, as though they caged something powerful, something ravenous, something waiting to pounce.

Anderson struggled to focus. This was not the first time powerful magic had held darker forces at bay. This was not the first time the truth had been veiled to protect the innocent. Next to Anderson, Serina now sobbed openly, and there seemed little need to silence her in the realm of the dead, in the space in between. No one listened to the tearful cries of a dead woman in a place where everyone mourned what had been lost.

Only Mr Ferris was a reminder that the world still lived and breathed and found cause to celebrate and love. Mr Ferris breathed living words, which were no longer silent, into the chilled night air. They were strange words, words Anderson did not understand. Words he was not entirely sure he ever wanted to understand.

Then the man removed a square of black silk from the pocket of his coat and shook it out. Still chanting, he straddled the stream, still careful that his feet did not touch the flow. And with the very corner of the cloth, he reached into the shallow water and extricated the mirror by the very tip of its handle. For the briefest of seconds, the wind rose to a deafening howl, and the water gave up the mirror with a roiling sizzle and a blinding flash of light, sights and sounds that none would have heard in the land of the living. Nor could any who lived have smelled the scent of ozone, which permeated the air as Mr Ferris wrapped the mirror in black silk, careful to hold it face down, careful not to touch it with bare flesh. The smothering weight of the silk deadened the feel of the magic so the mirror could be safely transported. By that time, amazingly, the cut on his palm had sealed itself, and the night was once again calm and ordinary. Somewhere close by, a tawny owl called.

Fiori was the first to heave a sigh of relief. 'Good. Now let's get the fuck out of here!' She turned down the trail and called over her shoulder. 'Anderson, you and Serina go on home, tell the others we have it.'

'My dear Fiori,' Anderson said, 'I think that under the circumstances, it is better that we all stay together.' Fiori gave no argument.

Anderson felt his heart swell at the sight of Cassandra, seated on the floor of the library, the fire long gone out, still perusing her pile of books, as she had been when he'd pulled her away to tell her goodbye. On the floor next to her, curled under the blanket from the chair, Alice slept soundly, and he smiled to himself, knowing what had happened as surely as if he had been here, knowing the poor woman's need, and knowing his beautiful Cassandra's compassion. He watched her for a long moment. Her lust for knowledge was nearly as enthralling to him as her lust for the pleasures of the flesh. She was stunning in her vulnerability, vulnerability belying the power of a goddess, power that many would give their lives for, and yet she wore it uncomfortably, cautiously, and more exquisitely than she could possibly have realised. He watched her until he could stand the space between them no longer, then he spoke.

'You have not been truthful with me, Cassandra Larkin. I have just returned from your room where I found your bed empty and cold.'

She smiled up at him. 'I didn't hear you come in.'

'Indeed you did not. Imagine my disappointment at not receiving the reward for which I have endured a cold night on the fell to bring back the prize.'

'Then you found the mirror?'

'It is safe within the walls of Elemental Cottage, my love.' Before she could stand and move into his arms, he seated himself on the floor behind her, legs spread on either side of her. His erection pressed hard against the small of her back as he scooted in close, running his hands up under the cashmere top to cup her full bosom, relishing the feel of her. She caught her breath and arched back into his embrace, so that his mouth found the hollow of her throat.

He slipped a hand up under her skirt over the solid

muscles of her thighs and found that she wore no undergarments. She shifted and grunted softly, opening herself so his fingers found purchase, first against the soft, golden nest covering her mound, and then in between the burgeoning folds of her womanhood to the warm, moist core of her sex. 'Oh my love, you are in need, as am I. I am full with the weight of my lust for you. But even now, I hear clattering in the kitchen. Our dear Fiori will not have it, the two of us missing breakfast after our night of magic and your night of –' he nipped her neck then nodded toward the sleeping Alice '– your night of magic. I fear we will have to manage with a quickie.'

She pulled away from him long enough to reposition herself and help him open his trousers and ease them down far enough that his manhood was free and anxious for her. Then she lifted her skirt, giving him just the tiniest, most exquisite glimpse of her glistening sex before she settled onto his lap, sheathed his member with delicious ease, and wrapped her legs around him.

'Take from me, but a little, my love,' he grunted, as she began to rock against him. 'It will be our secret, and it will make me stiffen in my trousers as I sit next to you eating Fiori's fine breakfast, and everyone will smell your delicious sex all over me, and they shall all long for you to take from them as you have from me. They shall all long to be the chosen lover of the succubus.'

He covered her mouth with a probing kiss, letting his tongue and his lips swallow back her protests, and when she relaxed against his mouth, he spoke. 'For that is what you are, my beautiful Cassandra. You are a succubus, a creature of exquisite, terrible and beautiful magic, and I long with all of my heart to be enthralled by you.'

The feel of her soft laughter against his mouth was ecstasy almost beyond words, and the deep pall of the night vanished in the sound of it, in the taste of it. And in her magic, he felt as though he were walking on a rain-washed fell in the sunrise.

'I'm not keen on facing Fiori's wrath if we're late to the breakfast table,' she said, 'So I'll only enthral you a little bit this time. She bit his bottom lip, then his throat, and his member surged almost beyond control at the pure wonder of her. 'It'll be a quickie, succubus style.'

And her womanhood tightened around him like a glove, and she surrounded him with such delight that he scarce could remember his own name, and it mattered not. It mattered not.

It was the trembling of her sex around him, and the shimmer of her power as she took her release that sent him tumbling to his, and he knew that if he were not already dead, he would happily die in the ecstasy of her love.

'I am undone, dear woman,' he whispered in his convulsions of lust. 'Each time you take me I am undone with such pleasure as I have never known.'

'That's my magic, Anderson. I undo people. Just like it says on the label.' She nodded to the pile of books on the floor.

He pulled her to him with such fierceness that she gave a little gasp. 'It is much more than that, my darling, and you know this to be true, as do I. It is so much more.'

When he pulled away this time, there were tears in her eyes, and his heart felt like it would burst from the sight of her so. 'I wish I didn't know what I know,' she whispered as he pulled her tight against him. 'And even still I need to know more.'

There was so much he wanted to say to her, so much he wanted her to say to him, but Sky knocked softly on the frame of the door.

'I'm sorry to interrupt, but breakfast is served and we all need to eat. There's lots to be done.'

The commotion woke Alice, who had slept through their lovemaking, and she hurried upstairs to dress while Anderson and Cassandra tidied and tucked as best they could, offering each other furtive smiles as lovers do when they share such secrets as their flesh allows them.

* * *

Tara refused to even examine Serina's mirror until they were all safe inside a circle of power, especially after hearing of the mirror's retrieval over breakfast. It had already been placed on the altar in the Room of Reflection and everyone was given until midday to prepare themselves, as midday would be the time of seeing most clearly.

That suited Cassandra just fine. When they would be dealing with two gruesome objects of power – Marie Warren's shattered, bloodied amulet and Serina's scrying mirror – she'd rather do it in as much daylight as possible. It also gave her time for a little more research. Anderson had not come to her since before breakfast, but she was sure he had his own preparations to make for the magic that lay ahead of them. She knew that next to Tara he was the most senior witch of the coven. She didn't know what her role would be. What did a succubus do in a magic circle? It was Sky who gave her the answer to that question.

She had just showered and was sitting wrapped in a towel, trying to comb the tangles from her hair, when the ghost knocked softly and entered. She held up a robe the colour of the sky at dawn. 'This is mine,' she said, motioning Cassandra into the robe. 'It was always one of my favourites, and it's fitting that the new Guardian of the East and of the Air should wear it.'

'What?' Cassandra tried to pull away but Sky held her, then settled her onto the edge of the bed and sat down next to her.

'I've been dead a long time, Cassandra, much longer than Fiori, though not nearly as long as Anderson.' She offered an apologetic smile. 'They both wear the flesh much better than I do. I've stayed among the living because Tara needs me, and I'll stay as long as she still does. But the quarters should be presided over by the living whenever possible.

'Marie's now Guardian of the West. That quarter was empty a long time before she joined us. She replaced Rayna, another one of our tragic losses to Deacon. Fiori still presides over the South, and Tara, as you can well imagine, is the

Guardian of the North. As long as I've known Anderson, he's watched over the Great Realm of Below, and Tim Meriwether now watches over all that's Above. It's clear to me, as it is to everyone else, anyone who rides the Ether as easily as you do is a fitting Guardian for the East, and it's time I gave it over.'

Sky leaned in and kissed Cassandra. Then she smoothed her damp hair away from her face and offered a smile. 'Oh, I know you haven't agreed to stay at Elemental Cottage yet, and you do have Storm Croft, but since you never stay there anyway … well, a girl needs a home, doesn't she?'

A girl needs a home. Cassandra felt the muscles in her throat tighten and ache. A girl needs a home. In all these years, she had never thought about a home, never thought about a place to settle, a place to belong. Somehow she had pushed it all away until now.

Sky's smile was suddenly tight, as though it bordered on tears. She squared her shoulders and offered a satisfied nod. 'And once Deacon is bound and all is safe, then I think I'll take a holiday. Somewhere really warm would be nice.'

For the first time, Cassandra had a feeling of just how tired Sky really was, and it was nothing a good night's sleep would ever be able to fix.

'You haven't even asked if I know what to do,' Cassandra said, when she could think of nothing else to say to her. 'If I know how to call the quarters and hold the magic.'

Sky gave her a hug as though she were a child who had just said something cute or precocious. 'I knew your grandmother. She would have never let you get away with not knowing how to call the quarters and hold the energy.'

Before she could respond, there was another soft knock on the door and Anderson stepped inside, dressed in a dove-grey robe, the first time Cassandra had seen him in anything other than the black suit. She felt the warm tumble of her insides at the sight of him, at the way his eyes took her in. The spark of his energy still lay against her skin and inside her body because she had taken from him, and because she had taken only a little he was marked as hers, marked with her magic, and through the eyes of a succubus, her mark veiled him from head to toe. Her insides tumbled again that such a powerful witch, such a powerful man should be so willing to wear her mark.

His smile was fleeting, but it was enough, then the look on his face became serious. 'The Room of Reflection is ready.'

Cassandra was a little surprised to find everyone in the room as she took up her position in the circle at the East. She had expected only the members of the Elemental Coven. It was as though Tara had read her thoughts. 'I wanted all of you inside the circle where it's safe when we unwrap the two mirrors,' she said. 'Besides, there may be questions, and each person here holds a piece of the puzzle that no one else may hold. I want nothing missing, I want nothing to keep us from understanding if and how these two mirrors may help us.'

Ferris stood to Cassandra's left and Sky to her right. Alice stood next to Fiori, and Serina, who had been given flesh for the duration of the magic, stood next to Marie, fidgeting from foot to foot. Anderson and Tim stood on either side of Tara, who stood at the head of the circle in the Quarter of the North.

It was Cassandra who began the ritual, and even though she had never participated in magic as a part of the Elemental Coven, she knew what to do as well as she knew her own breath. As the sun rises in the east, so is it in the east where the casting of the circle of power begins. Cassandra called forth the powers of the East and of Air and of intellect and of the mind newly opened. She felt the energy surge through her and hold firmly just below her breastbone where her ribs came together.

Then Fiori called the powers of the South and of Fire, then Marie the powers of the West and Water. Finally, Tara called the powers of the North and of Earth and of the dream time and the time before beginning. All of the strands of energy wove the circle from heart to heart, from head to head, then expanded and stretched and connected Above and Below, to the strands of power Tim and Anderson held until the circle became a bubble of power and energy, a safe place for magic, strong magic, to be performed and held.

The space effervesced and tingled with energy and potential that played over the skin and pulsated deep into the marrow. Cassandra's pulse quickened at the powerful pull of so much magic in one place, at the excitement she had not experienced since she'd stood with her grandmother's coven and felt the calling of the quarters, the gathering of the energies.

On the altar at the centre of the room lay the mirror and the amulet, both still wrapped in black silk, and even so, the air above the altar shimmered like heat waves rising from the desert.

Tara, herself dressed in black silk, addressed the circle. 'What we're about to do now is not formal magic. In fact, we're making up the spell as we go along. That means if anyone has anything to say, say it. It might make the difference as to whether the spell works or not. And we can't afford for the spell not to work.'

Then she turned, with Anderson and Tim flanking her, and opened the silk on the mirror and the shattered mirror of the amulet, taking care not to touch either. Cassandra felt a sudden ache along her jawbone and up behind her ears. No one in the circle looked particularly comfortable. Then Tara beckoned Marie and Serina forward. Both women looked like they'd rather be just about anywhere else, and Cassandra certainly couldn't blame them.

Tara spoke. 'These objects belong to the two of you and I'm assuming they have never been touched by another.

'It was my amulet,' Marie said. 'Everyone within the coven has touched it as we've bonded, just like I have theirs, but no one beyond the circle, and even Deacon didn't touch it. He crushed it in my hand.'

'Then it should be safe for any coven member to touch,' Tara said.

Though Cassandra was pretty sure no coven member wanted to.

Tara turned her attention to Serina, whose gaze darted

from her mirror to Marie. 'Other than me, she's the only one who ever touched it, and that touch released Deacon into the world.'

'I shouldn't have touched it,' Marie said. 'I didn't know at the time, but it made me feel ill, it creeped me out.' She chafed her arms.

Cassandra didn't think Marie looked particularly well at the moment, as she looked down at the mirror. That was certainly understandable.

'He mentioned several times that just because I'd released him, I shouldn't think I could return him the same way. And then he lied to me in the end. He told me he'd destroyed Serina's mirror,' Marie said.

'Then we shall assume he really did fear you could return him with it,' Tara said. She nodded toward it. 'Marie, I'm going to ask you to touch it. With the magic Ferris has done to it, you should be fine, though you might feel slightly nauseated at the first touch.' She laid a hand on Marie's shoulder. 'My guess is that you would have been fine anyway. My guess is that for some reason you're already attuned to Serina's mirror.'

'I don't see how that could be,' Serina said. 'I bought it at a car boot sale, and then I went through all the rituals to cleanse it and attune it to my touch.'

'I don't know how it can be either,' Tara said, 'but if I'm not mistaken, that's how it is.'

Marie, who was nervous enough, didn't wait any longer. She no doubt wanted to get it over with, Cassandra thought. She gripped the mirror by the handle and lifted it, face down. Cassandra was pretty sure everyone, including her, was holding their breath. Marie swayed slightly and both Tim and Anderson stepped forward protectively. Then she braced herself and lifted it. 'It's heavy,' she breathed. 'A lot heavier than I remember it.'

'It's not heavy,' Serina said. 'It weighs what you'd expect an ordinary mirror to weigh.'

'Marie's right,' Ferris spoke up. 'I also thought it very

heavy for such a dainty mirror.'

'Give me that,' Serina grabbed the mirror away from Marie. There was a sharp sizzling sound accompanied by the smell of ozone, and Serina yelped and dropped it as though she had been burned.

The collective gasp of the others in the circle was swallowed up in Serina's shriek. 'Oh Goddess, oh mother! There's not any place I'm safe from him, even in death!' She turned and practically knocked Marie over heading for the door, but Fiori and Alice stopped her, and held her as she sobbed into Fiori's shoulder.

Cassandra wasn't sure why she did it. In some ways it was almost as though she watched herself from outside, looking down on herself as she moved into the centre of the circle and knelt over the mirror, which had landed face up. For a second the pull of it was dizzying, and a wave of vertigo rolled over her, as though she were standing on a precipice about to fall.

'His face,' Serina wailed. 'I still see his face!'

Bracing herself, Cassandra leaned over and felt a strong wind from the depths of the space that opened just below the surface of the mirror. 'It's the void,' she breathed.

'What?' Tara and Anderson spoke in unison, and both knelt next to her.

'Goddess!' Tara said.

'Fuck,' Tim whispered.

Cassandra couldn't understand what Anderson said. It wasn't English. But she was pretty sure she could agree with the sentiment.

'His face,' Serina wailed. 'I swear it was his face.'

'It's only holding the last memory of the person who possessed it,' Fiori said, patting the woman gently on the back. 'He's not really there.'

Tara reached for the piece of silk to cover it again, but Cassandra stayed her hand. 'Wait!'

She leaned over as far as she could and stared hard into the emptiness, her fingers gripping the edge of the altar. Even though logic told her she couldn't fall into the mirror, the

165

tingle of her instincts told her otherwise. 'It's not the whole Ether,' Cassandra said. 'It's like someone captured a piece of the Ether inside the mirror.'

'How can that be?' Marie asked.

'We return from the void with small fragments of it each time we ride,' Anderson said. 'It would not seem possible, since it is not our physical self we send into the void, but it happens. Never is cleansing after magic more important than when one visits the void.'

'Do you suppose that someone has collected these pieces of the Ether, then, and captured them in the mirror?' Ferris asked, straining from his position in an effort to get a view down into the mirror.

'That would be a feasible supposition,' Anderson said. 'In fact, quite likely, as a part of our binding of Deacon involved just such a prison, a place set apart within the Ether, which I myself discovered. This space was a part of, and yet separate from, the void. When Tara and I were both certain that there was no escape from that place, that it would be an adequate prison for Deacon, then we set about enticing him there and trapping him within. I confess I had never before, nor since, come upon such a device in the Ether, but desperate times, as the saying goes, call for desperate measures. And the prison did, indeed, hold the demon. Although I do not see how there could have been an outlet into the World of Flesh through Miss Ravenmoor's mirror. Perhaps this device with the mirror is for a different purpose.'

Cassandra blinked and settled back on her haunches, fighting dizziness. 'No, it's a prison, and it must be the same one because –' She looked up at Anderson '– your energy is all over it.' There was a murmur of surprise around the room.

Anderson squatted next to her. 'How the prison could be connected to the mirror I do not know, for Tara and I were certain there was no means of escape once we sealed the only entrance.'

'If I were to venture a guess,' Tara said, 'whoever's responsible for the creation of the prison may have used the mirror as a magical way of monitoring the prisoner, though, sadly, they also created the means for his escape.'

'Wait a minute,' Serina said, now easing toward the place where the mirror lay on the floor. 'I saw Deacon's reflection in the mirror. I saw what he really looked like. I never got any indication that he was trapped there.'

'That's because you didn't shut the door,' Marie said, and then a shudder ran up her spine as though she had just awoken from a nightmare. 'I opened it at the psychic fair, back when I had no idea what I was doing, and you didn't close it when you jumped to your death, Serina, because you didn't know either.'

'But Serina just said she found it at a car boot sale,' Tim said. 'Whoever was supposed to be keeping an eye on Deacon was pretty careless with something so dangerous.'

'On the other hand,' Sky added, 'if it were not intended for Deacon, perhaps whoever it belonged to felt no further need to keep it safe.'

'It didn't come with an instruction manual,' Serina said. 'It was just a car boot sale. There were worthless trinkets, old paperback novels and some old videos and DVDs, nothing of any consequence really. I almost overlooked it.'

'But you didn't,' Fiori said. 'I don't think you weren't meant to.'

Cassandra shivered. 'Or is it possible that whoever the mirror belonged to wanted Deacon to be released? Goddess, that doesn't bear thinking about.'

'That explains why Deacon wanted it destroyed,' Marie said. She took a pinch of salt from the pot on the altar and let it fall onto the mirror. It sank like a rock dropped from a high place and disappeared into the void.

'Marie,' Tara said. 'Take your old amulet and hold it over the top of the mirror.'

Marie did as she was asked. The amulet had been secured in a thin piece of what looked like black bridal veil, which held all the broken fragments together. Cassandra didn't miss the trembling of the American's hands. But then she couldn't really imagine anyone not trembling under the circumstances.

What happened next caused a tremor to pass through the whole of the circle as though a filament of a spider's web had been plucked. The void in the face of the mirror vanished and all that remained was the reflection of Marie's destroyed amulet and the astonished faces of those looking into it.

'Great Goddess,' Tara whispered. 'You were both his liberator and his possible captor, Marie. And you,' she turned her attention to Serina, 'You were caught in the middle.'

'It feels lighter now,' Marie said, folding it back into the black silk. 'Just like an ordinary mirror.'

Once both objects were safely wrapped and placed back on the altar, Tara sprinkled a circle of salt around them. For a long time, she stood staring down at the black packets, which now seemed innocuous. Then she spoke. 'We have our prison. We have the perfect trap, a trap that seems to be designed especially to contain someone like Deacon. Now all we've got to do is figure out a way to get him back into that prison.'

Chapter Sixteen

ALICE WAS RESTLESS. SHE felt like her skin would crawl off her body. She wanted – no, she *needed* – to spend time with Cassandra. Being in Cassandra's presence made her feel at least a little bit more sane in the midst of this nightmare. But Cassandra had gone somewhere with Tara and Ferris. She didn't know where, and no one would give her a straight answer. Strange that she felt the woman's absence so. It was just the comfort of her. She was the only one who made Alice feel like she might survive Deacon and maybe even live a normal life again some day. Of course, that was if any of them survived Deacon. Serina Ravenmoor hadn't. Sky and Fiori hadn't. Tara's husband and sister hadn't. She shivered at the thought.

Anderson was in the Room of Reflection with Tim and Marie, trying to learn more about that horrible scrying mirror. The door was shut, the circle cast, and the room was off limits. Not that she wanted to be in there with that awful mirror and the broken, bloody amulet that had trapped Deacon. Jesus! Who would keep such creepy things? Sky and Fiori were in the library, Sky on her laptop while Fiori had taken up Cassandra's spot by the fireplace amid a stack of books. Even Serina Ravenmoor, who was still in the flesh, sat demurely on the settee, wrapped in an oversized robe that one of the witches had lent her and surrounded by several books on demons.

Alice was the only one who had nothing to do. Hell, her understanding of the Wiccan world, up until Deacon wrecked her life, had come from popular fiction and books she'd bought from the local mind, body, spirit shop. The thought made her angry. No one had prepared her for this. She had no skills for this. If she had a latent talent for – what was it they called it – riding the Ether, well, she sure as hell had no desire to pursue it. Who would want to go to such a horrible place on purpose? She would never have the skills for this. She wished she didn't know any of what she knew, she wished that she had never met these people – any of them!

She grabbed her jacket from the peg by the door and went outside to get some fresh air, but not before she was warned, like some ignorant child being told not to play in the street, that the protection spells extended only to the edge of the property and not to stray beyond it if she wanted to stay safe. Safe? What the hell was safe anyway? Last night, when she was in Cassandra's arms, that was safe. That was bliss. Damn it! If only Cassandra had taken more from her. She would have gladly let the succubus drain her dry if only not to feel this way, if only not to want Deacon so badly, while at the same time being so afraid of him that the very thought practically made her ill.

The protection spell went as far as the crossroads. She knew that from the destruction of Cassandra's books and Ferris's SUV. But strolling around the property wasn't much of a walk for someone who was used to long hikes on the fells every day. It was nothing, really, and she was itching for just a little more. She knew that Tim Meriwether's Lacewing Farm joined the property of Elemental Cottage at some point, and that Lacewing Farm had been as heavily magicked with protection spells as Elemental Cottage. That would give her a little more of a walk.

Alice was not a reckless person, so it made no sense under the circumstances that she would even be brave enough to leave the house. It made no sense that she would even be brave enough to come out of her locked bedroom in the heart of Elemental Cottage. And if her head had been clear, if she hadn't felt like insects were crawling over her with barbed feet, if she hadn't felt like someone had stuffed her head full of hot coals, she would have never done anything so foolish. But when she got to the boundary of the property, she just kept walking. After all, it wasn't terribly far to her bungalow. It would be a good walk, and she'd just pick up her car and drive back before anyone missed her.

It all happened so fast that she barely remembered doing it until she found herself walking along the River Derwent almost to Rosthwaite, almost to her bungalow. She felt light, almost euphoric. What had she been afraid of? It felt so good to be free of all that heavy oppressive magic. She felt as though she would suffocate under the weight of the protection spells and banishing spells and who knew what other kind of spells that surrounded Elemental Cottage. It was only Cassandra wrapped around her body, comforting her, making love to her, taking from her that made the whole dismal place bearable. How had she not seen that before? Elemental Cottage was a horrible place, a place keeping her from her home, a place keeping her from her life, a place keeping her from something ... something important.

Inside her house, she dressed in her best black jeans, the really tight ones, and a blouse that showed lots of cleavage, especially when she wore no bra. She would have put on lipstick and a bit of make-up, but her bag was over at Elemental Cottage. Well, she'd pick it up tomorrow, thank the witches for all their help, and move back into her lovely bungalow where she belonged.

Once she was dressed, she found the spare car keys and hopped in her car. She really didn't need to go back to Elemental Cottage now. All was well. She was fine. She didn't need their protection. What she needed was a quick drive up Honister Pass and a short walk around in the fresh air. If she hurried, she could almost make it before darkness fell. Then, when she got back ... She couldn't actually imagine what would happen when she got back ... if she ever came back. She didn't have to if she didn't want to, she told herself.

It had just begun to snow when she started the steep,

narrow ascent over Honister Pass, thinking of Cassandra, thinking of what it felt like to have the succubus take from her. She was rocking and shifting her bottom against the vibrations the motor made on the seat when there was a sharp crack of pain up the back of her neck and Deacon's voice filled her head. 'You are such a little whore, my darling.'

She yelped out loud, and the car spun out of control.

'We could have walked it easily enough,' Tara said, as she and Cassandra and Ferris climbed out of her Land Rover near the top of the treeless hill. The stone wall had crumbled, and the stone had clearly been cannibalised, a long time ago from the looks of it, for other building projects. There was a gap of about 15 feet opening the two properties on to one another before the stone wall abruptly began again then continued down the other side of the hill and disappeared into the scrub below. 'I know it's just a psychological thing,' Tara said, as she looked out over the fells, then back at her vehicle, 'but I don't like being this close to his body without a quick means of escape.'

Cassandra shivered at the feel of magic within the gap in the wall – magic so strong it made her jaw ache, magic that overlaid something dark and sinister. There was no visible mark on the earth now. There had been no stones erected, no marker whatsoever to delineate the place where Tara and Sky had buried Deacon's incorruptible body eight months ago. Anyone who walked this spot would never know, and yet, she wondered, how could they possibly walk over such a spot and not feel a shudder?

'We never thought he might be able to escape into the Ether, or at least a part of him, enough of him to do damage,' Tara said, looking down at the ground, which held its sinister secret. 'The body was incorruptible. It should have been the perfect prison for him. He shouldn't have been able to leave it. He couldn't go into the spirit world as he'd been able to do as a ghost. In essence, the demon that joined with Deacon all those years ago created his own prison with his perverted

172

version of the enfleshment spell.'

'But the Ether is neither flesh nor spirit,' Cassandra said. 'And who can say what a demon really is?'

Tara nodded. 'The best we can tell is that the magic Marie and Tim used did trap Deacon in his body in the beginning, but Deacon is endlessly resourceful, and we basically left him with nothing but time on his hands.'

'And he found a way into the Ether,' Cassandra said.

Again, Tara nodded. 'And from there, he can affect some situations, he can do enough damage, assert enough control to get attention, to cause pain and suffering. From there he could bide his time until he found a way out.'

'And that's when he discovered me,' Cassandra said.

'I think it more likely that he always knew about you. Certainly he would have suspected, if he knew your father, as he said he did. But you gave him something extra to use when you shanghaied Anderson into the Ether. You gave him not only the means for escape he already expected you could be, but also a way to get back at me – a strong connection to the Elemental Coven.'

Tara walked a wide circle around the site, then she spoke again. 'Ultimately, he needs this body to interact with the living in any way more potent than driving a few vulnerable people nuts and destroying a few riders of the Ether who get too close. Just for fun. That being the case, this is where he'll want you to bring him, Cassandra. It's the boundary between Lacewing Farm and Elemental property. Because it joins the properties of witches, it's a particularly strong, particularly safe area for such an unnatural grave. But none of that will matter if he makes it back to this spot. If, somehow, he's returned to this spot, there'll be no stopping his enfleshment, and it'll be as though nothing had happened to him, as though his body had only been sleeping. The body's not flesh and blood. It shouldn't even exist in the natural world.'

Cassandra chafed her arms as the first snowflakes fell and began to stick to her hair. 'I won't bring him here. I'll die in the Ether with him before I do that.'

173

Tara took a step closer to her. 'Believe me, if we can find another way, we will.'

Cassandra looked down at the snowflakes falling and melting on the unmarked grave. 'There is no other way. You don't have to cheer me up, Tara. We both know there's no other way. If you'd thought there was, you wouldn't have brought me here.'

'You asked me to bring you,' the coven leader said.

'I need to know where not to bring my hitchhiker when I return from the Ether.'

Tara studied her for a long moment, so long that Cassandra began to feel uncomfortable. 'The decision hasn't been made yet. At the moment, we have time, and I plan to take every second we have.'

'Perhaps Anderson and the couple from Lacewing Farm will find something out about the scrying mirror that will help us,' Ferris said. And once more Cassandra was reminded of just how easily the man could make his presence forgotten.

'It's a prison,' Cassandra said. 'The scrying mirror is a prison, nothing more. It won't do us any good until we can get our prisoner there.'

Alice had barely regained control of the car before it went off the steep edge of the road. She sat with her heart racing and her head resting against the steering wheel, trying to stop shaking.

'I am not surprised that you would long to experience the embrace of a succubus.' Deacon spoke as though nothing out of the ordinary had happened, as though they had just met at the coffee shop for a cuppa and a chinwag. 'I have heard few can refuse such powerful lust. Did you like it, my darling?' He whispered close to her ear. 'Did you like the way the succubus lapped at your cunt like a starving dog? Did it give you pleasure to be so used? I knew that in the end, so deep is your debauchery that even a succubus, especially one with such a tender conscience as our Cassandra seems to have, would never be enough for you.'

He spoke using her voice, using her mouth for that which he did not have, and when she was herself, she knew how much he loved making her vocalise the depths of her depravity, depravity she hadn't known she had. He took pleasure in embarrassing her, humiliating her by making her speak words she could barely even bring herself to think, making her speak them out loud as though they were her own words formed from her own thoughts, and then he made her believe that, indeed, they were straight from her very soul.

She didn't know when it had happened, but she had eased the car on to the road again and found herself once more ascending Honister Pass, with Deacon so close to her that she felt almost as though he caressed her, almost as though he had wrapped himself around her. 'I have something planned for you,' he said. 'Something far better than letting a weak-willed succubus sniff at your gash.'

And the whole of his plan appeared in her head as though it were her own plan, as though she wanted nothing so desperately, and even as it sickened her, it aroused her. Had she really always been this depraved? Had Deacon only brought out that horrid side of what was already there? The man she was to meet lived in Cockermouth. She knew exactly which pub he would be in, knew that he'd be hunched over his pint and his copy of the *Telegraph*. And she knew he liked pain.

'He likes it very much indeed,' she was saying out loud, or rather Deacon was saying it through her lips. 'He will completely delight us, my love. He is utterly insatiable. None of those he has rutted with have ever satisfied the depths of his perversion. They are always frightened by his demands, when he is brave enough to ask, which he seldom is. Can you imagine such a thing, my dear woman? Afraid of a little pain? But you aren't afraid of pain, are you, Alice? You are not squeamish, no matter how debased one's pleasures are. Together, we shall give the dear man exquisite pain, pain he has never imagined he could feel. And you, my darling Alice, such a release his pain shall give you, a release as you have yet not known.'

Alice's stomach clenched tight, and for a moment she thought she'd be sick. She knew what she would do to the man, and she knew there would be no turning back. Even as the horror of it filled her, and her stomach roiled, her pussy felt heavy and needy.

With the snow worsening, she quickly pulled into the deserted car park at the Honister Slate Mine. She needed some air. Dear Goddess, she needed some air. She threw open the car door and practically fell out onto the pavement, grabbing the side mirror to steady herself as the world spun around her and nausea clawed at her insides.

'Do not you worry, my love, the place where you shall take him is deserted,' she heard Deacon saying, or was she saying it out loud in the howling wind? 'And this one always carries a knife. He will be pleased to let you use it on him in this place. No one will find you there, and you can take your pleasure without fear of interruption. It will be as though you are avenging yourself on your letch of a husband. Or, you may imagine that you are the succubus draining away his life force to give you pleasure. Does that thought not make your cunt wet, my darling? Of course it does. Oh, how you shall delight in punishing this one. I think that perhaps he even resembles your ex-husband a little. And when you are done with him … Well, what happens when you are done with him is of no consequence, is it? Oh, do not worry so, Alice. He shall not be easily found in the place I have chosen for your little tryst. Only you and I shall know. It will be our little secret.'

Just when she was certain she would vomit, the cold clean wind cleared her head, and her stomach settled. She could make out the pale halos of the security lights at the tourist entrance to the gift shop. Beyond that, she knew, was the path that led to the dismantled tramway line, then out on to Moses Trod, out across the desolate, high, open space of Fleetwith Pike.

After her divorce, she had moved to the Lake District

intent upon exploring it on foot, and this area, because of its history of slate mining and legends of whisky smuggling, had fascinated her in particular. She zipped her jacket. For a second, her mind was her own, if only for the briefest moment. But it was enough. From the boot of her car, she took out her walking boots and slipped into them. If she were going to go to Cockermouth and do this horrid thing, she would not do it without a walk first. A very long walk without a compass. For a second, she felt a deep sense of empathy with Serina Ravenmoor. Now she understood completely why the woman had done what she did.

'Anderson,' Marie called. 'You've been in there long enough. You're making me nervous. Come out now – I mean it.'

Anderson gave one last glance around and returned to the Room of Reflection. Marie jumped and Tim cursed under his breath as he materialised in between them. 'There truly is no way out,' said Anderson. 'I do not understand how we entered into this place from the void, and yet I have no doubt that this is the very space in which Deacon was confined, for it contains the magical imprint of our energy, Tara's and mine. And, of course, the energy of the demon is also within.'

'Jesus,' Tim cursed. 'That's creepy. And the seal?'

'The reflection of a reflection,' Marie said, clenching her amulet in her fist – not the ruined one, but the one she now wore around her neck.' To prove her point, she moved the ruined amulet above the surface of the mirror. The void vanished and the surface looked, for all purposes, just like the surface of any ordinary mirror.

'What's it like in there?' Tim asked.

'It is just like the void, my dear man,' Anderson said. 'Nay, it *is* the void, or at least a small portion of it, captured somehow by magic that is beyond anything of which I have understanding. However, the space within the mirror is finite – I would guess it to be no larger than our Room of Reflection. In every other way, though, it is the void. If either of you would like to view the inside, I can instruct you in a simple spell that will allow your fetch to pass through.'

They both shook their heads.

Anderson chuckled softly. 'Though I was attempting to be polite and meant the offer as a kindness, I do indeed understand your lack of desire to venture inside. There are more pleasant places in which to entertain oneself and one's friends. And now there is one more thing I should like to try, and I will need your help, my dear Marie.'

'No,' Marie said.

Anderson raised an eyebrow. 'I believe it is customary to at least listen politely to the request.'

'I know what you want,' she said, clutching her amulet with a white-knuckled grip. 'And the answer is no. I won't lock you inside.'

'Fuck! You want her to lock you in?' Tim said, shaking his head violently.

'Only for a brief time. I only desire to test our theory.'

'No.' This time both Marie and Tim said it in unison.

'We can't be certain that I can unlock it once someone's inside,' Marie said. 'For all we know, it's designed to stay locked once it's received its prisoner.'

Anderson studied the mirror with his arms folded across his chest. 'I suppose that is possible, but I consider it highly unlikely, since you were clearly able to open it with no trouble, nay, without even knowing what you had done. So, my dear Marie, I believe your power would be much stronger when working in tandem with your will'

'No,' she said again. 'I don't care what you believe. I won't do it.'

'My dear woman, it is important to know that we may close the prison and keep it closed before we attempt to lure Deacon into it.'

'I don't care. It's not happening. I'm not locking you in there and that's final. Tara wouldn't do it, and I'm not doing it either.'

Anderson was making a futile attempt to explain to Marie that what he was asking of her would not put him at risk when

178

there was a sharp knock, and Sky threw open the door with a reckless disregard for protocol that only an emergency would demand. 'It's Alice,' she said. 'She's gone.'

Even before Tara answered her mobile, Cassandra felt a cold sense of urgency in her belly. When Tara put the phone back in her pocket, Cassandra was already heading back to the Land Rover in a trot. She didn't need to hear Tara inform them that Alice had gone missing.

Cassandra felt an icy chill down her back, and the connection that had forged between her and Alice when she had taken from her felt like a flashing red light with a siren going off at the base of her spine. 'Honister Pass,' she called over her shoulder as Tara and Ferris raced to catch up. 'She's on Honister Pass, and he's with her. We have to go now.'

Tara barely had the engine started before Cassandra sent her fetch out into the beginnings of snow. She didn't find the usual gossamer threads of the Dream World but followed, in their stead, a dark, hollow emptiness that felt like what was left after a firestorm.

There had only ever been three others she had done any form of dream magic with – Anderson, Tim and Deacon. That the path was Deacon's she had no doubt, but the nightmare was not his, and the very worst of a bad situation was that the dreamer was not asleep. It was Alice's essence she felt, weak and filled with despair. So bad was the nightmare, so horrific had it become that the dreamer now openly and actively sought release from the world of the living.

'Jesus,' she gasped, reaching out to touch Tara's arm. 'Hurry. Please hurry.' And her fetch moved effortlessly up Honister Pass, past the deserted slate mine and up onto the dismantled tramway line. It was there she saw Alice struggling against the brewing storm, a small torch grasped in an ungloved hand making a feeble attempt to fight back the quickly descending darkness.

'Leave me alone,' the woman gasped, fighting her way along the rocky path above the slate mine. 'Stop tormenting me. I won't do what you want. Not this time. Not ever again.'

Even though Cassandra expected him, even though she knew he caused Alice's suffering, she could not fight back the sudden wave of horror at the sight of him. Though Alice couldn't see him, Cassandra's fetch saw as plainly as day. There, mantling the struggling woman like some obscene raptor over its prey was Deacon. She had no way of knowing if he really hadn't noticed her own presence or if, at least for this moment, it was of no consequence to him. As much as she wished otherwise, she suspected it was probably the latter, but it really didn't matter. There was little choice.

'It is not my wish to cause you suffering, my dear.' As he spoke, Cassandra realised with horror that his words were being forced through Alice's own mouth in her own voice, sounding raw and unpractised. He continued. 'If you prefer death over the pleasures of the flesh, I certainly shan't keep you from it. You will accomplish my purposes either way, and it is not as though you are irreplaceable, is it?'

As Alice battled on, nearly bent double in the force of the wind, fully awake and yet fully in the grip of the most horrible of nightmares, the situation got worse. For a short time Cassandra had forgotten about anything other than rescuing Alice. But at the moment, Alice was one giant adrenaline surge overlaying thick, palpable lust. And because Cassandra had already tasted of the feast last night, the pull was even more irresistible. In the onrush of the storm, in the realm beyond the flesh, Cassandra sensed the bright tendrils of connection that now linked her to the Elementals, to Tim and Anderson and Tara and the others, tendrils like strands in a spider's web, sensitive to the slightest motion. 'Stay with her,' she heard Tara say from far away in the Jeep. 'Stay with her, Cassandra. I know it's hard, but you're all she's got until we can get to her.'

And her attention was once again with her fetch, focused on Alice Hartley and her tormentor.

Cassandra had never felt such a powerful pull. When Tara drove into the deserted car park at the slate mine and parked next to the only other vehicle there, Cassandra's fetch returned instantly to her body, which she now needed in order to get to Alice. She was out of the car and heading up the steep, treacherous path behind the tourist centre at a pace she would have never managed without the powerful sexual energy that saturated Elemental Cottage at all times. 'Wait for Tim and Anderson,' she yelled back to Ferris, who had started up behind her but was unable to keep her pace. Even Tara, who was strong and fit, could not keep the pace of a succubus well nourished. And soon she was alone, following the path of the nightmare laid before her like a luminous trail of breadcrumbs.

Cassandra sent out the majority of her energy to seek Alice. Whatever was happening inside the woman's mind was sexual and horrific at the same time. The adrenaline in her brain spiked with fierceness, and the nightmare flashed both bright and dark, more terrible than anything Cassandra had ever experienced. It was more delectable in its temptation and, even well-sated from the energy at Elemental Cottage as she was, Alice's own energy would have drawn her with an irresistible force. Cassandra had strength Alice didn't possess, and the closer she drew, the more aware she became of the woman's weakened physical condition. She had already suffered at Deacon's hand. It was truly only the power and the threat of the waking nightmare that now drove her.

If anyone had been able to see, they would have assumed that Deacon was embracing Alice from behind, his powerful arms folding around her waist and her leaning back against his broad chest, taking a rest. But Cassandra knew with a chilling certainty that though Alice was aware of all that the demon did to her, she was only his puppet, with very little control left to her.

In spite of the terror, the beast within Cassandra ached for such a feast, even as everything human and ordinary in her cried out at the horror of what was happening. It had to stop. Almost by instinct, Cassandra sent out a thought to Anderson, a touch of consciousness, all she could offer at the moment.

181

But it gave her strength when she felt it brush against his fetch, felt his fetch stretch out to her in response. That was all there was time for. Then she stumbled forward, and scooped the trembling Alice away from Deacon and into her arms, knowing as she did so that if help didn't come soon, her own control might be lost and Deacon would win anyway.

Deacon only smiled and yielded Alice up, the weight of her nearly unbalancing Cassandra. Almost immediately the woman calmed in Cassandra's embrace, a condition that Cassandra knew meant nothing.

Deacon chuckled softly. 'Such a glutton you are, little succubus. I can still smell your lust on this one's worthless carcass. Ah, but perhaps that was nothing more than the appetiser, hmm? Perhaps you are not finished with her yet?'

The snow had grown to near-blizzard force around them now, and even Cassandra was beginning to feel it. She feared for the woman in her arms, in more ways than one. She seemed so frail it was amazing that she had made it this far.

Deacon raised a dismissive hand to Alice. 'She means nothing to me. I would happily give you such a meal, Cassandra Larkin. In fact, she is only the bait for what it is I really want.' He was suddenly close to her, so close that she could feel the heat of his breath and the rise and fall of his chest against her shoulder, as he spoke next her ear. 'And you, my dear woman, are not stupid. You know what it is that I desire. We have already had this conversation, and I grow tired of talking. Therefore, I shall demonstrate my intent.'

With one flourish of his hand, Alice caught a deep breath that was nearly a shriek in its effort, her back stiffened and arched, and then her whole body went limp. Before Cassandra could take in what was happening, Deacon looked out over the snow-ravaged fell, back toward the Honister Mine, and lifted his hand again. Then he sighed his satisfaction.

'Actions speak louder than words, it is said, my dear succubus. Therefore, I have spoken volumes.' He nodded down to Alice, now limp against Cassandra's body. 'Am I not correct in assuming that neither this one nor your eunuch, Mr

Ferris, are riders of the Ether?' He shrugged mightily. 'Even if I am mistaken, and they both know their way to the void and back, they shall not find their way home from where I have hidden them, nor shall you find them either, my darling, no matter how well you may ride the Ether.'

Cassandra fell to her knees, lowering Alice onto her lap. Even beyond the driving bite of the cold wind, the chill inside her went to the marrow. She could already sense the coma-like symptoms manifesting in Alice, the symptoms that happened when the fetch was in the Ether.

'She's not a rider. You could kill her,' she said between chattering teeth.

'I could indeed, if I choose to, Cassandra Larkin, but at this moment I assure you I do not choose to damage either her or your Mr Ferris.' He loomed suddenly close to her and she felt as though the skin would scorch off her body as she bent protectively over the comatose Alice.

'Give me my freedom, succubus. That is all I ask. Give me but that small boon and these two shall I happily return to their flesh, hale and hearty and none the worse for wear. That one is already weak –' he nodded to Alice '– and though I cannot vouch for the condition of your Mr Ferris, I would not wait too long before you make your decision. Their lives are in your hands, succubus, and it would be such a tragedy if your indecisiveness would cause their death, or worse yet, their further suffering.

'When you have made your decision, all you need do is come into the Ether. I shall not be hard to find. Oh, and one more small thing, my dear succubus. Come alone, or I promise they shall both suffer for it before you even cross the threshold.' Then he vanished, just as Anderson materialised at her side. Tim and Tara weren't far behind.

Cassandra eased Alice onto the ground then stood, trembling far more with rage than with cold. And when Tim knelt to examine Alice, Cassandra walked into the blizzard without looking back, already forming the spell that would take her to the Ether, already seeing the void open before her, already feeling the silent pull of it.

'No!' Anderson lunged at her and pulled her tightly into his embrace, shaking her hard. 'You cannot do this. Not now. You cannot follow him. If you do this thing you will die, so will Alice, so will Mr Ferris, and nothing will have changed except that you will have caused me more grief that I could possibly bear, my darling.'

'I can't let him do this! I can't let the bastard do this!' She screamed into the wind. 'I won't let him get away with hurting them. I won't!'

Anderson held her face in his hands and forced her to focus. 'He shall not get away with what he has done, my love, I promise you he shall not. But this is not the place to stage the battle we must fight. We must get Alice and Ferris down off the fell. Now.'

Chapter Seventeen

'VERITY'S WITH ALICE AND Ferris in the guest wing. There was no need to send them to the hospital when there's nothing that can be done for them there.' Tara spoke to everyone gathered around the breakfast bar in the kitchen. Fiori had ladled up the carrot and coriander soup that had been intended for dinner's first course as emergency rations along with home-made focaccia bread. 'This will all be over in a few hours. We've had enough of Deacon's bullshit.' Tara met Cassandra's gaze.

Cassandra knew the remark was intended to reassure her, but a few hours seemed like an eternity, and the fact that she would have to go alone with no one knowing made her all the more anxious to get on with it.

Anderson laid a steadying hand on her arm, and nodded to her soup. He had done everything but force it down her throat to get her to eat. And indeed she had eaten because she feared he might do just that, and because she knew that she would need her strength for what lay ahead.

'The prison and its lock are ready,' Anderson said, 'although it is untested as my two esteemed colleagues would not afford me that honour.' He offered Marie and Tim a teasing smile. They both glared back at him. Tim flipped him the finger.

'It's all right,' Tara said. 'It's been tested. The lock works just fine.'

Marie and Tim shot each other a surprised glance. 'You tested it?' Tim asked.

Tara nodded, ripping off a chunk of bread. 'It works. It'll

hold Deacon just fine.'

The very thought of Tara allowing herself to be locked in that tight, horrible place made Cassandra shiver, and her respect for the coven leader, which was already substantial, went up another notch.

'I do not like Cassandra bearing the dangerous burden of delivering Deacon to his prison,' Anderson said.

'I don't like it either,' Tim said. There seemed to be a general consensus around the table.

'I'm the only one that can do it,' Cassandra said. 'Besides, I'm the one who got you all into this mess in the first place.'

'Bullshit,' Tara said. 'You only forced Deacon's hand, made us aware of what he was up to. You may be the only one who can do it but I assure you, we won't be sending you in alone. Anderson and I'll be going with.'

Before either Anderson or Cassandra could raise a protest, Tara continued. 'Yes, I know how much time the preparations take for me to go into the Ether, Anderson. You've told me *ad nauseam*, and with that in mind, figuring that in the end we would be left with the choice we now face, all the preparations have been made. What's left to do Sky and Fiori will help me with, while the rest of you prepare.'

'It seems to me, then, that if Cassandra will be our bounty hunter, returning Deacon to jail, the rest of us could best prepare by giving her as much energy as we can spare to make sure she's strong for the task,' Tim said. Marie nodded agreement.

'No!' Cassandra said. 'No. Everyone here will need every bit of energy they can muster if we're going to get through this. I'm well-nourished and strong just on the residual energy from being here at Elemental Cottage. I won't need to take from anyone. Honest.'

'That seems a bit presumptuous,' Fiori said, from where she stood cutting apples for the apple crumble as though nothing out of the ordinary were going on, as though dinner at eight would not have to be rescheduled. 'I've never worked any magic where I wouldn't have happily taken a little extra energy for the task.'

Cassandra shifted uncomfortably in her chair. 'I didn't say I wouldn't be happy for the extra energy, just that I'm not the only one doing battle here. And you've all dealt with this bastard enough to know that he'll go for the weakest point in our defences. And I don't want that weakest point to be the place where I've been a glutton.'

'Still, I don't like it,' Tim said.

'Believe me,' Cassandra said, 'I don't much like it either, but I'm right. You know I'm right.'

'No.' Tim shook his head. 'No, I don't know you're right. I don't know that at all. I've done battle with him and he'll never do what you expect.'

'It doesn't matter.' Cassandra held Tim's gaze. 'I won't take anyone's energy for this task, and as far as I know, there's no one here who can force me to.'

'That's right,' Tara said. 'No one can force you to. However, we can do our best to make sure there's plenty of residual energy in this house for the taking.' She looked down at her watch. 'Everyone could use a break and a rest. I want everyone fresh when we begin the ritual. And no one sleeps alone, is that clear? No one.'

Strange that this remark should make Cassandra blush. Tara had just told everyone in the room to have sex for her benefit. Not only did she blush, but she felt deeply moved.

'That goes for you too, Serina,' Tara said. And the coven leader surprised everyone by reaching out her hand and enfleshing the ghost, who in life had not been her friend. She now stood quietly at Cassandra's side. 'You deserve a piece of revenge on this bastard at least as much as anyone else in this room,' Tara told her.

Tim excused himself from the table and took Marie by the hand, making no effort to hide what their intentions were. Then, before they headed off to the room reserved for them at Elemental Cottage, they both turned to Serina. 'The bed's big,' Tim said. 'You're welcome to join us if you'd like.' He reached out his other hand to her. For a brief moment she looked up at him incredulously, then her lip trembled slightly and she offered him a self-conscious smile, took his hand and disappeared down the hall with the two of them.

'Cassandra Larkin, I shall ravage you here and now if you do not come with me – do not think that I won't.' Anderson shoved his way into the library. 'I am at least as much a lover of books as you are, but I assure you, my dear woman, now is not the time for research.'

Cassandra turned from the stacks, her heart racing at his sudden intrusion. 'I don't think this is a good idea, Anderson. We don't know what will happen and besides, there's still something I'm missing, something I don't –'

It took him all of three strides to get to her from across the room. He shoved her up hard between his body and the shelf of books, while his mouth crushed hers before another word could escape. His tongue forced its way in between her lips as though it would not only lap up any words that might threaten to spill out, but also any thought that didn't involve Anderson wrapped around her body, kissing her brains out, leaving her knees weak, and kicking her pulse rate up into overdrive.

At last he pulled away, just enough to speak against her mouth. 'What is missing you will not find in books, my love, and it shall not be tolerated, such unacceptable behaviour in this household, in this bastion of sex magic. It shall not be tolerated that the high priest and the resident succubus shall be left unsatisfied while all others do their duty and partake of the pleasures of the flesh. I shall not be denied, Cassandra Larkin. Nor shall you.'

Then he practically ripped open her jeans, yanked them and her panties down, turned her to the wall and fingered her open. It was that unceremonious, and it was a side of Anderson she had never seen before.

'Ah, I see it is as I suspected,' he breathed. 'Your womanhood is in as much need as my manhood, and yet you deny us both. It shall not be.' He reached upward to tweak her clit, making her wet herself and his hand with the pleasure of his efforts until the library smelled of her heat. She heard him open his fly and the whisper of cloth against flesh, but little else before he forced her forward just enough, then pushed into her with a harsh grunt.

She yielded and grunted back.

She could feel his hot breath coming in tight gasps against the back of her neck. 'Oh, I have so needed to be sheathed in your warm depths, my darling, and how you have tortured me so cruelly.'

'I didn't mean to torture you. I wasn't trying to be cruel,' she gasped. 'It's just –' She completely lost her train of thought as both his arms tightened around her for the first hard thrust that had her cheek pressed up against the spines of the books. He found her clit and pinched and stroked until she was forced to bite the knuckles of her fist to keep from crying out as she drenched both of them with her pleasure.

'There is no need to keep your passion silent in this house, my love. These walls are not unfamiliar with the sounds of lust.' Anderson bit and kissed and caressed her nape, moving her hair to one side to expose and nibble her ear, all the while thrusting and grinding deep into her, breathing like a windstorm on the fells, every muscle tensed with need.

'I shall give you your release now, my love, and take mine for I can wait no longer.' Two more hard thrusts and he grunted his ejaculation, and she banged her knee on the shelf as she convulsed in her own orgasm.

They were barely finished coming when he pulled away, tugged up his trousers, and lifted her into his arms, her jeans still around her knees. 'Now, my love,' he breathed. 'Now that we have taken care of our most urgent needs, we shall adjourn to my bed where we may pleasure each other with abandon, as is fitting under the circumstances.'

He mounted the stairs with her in his arms as effortlessly as if she weighed nothing. He pushed open the door into the darkened room, and carried her to his bed. Though she felt his presence in the space he had made for himself, felt his personality like a warm blanket, she wished desperately that she could smell him. The fact that she could enter the sleeping-room of the man she loved and not smell his scent saddened her. She wondered how often he actually used the room when he had no real need to sleep. The man she loved. Did he know that? Did he know how she felt about him? Did he know that she had already loved him long before their first encounter in the Ether? She wondered if she should tell him or if that would only make matters worse.

His room was a study in monochrome simplicity. In the winter moonlight, shades of silver and grey flooded his window. The wardrobe, the dresser, the desk were all clean, straight lines, simple and unadorned wood. He eased her down on the big bed and helped her out of her remaining clothes. It was not a four-poster, like hers, but a simple bed, little more than a futon raised on a platform.

She watched him undress with an excitement in her body that was so much more than just arousal. She watched the superfluous rise and fall of his chest. She admired the hard flat of his abdomen, the curve of his thighs, the rounded muscles of his buttocks. The body he wore was a body that, in its power and rugged elegance, matched his spirit so well.

She had been a voyeur in his life long before she'd met him in person. Some day she would tell him that, tell him how she had studied him, how she had stalked him through history, stalked him through the pages of the obscure documents in her grandmother's library, and the other documents, the ones she had tracked down and spent a good bit of her own money on. One day, if they survived that long, she would tell him how she had fantasised about being welcomed into his bed, how she had dreamed about being wrapped in his arms.

She hadn't realised how badly she was trembling until he lay down next to her and pulled her into his warmth – such an amazing warmth for a ghost, she thought. She whispered against his throat as he pulled her tighter to him. 'You have to understand, I don't trust myself when I want you so badly.'

'I trust you, my darling.' He rose on his elbow so that he

looked down on her where she lay next to him. 'And I would not have taken no for an answer.' With his other hand he stroked her breasts, lingering to run his thumbs over her burgeoning nipples. He lowered his lips to each in turn, suckling and running his warm tongue around them until they were hard with the pleasure of his kisses.

Then he rolled with her and pulled her on top of him, running a hand down between their bodies to splay her wet pussy, while she shifted her pelvis until his cock was where she needed it. Then she settled onto it, and with her knees against his hips, she lay forward so that her breasts rested against his chest, nipples to nipples.

He kissed her ear, and moved his hips gently. 'Would that I could stay inside you forever, my love. That would be the deepest joy of my heart.'

She laughed softly. 'How can that be when surely there've been so many joys in your heart?'

He kissed her with emotion that tightened his whole body around her. Then he pulled away enough that he could see her face. 'I do not know how it can be, Cassandra Larkin, but I swear to you by the love of the Goddess that it is true. From the moment you pulled me so unceremoniously into the Ether, my heart has been yours.' His dark eyes shone in the moonlight, and she could see the shudder of his pulse against his throat. 'And whatever happens, my darling Cassandra, you must know that it will be yours until my days have ended.'

Cassandra felt like her chest would explode with feelings she'd never thought she could have. There was so little time before she would do what had to be done, and that she would have to keep it from him tinged his revelation with sadness and made her desperate to tell him all that was in her heart before it was too late, and tomorrow it could very well be too late.

It was then that she noticed Serina Ravenmoor standing naked at the foot of the bed. Crying.

Anderson spoke first, and it was probably a good thing. Cassandra doubted if she would have been so civil.

'Miss Ravenmoor, you are distressed.' He rolled slightly to one side and Cassandra discreetly dismounted. 'Is there anything we may do to ease your discomfort?'

Cassandra heaved a sigh and threw back the duvet for her to join them.

'Come – come, dear woman,' Anderson said. 'You shall catch your death wandering about this draughty house unclothed in the Cumbrian winter.'

She forced a laugh around a sob as she climbed into the bed next to Cassandra. 'I'd be much more concerned about that, Mr Anderson, if I weren't already dead.'

'Still, my darling. The cold is no more pleasant, living or dead, when you are in the flesh. Please, do not worry so. The end has not yet come, and we may yet prevail. Now do you wish to share pleasure with us?'

Serina sat upright in the bed, her spine straight, her eyes bright in the moonlight. 'I had hoped for something more than pleasure, actually,' she said.

'What do you need?' Cassandra asked, trying to keep the frustration out of her voice.

'It isn't so much what I need as what I can give.' She reached out her small hand and smoothed Cassandra's wild hair. 'I want you to take me. All of me.'

'What? Are you crazy?' Cassandra slapped her hand away, and scooted as far back as she could get in the bed without shoving Anderson out onto the floor.

'No. No, listen to me, please.' Serina moved closer. 'I'm not crazy. I've never been more sane. I know exactly what I'm doing. I want you to take me. I'm offering you my energy. All of it.' She wiped frantically at her eyes. 'It does me no good any more. Please. The others.' She nodded toward the bedroom door. 'They're all powerful witches, they all have something to offer. This –' she opened her arms wide and nodded down to the flesh she now wore. 'This is all I have.'

'I'm not listening to this. This is rubbish. You know how I feel about this.' Cassandra pushed her way toward the foot of the bed for a quick escape, but Serina grabbed her arm in an amazingly powerful grip for one so small.

'I never wanted to be a ghost. When I jumped from Raven Crag, I thought that would be the end of my suffering. Don't you see?' This time she made no attempt to stop the tears. 'I never wanted this. Endless hours of nothing, no purpose, no physical contact, no human contact unless you or one of the Elementals has mercy on me. Don't you understand? I don't want to be this way.'

She squeezed Cassandra's arm until it was nearly painful. 'This is something I can do. Something that might make a difference. And who knows? All that rubbish about unfinished business. Perhaps that is the reason why I didn't pass on, the reason why I remained on this plane as a ghost.'

'Jesus!' Cassandra shook her head. 'I don't believe we're having this conversation. Do you have any idea what you're asking of me?' This time Anderson gently restrained her when she tried to get out of bed.

Serina surprised Cassandra by leaning forward and kissing her tenderly. 'I'm not asking anything of you, Cassandra. I'm giving you a gift, a gift that, you've said it yourself, no one else in this house can afford to give you right now. But I can, Cassandra. I can and you know it's true. You know it. Plus, no matter what you tell everyone, you need all the energy you can get to face Deacon. We all know it's true, and I'm the only one who is free to do anything about it.'

'Dear Goddess, Serina, don't ask me to do this.' Cassandra hauled the little ghost bodily into her arms and held her. It was difficult to tell who was trembling the harder.

When Serina calmed a bit, she wiped her eyes and sat back on her haunches. 'It's not like I'm asking you to take my life. I'm already dead. Deacon took care of that.' The venom in her voice sent a chill down Cassandra's back. 'All I'm asking is that you use what's mine to give. Take from me, use my energy.' Her eyes brimmed again. 'Take my energy, set me free. And then, make that bastard pay for what he's done. Make him pay. Make him pay for all of us.'

Even when the decision was made, it felt like a hard bruise

added to a fresh wound. The three settled into bed together, with Anderson pushing open the little ghost's legs and laving the length of her pout with his tongue. Cassandra watched as he strummed her clit with his thumb. She could see that his cock was heavy again, that it would be ready when the time came.

She cradled Serina's head in her lap, watching the pleasure on her face while Anderson ate her pussy. She caressed and cupped the ghost's small, high breasts, kneading her nipples between her thumb and forefingers, allowing Serina's hands to move up to her own breasts, even allowing her to rearrange herself until she could nurse like a baby. And Cassandra cradled her there next to her heart, opening her own legs and shifting to accommodate the little ghost's hand as she stroked and fingered Cassandra's pussy.

She raised her head long enough to kiss Cassandra and whisper against her mouth, 'I love you, Cassandra Larkin. You kept me sane these past few months.' Her face was pearlescent in the moonlight, her eyes large and wet.

Cassandra stroked her face, then her flank. 'You've been a companion to me, Serina, when I was most alone. I'll miss you.' Cassandra choked out the words. She could barely believe what was about to happen and yet, at the same time, it seemed the right thing to do.

Anderson now rose on his haunches, kissing both women in turn, cupping Serina's face in his hand. 'You are very courageous, Miss Ravenmoor, and it has been an honour to have known you. I wish you a swift journey to the peace you so richly deserve.' His words ended in a grunt as he pushed into Serina, and Cassandra scrambled to reposition herself for what she knew was to come.

The power of sex, the flood of adrenaline and arousal in the room had heightened Cassandra's senses. The animal in her rose and sniffed and hungered. That which was less animal found a quiet corner, to watch in wonder and terror and sorrow and hope. Cassandra rose naked over the writhing Serina and kissed her long and tenderly, and while she kissed her, she found the pulse of her lust, the thrum of her essence, and tasted its sweetness, its need.

Serina whimpered softly and her eyelids fluttered. 'My beautiful friend, my powerful succubus. Take me now, and don't let Deacon ever do this again.'

'Move away.' Cassandra spoke to Anderson, barely able to hear herself over the pounding of her raging hunger. 'Move away or you'll get pulled into the vortex.' She nodded to a chair at the foot of the bed. 'Stay there until it's done.'

When she was sure he was safe, she slid down into the duvet next to Serina and took her into her arms. 'I am so sorry, Serina,' she whispered, as she kissed the woman, who was already in the ecstasy of the succubus's magic. 'I am so sorry that this happened to you. I won't let him do it again. I promise.' She hoped desperately that it was a promise she could keep.

And she took. As she had never taken before, she took. The room flashed silver, then became too bright to look at through human eyes as she pulled Serina Ravenmoor into her, caressing and kissing and fondling. She pulled into herself all that Serina was, all that she had ever been, her hopes, her dreams, her very secret fantasies.

There were fantasies of being a powerful witch like Tara Stone, fantasies of finding a powerful lover. And, for a brief flash, Deacon's face was the face of that lover, a fantasy that turned to a dark and sinister nightmare. There were fantasies of beauty and love and magical fairy-tale powers, and Cassandra took them all into herself. And when those were gone, she took into herself the woman's fears and sorrows, and failures.

She took into herself Serina Ravenmoor's bitter jealousy at Tara Stone's dismissal of her, jealousy of the loyalty and love Tara Stone commanded so effortlessly as she never could. Then she took into herself the woman's very darkest nightmares, the face of which was Deacon, able to offer her both pleasure and terror as she had never known, able to make himself indispensable in her heart, able to force her in her moment of sanity from the precipice on Raven Crag at the horror of what he had made her into.

And when even those very worst of living nightmares were drained to nothing, with one last kiss Cassandra took the very heart of the enraptured woman, the very essence of one who would give herself up in such a way for such a cause. And finally, there was nothing left of Serina Ravenmoor that did not now rest close to the heart of the succubus.

Somewhere far away, she sensed Anderson ejaculating in the power of the magic that overflowed from the taking of Serina Ravenmoor and flooded Elemental Cottage and, no doubt, the fells beyond. All that remained was a reflection of a reflection, peaceful as the summered surface of Derwentwater at dawn. Cassandra brushed a final kiss on Serina's pale lips, and with one last ecstatic utterance, Serina Ravenmoor vanished and Cassandra's arms were empty.

Anderson stumbled to the bed and pulled Cassandra into a tight embrace, but that was about all he could manage before he fell into a deep sleep. The residual of what had just happened was like a powerful post-coital soporific. She knew he could do no more.

For a long moment she held him close to her, feeling power surge through her body as she had never felt before. She could feel the heartbeat of each person in the house, she could follow the flow of their blood through their veins. She could see and understand the magical flesh the ghosts wore. She could tell the difference between Anderson, who rode the Ether, and Fiori and Sky, who enfleshed ghosts. More than that, she could feel their dreams, their hopes, what excited them, what aroused them, what was their worst nightmare – not details, more like hot spots on an infrared camera. The house buzzed with energy and magic and lust. The only placed that wasn't filled with it was Serina's scrying mirror, which contained only the cold emptiness of the void waiting to be filled.

When she was certain Anderson slept, and she was pretty sure the surge of energy from her taking of Serina had had the same effect on everyone else in the house, she settled herself into Anderson's arms and kissed him. 'I love you, Anderson,' she whispered against his lips. 'And I'll be back as soon as I can.'

He shifted slightly and pulled her tighter against him. It didn't matter, her fetch had already slipped her body and was wending its way toward the Ether, empowered with Serina Ravenmoor's gift.

Chapter Eighteen

SHE CAME TO HERSELF walking in a graveyard, a graveyard that stretched endlessly into the Ether. Had she not known where she was, had she not been able to see the way the green shimmered and faded into nothingness just at the edge of her peripheral vision, she would have thought herself in an old cemetery somewhere in London, a cemetery that extended quietly outward in all directions toward the noise and bustle of the city.

Moss-covered branches mantled the footpath and hung low enough to snag her hair as she passed beneath them. Gnarled tree roots toppled headstones that slanted from shifting earth that wasn't really there and cracked from age that hadn't really happened. It was outrageously elaborate. No Ether rider would have wasted energy so lavishly. With a chilled certainty, she knew it was Deacon's doing and entirely for her benefit.

She followed the uneven stone footpath up the steps to an aging mausoleum with crumbling Corinthian columns. Heavily carved doors creaked open before her, as though invisible doormen had anticipated her arrival.

Though she was prepared for it, the sight of him, as ever, left her feeling as though she were turning to ice from the inside out. Deacon stood beside two open stone caskets on ornately carved plinths. His feet were planted firmly apart and his hands were folded in front of him as though he were the vicar readying himself to offer a prayer for the dead.

'You are quite a lovely sight to behold when you have taken to the dregs, my lovely succubus. And yes, my darling, it is indeed that obvious. Though I must admit I am surprised that someone of your sensitive nature would have had the courage to do what you were always meant to do.' He clapped large hands together slowly in applause. 'Well done, my lovely. Well done. At last Serina Ravenmoor has done something worthwhile.' He came to her side and walked around her as though he were examining her. 'I felt the surge of your energy long before you entered the void, my love. You were not subtle.'

'I wasn't trying to sneak up on you, Deacon, if that's what you think.'

He nodded to the open caskets. 'In a gesture of goodwill, I have chosen to reveal to you Alice and your Mr Ferris. As you can see, their fetches are undamaged. It is as though they are in a peaceful slumber, my darling. And once you have returned me to my body, they will wake as though it has been only that – just sleep, restful dreamless sleep. He laughed softly as she stared down into the caskets at the unmoving fetches.

'As I am sure you must have guessed, my darling, I have chosen their resting places as a reminder to you of what shall ultimately await them if you do not uphold your part of the bargain.' He shrugged. 'After I have toyed with them for a time, of course. Most likely for a very long time.'

'There was no bargain, Deacon. As I recall, you've left me with little choice.'

He offered her a disappointed pout. 'Oh, my dear succubus, there are always choices. Surely you know that by now.'

'If you don't mind, I'd like to get this over with,' Cassandra said, sounding much calmer that she felt.

Deacon raised a dark eyebrow and circled her again, slowly, pausing to run a finger along her cheek. She didn't flinch. 'You seem rather nonchalant about returning me to my body, to the land of the living, the place you were willing to sacrifice your very life to keep me from last time, as I recall.' He moved behind her, almost as though he were going to embrace her, pulled her hair to one side and spoke against her ear. 'Tell me, my beauty, what has changed your mind?'

'I want this mess over with,' she said, the hairs rising along the back of her neck as she felt his magicked, unnatural breath.

'I am hurt that you esteem my companionship so little, my dear Cassandra.' His lips grazed her ear, and his voice became a low purr, or perhaps a growl. 'Now tell me, what has changed your mind?'

'You know full well what's changed my mind, Deacon. You have my friends and I want them back safe and unharmed,' she said.

He looked over at the two unconscious fetches in the caskets as though he had only just realised they were there.

'Can we just get on with it?'

He took a deep, unnecessary breath and studied her thoughtfully for a long moment before he finally spoke into the silence. 'As you wish, my dear. I am certainly not anxious to remain here in this dreadful place any longer than necessary. I find cemeteries so depressing, don't you?'

She didn't answer.

'There is one condition before you take me home, my lovely,' he said.

'What condition? I came alone, exactly as you said. At your threats, I told no one. You said nothing about further conditions.'

He laughed softly, and the feel of it crawled up her spine like a living thing. 'Ah, but that was before I imagined that you might actually use your gift and come into the void a well-nourished succubus at the height of her power. Surely you didn't think that I wouldn't notice such a thing.' He looked down at his hands clenching into fists, then relaxing and clenching again.

'Power is not a thing to be trusted, my dear Cassandra. Though you have not had it long enough to understand this.' He lifted his hand to her cheek, stroked tenderly, then settled it onto the nape of her neck in a caress that anyone watching

200

might have believed to be the epitome of loving gentleness. 'I, on the other hand, know this to be true through experience, my darling.' His grip tightened slightly. 'Therefore I cannot allow you more power than what is essential to return me to my body. I am sorry. For truly, you are beautiful at your peak.

His fingers barely moved but Cassandra felt as though he were ripping her throat open, as though he were bleeding her like a slaughtered lamb. She didn't cry out but held herself tight against the pain, held herself tight as she always did in the Ether. But mostly she held herself tight lest Anderson hear and come to her aid.

Deacon took her mouth in a kiss – she was too paralysed with pain to deny him. And when he pulled away, his voice was breathless. 'You are only a half-blood, my darling, for that is what a succubus is, the bastard of your father, and by no means my equal. Nor his. A foolish girl-child of questionable parentage. I'm sure your father never imagined he would get a child on a weak little Ether rider with gifts disappointing. I'm sure no one was more surprised than he.'

Again, he tightened his grip. 'Nevertheless, no matter how strong your father was, your mother was weak, and sadly it is her lack of ambition and her weakness that you seem to have inherited. Never mind that, my love. Your life force will serve me well, a fitting sacrifice to return me to my flesh. I am sure your father, wherever he is, will not mind. You were as nothing to him, the emission of his loins, no more, an embarrassing accident on which he hadn't counted. Contraception is, as you can imagine, a thing not much thought on among demons.'

Cassandra felt as though she were being suffocated, crammed into a space much too small for the expansion that had occurred with Serina's gift. An overwhelming sense of claustrophobia drove her to her knees and this time she cried out, but it was barely more than a breathless gasp.

He yanked her back to her feet and spoke again, close to her ear. 'Oh do not you worry, little succubus. I will keep my promise. I will return these two to the World of Flesh. I quite like the idea of the guilt your death for their life will cause them. Especially with the promise that binds your Mr Ferris. And Alice shall suffer so deliciously at your loss. Of course that is as nothing to me. Ultimately, it is the anguish your death will cause Tara Stone and her ghost, your lover, in which I shall find endless delight.'

He pulled her close, pressed his lips to hers and a chill ran down her spine. 'I am sorry, dear succubus, truly I am. But I cannot allow you to make this journey glutted with so much power. And you *will* make this journey if you wish for these two to live and not suffer.' He held her arm behind her back and kissed her nape, then with his other hand cupped her breasts in turn, as though he were the most gentle, most considerate of lovers. 'And now my darling, kiss me and take me home.'

She had barely the strength to stand and everything in her ached. She didn't mind dying. That was inevitable. But the thought that she would not be able to fulfil her promise to Serina was nearly unbearable. That the little ghost had given her essence for nothing was anguish.

In spite of all that she had done, all that she had fought for, in the end he would win, in the end he would be returned to his body. She had no choice. *She had no choice.* And yet, even he himself had said, there were always choices. As her energy drained away to only enough to do what had to be done, as he took it from her as though it were nothing, as though it didn't matter, she racked her brain trying to think, trying to understand what she was missing, how she could make it right. It didn't matter that she wouldn't survive it. It only mattered that her friends would, that the people she cared about would, and that this monster would do no more damage. That was all she asked, and yet, how?

There was a sudden ear-splitting crack, and the Ether trembled and shook like water. 'This one you shall not have, demon!' With a voice loud enough to silence thunder, Anderson burst into the Ether in a flash of lightning that caused the whole void to shake. 'That you toy with one who is only just coming into her power, who has yet to learn her full abilities proves what I have always known – that you are a coward, demon, and a weak one at that.' Anderson raised both hands, which seemed suddenly enormous, and the void trembled again, and Deacon struggled to stand.

'It is true, I am only a ghost of my former self, demon, but I am not weak, and I am no stranger to the Ether. Perhaps you would prefer to toy with someone who is more in his element? Perhaps you would find my powers more of a match for you, more of a challenge?' With each sentence, Anderson lifted his hands and the Ether trembled as though there were an earthquake, until at last, Deacon shoved Cassandra aside just to keep his balance.

'You were not invited to this party, ghost! And you, Cassandra Larkin, have broken your promise. However, I will keep mine.' He raised a hand and turned to the stone caskets, then roared with enough rage to split the Ether.

They were both empty.

Cassandra struggled to her feet, relief washing over her at what she knew were the blessed doings of the Elemental Coven, though how they had managed it, she couldn't imagine. Then her focus returned to Anderson and Deacon, standing in the midst of the tremor and twist of the graveyard threatening to be swallowed back into the Ether at any moment.

With the whole void trembling as though it would collapse in on them, and with a rain of lightning that was far worse than any thunderstorm Cassandra had ever seen, Anderson forced Deacon back against the first of the caskets. It juddered then vanished into nothing, and the demon fell onto the plinth that remained.

'Have you not yet learned that you are no match for Tara Stone, demon?' said Anderson. 'Have you not yet learned that she will take back what is hers, all of what is hers, and leave you to rot for the loathsome piece of corruption that you are? Even now, she has returned the fetches of Alice Hartley and Mr Ferris to their waiting bodies, and that right from under your nose.'

He raised his hand again. Thunder cracked and lightning split the Ether with the harsh scent of ozone, and struck Deacon square in the chest, sizzling through his ethereal body and tossing him like a rag doll against the second coffin which dissolved into nothingness beneath him. All around them the graveyard disappeared until once again they stood in the nothingness of the void.

Anderson barely had time to pull Cassandra into his arms before Deacon rose above them to a terrible height, and the banshee shriek of rage let loose from his lips would have raised goose bumps on flesh and caused hearts to pound with terror. With an upward flourish of his hands, he ringed them in a fire so hot that had there been flesh, it would have melted away.

Anderson shielded Cassandra from the intense heat with his body. 'We do not fight this battle alone, demon. Surely by now you must know that you shall not prevail, that our allies are powerful, and as we have defeated you before, even now Tara Stone and the Elemental Coven are weaving the spell that shall destroy you, that shall make it as though you had never been.'

Then Anderson, still holding Cassandra to him, raised his other arm into the air. 'I call upon the powers of the elements, the powers that set the world in motion and keep the balance of life and death, the powers that will not be manipulated by a demon who exists only in the vileness of his own pride.'

Cassandra felt the power of the elements surge through her, saw in her mind's eye the Elemental Coven gathered in the Room of Reflection, focused, powerful, weaving magic that was terrible and wonderful and unlike anything Cassandra had ever witnessed. They stood in the circle, united as one, shining like the sun. And suddenly, the heavens that did not exist opened into torrential rain, a wall of water that would have dwarfed Scafell Pike consumed the fire, the earth that was not there trembled, wind raged with a hideous scream, and it all vanished again in an instant, leaving Deacon on his knees in the ravaged void. Then fire erupted around him and engulfed him like a prison.

Anderson scooped Cassandra into his arms and lifted her face to his. 'You must finish this, my love.' He held her gaze. 'Only you can, or others will suffer. I have a gift for you, one you must take.' He took her mouth, and in a deep kiss that felt more physical than anything Cassandra had ever experienced in the World of Flesh, he did the impossible. He forced his energy into her.

'No! Anderson, don't do this.' She tried with all of her strength to pull away but she was already weakened from her efforts, and he held her and kissed her, and her struggle was useless.

He spoke against her mouth as his energy flooded her in waves and flashes of power that would have been exquisite, that would have been sheer ecstasy and delight under different circumstances. 'I have long ridden the Ether, and in this place the laws are mine to command. In this place, my love, I am indeed able to force you to take my energy, and force you I shall, for I could not bear to lose you, my darling. I could not bear it.'

First, she felt as though her head was expanding, as though everything wonderful and amazing and moving and beautiful that Anderson had ever known was now pouring into her mind. Then she felt as though all of her expanded to fill the entire Ether, as she took from Anderson. She struggled to stop but was unable, as he wrapped himself around her and fed her from his dark, rich, potent essence. The world that danced before her eyes was bright and beautiful and old and frightening, and so very powerful.

She saw the boy with dark eyes who was not the daughter his mother had so longed for, who sneaked into and out of the Ether at will when she was away, until she finally gave in and trained him. She saw the man, already a ghost, who held Tara Stone in his arms while she mourned the loss of her husband, the man who loved her enough to submit himself to her cause and be her ally through so much suffering and loss and battle.

She saw the man who fell to his death from the crumbling ledge of a cliff while fighting for the life of a friend. The friend he was able to save. Himself, he was not.

Cassandra clawed at his shoulder, trying desperately to get away. 'Anderson, don't do this. Please.'

'Just a little more my love. Then we shall do what we must and go home.'

And in truth, she felt as though she could contain no more, she felt replete in ways she could have never imagined, she felt as though she had consumed the world and everything in it. When, at last, Anderson pulled away, for the tiniest of moments the whole universe felt suspended in a single rich breath, a superfluous breath that they shared, and she had never seen anyone more beautiful than the man holding her to him, feeding her with his essence. 'Anderson, I love you,' she whispered against his lips. It took no time to say the words, and yet it was all the time left to them.

The Ether convulsed mightily and Deacon, unharmed, walked through the wall of flame as though he had barely noticed it. His arms were folded across his chest, the bullwhip he carried was curled in one fisted hand. 'Surely you cannot believe that I will allow myself to be so trifled with by a ghost and a bastard succubus. You are, both of you, beneath my notice, toying in realms I mastered long before either of you was even an emission in the cunt of your mother.'

He unfurled the bullwhip with a single, swift motion and cracked it hard and loud, and where it crossed the Ether, it left an angry welt, much as it would have done had it been expertly wielded against human flesh. But the welt expanded and split open, consuming the void around it into black emptiness, racing toward Anderson and Cassandra at terrifying speed. And just as it opened into a chasm, Anderson shoved Cassandra aside. 'Do what you must, my love. We shall yet prevail.' Even as he said it, the chasm expanded beneath him, swallowing him whole, and would have done the same to her if Deacon hadn't grabbed her arm and pulled her to him, his laughter still shuddering through his body.

Even as she cried out Anderson's name and fought to escape, the chasm sealed itself as though it had never been.

Deacon held her as she raged, steeling his grip so that, in his arms, she couldn't move. And when at last the pressure of his hand against her throat silenced her, he spoke close to her ear. 'Oh, do not you worry, my little succubus, I did not destroy him. However, it is well that he is a master of ethereal magic, for I do not know where in the whole of the void I have sent him.' He shrugged and offered a wicked smile. 'However, it does not matter for one such as him, does it? He has all of eternity to find his way back to the World of Flesh. If there is any flesh left to find his way back to by then.'

He raised an eyebrow. 'I do not know, my dear, for your father did not tell me. Are your kind long-lived?' He shrugged. 'Of course it does not matter, since you shall not live past the time it takes you to deliver me to my body. And oh, how I shall rejoice at watching Tara Stone suffer the loss not only of her little succubus but, a coup I had not counted on, the loss of her dear Anderson too. Why, it is as though in one fell swoop I have cut off the witch's right arm. Yes, I think I shall enjoy my homecoming very much indeed.'

In her rage and grief it was then that Cassandra remembered, and what she remembered was the very thing she had longed to forget all of her life. She was a succubus. Her voice, when it came back to her, was clear and powerful. 'And take you home, I shall, demon. Oh, indeed I shall.'

With Anderson's power and Anderson's essence still coursing through her, she pulled Deacon into her arms and kissed him. Oh yes, he felt it all right. Though he would deny it, Cassandra could tell that the demon was not immune to the power of a succubus – in fact, as a demon driven by lust, he was particularly vulnerable. His whole body quivered with first contact, he dropped the bullwhip at his feet, and for a second it was unclear if he were trying to push her away from him or pull her still closer.

She curled her fingers in his hair until it would have caused pain in a fleshly body, and she hoped he felt it as such.

She certainly meant it as such, as she deepened the kiss until she found what she was looking for, the darkest abyss in his psyche. And just as she had suspected, even a demon had one, especially a demon who had once been, at least in part, human. There was a man bent over in a filthy alley, his own bullwhip tight around his neck, surrounded by the women he had caused so much suffering. And leading them was Rayna Stone, Tara's mother, shining with rage.

'What are you doing, succubus?' Deacon tried to push her away, but it was too late. She had found what she needed, and her rage and her anguish knew no bounds. 'I told you, I'll take you home now.' She settled in close to him, wrapped her arms around him and took his essence into herself. And she gorged as she had never dared allow herself before. Her rage bloomed bright, blood red before her eyes, hot enough to scorch the Ether and beyond, hot enough, at least for the moment, to burn through the grief that burned in a different way, a much slower, much more torturous way.

'Cassandra Larkin? What are you doing?' She heard him roar inside her but she ignored his rage. It was as nothing to hers.

'A slight detour, Deacon. Remember my nightmare? Well, this one has your name written on it, and I want you to relive every terrifying second of it.'

She felt his struggle, but she was well into the space that he most wanted to avoid, and she was gorged on his darkest fears. She held him tight.

'I will not tolerate this, I will not allow a bastard cunt of a succubus to do such a thing!' he raged. 'Oh, how I shall make you suffer for this!'

'You have no choice, demon, not this time, and you know it. You'll go exactly where I want you to go.'

His attempt at a chuckle was warm and cloying against her ethereal heart. 'I underestimated you, my darling succubus. Only return me to the Ether, that is all I ask of you. Return me there and not only will I do you no harm, but I will tell you what you so long to know about your father. I will tell you everything. Everything, and oh, what gifts I can offer you, what power.'

With a pain that felt as though it would break her apart, she recalled Anderson falling into the void, and she tightened her grip. In her mind's eye, her ethereal body was a giant serpent of rage and pain and anguish squeezing the demon, holding him captive, and then she let his nightmare wash over both of them, as the serpent was transformed to a bullwhip, tightening endlessly around his neck, and the woman with the lead pipe held back from him what he most needed for his power. His manhood remained hard and unsatisfied, his seed retained, his death imminent, his helplessness complete. He struggled mightily, but the nightmare was his own, and the realm of such dreams belonged to the succubus. The realm of such dreams belonged to Cassandra Larkin, and her rage was rage beyond appeasing.

'You may leave at will, demon,' she said. 'We've prepared a place for you.'

She followed the bright thread back to Elemental Cottage, back to the Room of Reflection. And when she released Deacon from the nightmare, there was only one place for him to go. When she released him back into the depths of Serina Ravenmoor's scrying mirror, she settled one last kiss on his lips. 'You've taken from me and mine for the last time,' she whispered. And just before Marie Warren sealed his prison with her broken amulet, Cassandra said, 'The mirror and your return to it are compliments of Serina Ravenmoor.'

Then she fell back into her body, and into more pain than she had ever known it was humanly possible to bear. The physical was but the least of it.

Chapter Nineteen

ALICE FOUND TARA IN the greenhouse, a place she had spent the majority of her time since Anderson had been lost. She stood outside watching the coven leader move about mixing compost and transplanting seedlings. And when it got too cold to stand there any longer without a jacket, she gathered her courage and stepped inside, clearing her throat loudly, not wanting to startle the woman. She was still not all that comfortable with anyone who had such power at her fingertips. Even though Tara had been kind to her, she could no longer think of power with an innocent's naïveté after all that she had been through.

Tara laid down the trowel she'd been using to mix the compost and wiped her hands on her jeans. She offered Alice a smile that was warm enough, but tinged with sadness. Alice suddenly realised all of Tara's smiles were that way.

'You all right, Alice?' she said. 'You're looking better. Still a bit thin, but I'm sure Fiori's doing all she can to solve that problem.'

'I'm fine, I'm getting stronger every day, and Fiori's cooking's definitely helping.' Alice shifted from foot to foot and took a nervous look around the greenhouse as though it might help her find the right words. 'I ... I just wanted to thank you for all you've done for me.' She blushed and looked down at her walking boots. 'I owe you ... I owe you my life.'

'It was Cassandra's essence on you that led me to you. And to Ferris. I could never have found either of you otherwise,' Tara replied. 'Strange that, Cassandra's essence on Ferris, since the two have never been lovers. And she can't explain it either. I still reckon it's some connection to her father.'

Alice nodded, feeling more uncomfortable than ever. She'd heard the discussion about why Cassandra's essence was on Ferris, and she didn't care why. She was just glad it was there. She swallowed hard and found her voice. 'I need to go home.'

Tara studied her for a moment, the smile softening to a look of concern. 'You know you're welcome to stay as long as you want, Alice. I understand you're not comfortable with the idea at the moment, but you have real potential to practise magic.'

Alice nodded. 'Perhaps I may take you up on the offer some day. I love Elemental Cottage and you've all been so kind to me, but I really do need to go back home and try to put my life back together. I'll start seeing the psychologist again, this time the one you recommended, since she's probably the only one who won't think I need to be committed.' She forced a soft laugh. 'Or maybe she will. I'm still not sure I don't think that's what would be best.'

'I've often wondered that about myself,' Tara said. 'But I've decided I don't really want to know.' Both women were silent, lost in their own thoughts.

Shaking like a frightened schoolgirl, Alice took a bold step forward, and said what was really on her mind. 'You need to make peace with Cassandra.'

She saw the muscles along Tara's jaw tense and relax again, but the expression on her face didn't change. At last, she spoke. 'My relationship with Cassandra is not your business, Alice. I'm sorry you got dragged into this but –'

'I'd be dead, and so would Mr Ferris if she hadn't done what she did. No, worse yet, we wouldn't be dead, and that would have been far worse.'

'She went off half-cocked on her own.'

'Only because Deacon would have tortured us before he killed us if she hadn't. Did she tell you that? No, I suppose

211

not. I suppose you didn't bother to ask.'

'Alice, I –'

'You'd have done the same thing.'

'Alice, you –'

'She's packing to leave, did you know that? She thinks you don't want her here. And no, she didn't tell me that. I'm not stupid. Any fool could have figured that out.'

For a moment, the only sound was the trill of a robin outside on the bare hawthorn tree. Then Tara pushed past Alice and out of the greenhouse door, heading for the house like a woman with a mission.

Cassandra ignored the knock on her door. Maybe whoever it was would assume she was sleeping and go away. They didn't. She heard the door latch click, but she kept on packing and didn't look up, still hoping they would go away.

'Sky tells me you were in the Ether again yesterday.'

Cassandra was surprised to hear Tara's voice and felt her stomach knot at the sound of it. The woman had barely said a dozen words to her since Deacon's capture. She shot her a quick glance and went back to packing. 'That's right.'

Tara came into the room and sat down on the edge of her bed opposite the side she was packing on. 'It was too soon. You know that. It was dangerous and stupid.'

Cassandra swallowed the lump in her throat, recalling her desperate effort and how she had cried into her pillow when she had returned weak, disorientated and alone. 'Sky told me *you* made an attempt to go into the Ether too,' she said. Then, when she was sure she wouldn't cry, she added, 'That was even stupider.'

'Sky has a big mouth,' Tara said, then she offered a wry smile. 'Anyway, I couldn't get past the threshold.'

Cassandra tossed several pairs of socks into the suitcase. 'Surely you didn't expect to after all I took from you.' She wiped her suddenly sweaty palms on her jeans and moved to look out of the window into the back garden with its blanket of newly fallen snow. She didn't want Tara to see how close

212

to tears she was.

'You took from all of us,' Tara said. 'You were in a bad way when you came back. We were afraid we'd lose you.'

'But I took the most from you.' Cassandra's voice was barely more than a whisper in the quiet room.

For a long moment neither woman spoke, then Tara said, 'I had the most to offer.' Her laugh sounded more like a sob. 'He could have offered you more, Anderson could have.'

Cassandra gave up trying to stop the tears as she recalled how he had brought her back from the brink after her first encounter with Deacon.

Tara stood and moved to her side. 'I came to ethereal magic late, you know? It was another way to fight Deacon. My first attempt to ride the Ether, I got hopelessly lost. I wasn't even supposed to be there, didn't really think I could make it past the threshold, and stupidly hadn't planned what to do after I did.' Tara stroked the amulet around her neck and smiled out of the window. 'I would have died if he hadn't found me. He was young. His mother still didn't know that he could ride the Ether, would have never believed it of a son. But he found me and guided me home.'

She laughed softly. 'He had long been dead when we finally met in the flesh. By then, we'd been friends for several lifetimes.

'He didn't have to stay. It wasn't his battle. It was never his battle. He's the only one who had no reason to fight Deacon.'

The scene outside the window was blurred through Cassandra's tears. She blinked hard and turned to face Tara. 'How could you possibly think such a thing? Everything Deacon did to hurt you, Anderson felt like it was his own pain. You can't have known him all these years and not understood that about him.'

To her surprise, Tara's eyes were full of tears. The coven leader bit her lip and wiped her nose on her hand. 'Thing is, I could never figure out why. He knew the darkness I held inside me. He knew. And still he stayed.'

'I could tell you a few things about darkness,' Cassandra said. She hiccupped a laugh. 'Maybe he just likes neurotic women.' She took Tara's hand. 'I won't stop looking. We'll find him. I know we will, or he'll find us. No one's better in the Ether than Anderson, and this coven is a beacon that shines out through any part of the Ether I've ever been in.'

'Then don't go, Cassandra.' Tara nodded over to the half-packed bag. 'Here is his home, here is where he'll come back to. And when he returns, here is where he'll expect to find the woman he loves. At home.'

The full moon ritual that night was much more solemn than usual. Neither Cassandra nor Tara had enough strength to go into the Ether to set the coven spells that would amplify their search for Anderson and serve as a constant beacon to help him find his way home. It would be the next full moon before that could happen. All that could magically be done was done. Fiori had made sea bass grilled in fresh herbs, one of Anderson's favourite full moon meals. And after the circle had been opened, everyone had huddled in the library around the fireplace over Anderson's favourite champagne, an obscure vintage that only he knew how to get.

They shared stories of the man they all loved, and promises that they would find him and return him to his rightful place. One by one, everyone drifted off to bed, except for Cassandra, who couldn't bear the thought of her bed without Anderson to share it. Most often these days she slept on the sofa in the library, when she was able to sleep.

She wasn't sure how long she had sat there, nursing a cup of Fiori's hot chocolate and staring into the flames, but when she looked up to find Tara standing next to her, wrapped in a dark blue robe, the fire had died to embers and the cocoa was cold. The high priestess reached out her hand. 'Come to bed with me, Cassandra. You and I, we love him most. For tonight, let us hold that love between us.'

Cassandra followed Tara up the stairs in the silent house. She could hear soft moans of pleasure coming from Tim and

Marie's room. Alice had gone home, and Ferris had been taking his pleasure with Fiori or Sky, or sometimes both. She'd have never thought such an unassuming man would have such a powerful libido.

Tara led Cassandra into her room and shut the door gently behind them. She let the robe slide off her shoulders onto the floor and stood naked. Then she moved to Cassandra and kissed her gently. 'I need comfort, Cassandra. We both do. We need his comfort.' She cupped Cassandra's cheek and then her neck and opened her blouse to caress her collar bones. 'And we wear it all over us and in us, deep in us. His essence is so much a part of both of us.

'This is one of my shirts,' she said, smiling as she cupped Cassandra's breasts and pushed the shirt aside. Cassandra still hadn't had time to shop. 'My shirts are the only ones big enough for your lovely breasts.' She laughed a laugh that seemed almost carefree. 'Good thing Anderson has such big hands.'

Cassandra had taken Sky's advice and not worn any underwear, since all that she owned was practical and not very pretty. Tara ran her thumbs over her nipples and then guided Cassandra's hands to hers. 'I thought you don't make love with the living,' Cassandra commented. 'That's what Tim said.'

Tara eased open Cassandra's jeans and slid them down over her hips. 'What we did together after you got back from the Ether was far more intimate than lovemaking, Cassandra. You've already had more of me than any living person will ever have.'

Cassandra groaned. 'Me taking your life force – I'd say that's pretty intimate, all right.'

Tara took her face in her hands and kissed her, deeply and hungrily, as one who hadn't partaken in a while. Then, when Cassandra pulled back, she bit her lip playfully. 'I had to practically force you to take me. You're not going to make me do that now, are you?'

'You trust me, then?'

In the silver moonlight shining through the window, Tara's eyes were wide, dark and unbelievably bright. 'I trust you with my life,' she breathed, 'and the lives of all of those I hold dear.'

She guided Cassandra down on sheets that smelled of lavender and geranium, and of the powerful woman who had, no doubt, tossed and turned in them as unable to sleep as Cassandra had been. Tara's was the scent of the high fells and woodland earth with just a hint of the sea.

It was the scent that had bathed Anderson that first night her fetch had found him in Tara's arms – the scent that had lain against his sleeping body, next to Cassandra's own. It was the scent of Cumbria, Cassandra thought, and she buried her face in the hair of the woman who laved her nipples and areolae with a skilled tongue. And now, Cassandra wore so much more than just this woman's scent. She wore her essence, the deepest darkest part of her, offered willingly when Cassandra was at her weakest, at her most vulnerable, when Cassandra could have done the most unthinkable of things to her.

'At the time, I desperately wished you had taken all of me.' Tara spoke the words in soft kisses against her sternum. I wanted you to take all of me, Cassandra.' She slid up Cassandra's body and rested one hand on her pubic curls, caressing and wriggling her fingers until she found Cassandra's clit. Instinctively, Cassandra shifted into her touch, and Tara smiled down at her. 'I wanted to die in your embrace and forget the battle forever, forget the loss and the pain and the suffering. And you.' She dropped a kiss on her lips. 'You didn't want to take from me because you wanted the same thing.'

A single tear, sparkling diamond-bright in the moonlight slid from Tara's cheek and onto Cassandra's breast. 'But we're the only two who can ride the Ether, Cassandra. We're the only two who can look for him.' Her eyes were fierce. 'And we will find him. We will.'

They kissed for a long time. Just kissed and held each

other. But in a house so saturated with sex magic, need took its toll. 'Make love to me, Cassandra,' Tara said. 'And let me make love to you.'

The coven leader rolled to one side and opened her thighs, but as Cassandra fingered her swollen lips apart to settle in with her tongue, Tara rearranged her. With splayed hands, she guided Cassandra's hips until she squatted low over her face, until Tara could skim her open labia with her tongue, until she could nibble and suck and lick at her clit. With a sigh that vibrated warm and moist against Cassandra's pussy, she explored with her hands, fondling the Cassandra's buttocks, kneading and pulling them apart like freshly made bread until she could finger her anus while she tongued her.

Cassandra moved against Tara's face, riding the delicious feel of her tongue and lips and the tight friction of the finger invading her back hole. She took Tara's heavily swollen clit into her mouth, bathing her nose in the woman's creamy wet pout, taking in the powerful scent of her lust. Then, as she carefully allowed herself to nip and suckle and taste daintily, Tara whimpered and trembled beneath her.

With the build-up of pleasure brought on by the succubus's touch, the moonlit room danced and crackled and buzzed with the stretched-tight, aching hunger of the two women. They growled and clawed their orgasms from the depths of pain up into the bright world of moonlit snow and sex magic, into the house filled with love and lust that would heal the gaping hole rent in the fabric of their family. It was that lust and love and hope that would conquer whatever demon had to be conquered and traverse the most remote corner of the Ether to take back what belonged to them. And Elemental Cottage, as always, accepted the cries of love and joy and pain and pleasure back into itself, and the two women slept in each other's arms.

At first, Cassandra thought it was nothing more than the breeze of the heater rustling sheer curtains, the thinnest of gossamer making the bright moonlight shimmer and dance.

But then the image shifted, and even as it took form she knew she walked the Dream World. Her heart practically leapt from her chest as the shimmering mist coalesced and shifted and changed, until Anderson stood beside her, close to the bed, his hand brushing her forehead with a touch she could almost feel.

'It pleases me to see the two women I so love offering each other comfort and pleasure.' He laughed softly. 'It does not please me, however, that the bed is so very large and I am not there between you sharing your pleasure. When I am once again returned to Elemental Cottage, I shall have such a need as you can scarcely imagine, my love. I am sure that my demands upon the two of you shall be very great indeed. It shall be very difficult for you to satisfy such a lust.'

Cassandra swallowed back a sob and laughed out loud. 'I'm a succubus. I can handle your lust, Anderson.'

'And so you shall, my darling. And so you shall.' The apparition wavered and faded, but before it vanished completely, it said, 'I shall be anxiously awaiting your skilful handling of my lust, Cassandra Larkin.'

'Anderson!' Both women called out simultaneously and, at the same instant, both sat bolt upright in the bed.

There was no going back to sleep and, downstairs in the kitchen, it quickly became evident that Cassandra and Tara weren't the only ones whose sleep had been disturbed by the apparition. Fiori had already made a pot of tea and was busy mixing up Swedish pancakes, which were Anderson's favourite.

'It wasn't his fetch,' Sky was saying. 'It couldn't have been his fetch. If he could send his fetch, then he could find his way back home.'

'It was so real,' Marie said. 'I checked his room just to make sure. But …'

'Oh, it was real, all right,' Fiori said. 'I don't think any of us would argue that it wasn't.'

'I don't know how he did it,' Tara said, holding her

steaming cup between both hands, 'But I think none of us would deny that it couldn't have come at a better time. Once Cassandra's strong enough and I've recovered enough, we'll start regular forays into the Ether. We'll cover every last inch of it if we have to. At the next full moon, we'll set the magical beacons, and each full moon after that, we'll set new ones deeper into the Ether until we have him back.'

'I think we might be able to come up with a spell that would allow us to set beacons in the new moons as well.' Everyone was surprised to find Ferris standing quietly by Sky, dressed in his black suit, looking as though he had never gone to bed. He shrugged. 'I remembered a few things after my unexpected excursion into the Ether – things I didn't remember before, things I can't imagine how I could forget, lots of spells. Spells I don't know why I should know, but I do.'

'Something about Cassandra's father? Tim asked.

The man shook his head, 'Nothing as specific as that, but spells, histories, incidents that might ultimately be helpful to us in our search for Anderson.' It was then that Cassandra noticed, his hand resting on Sky's butt, and she felt hopeful. She felt truly hopeful for the first time since she had lost Anderson in the Ether. They would find him.

As Fiori served up the piping-hot pancakes smothered in whipped cream and lingonberry jam, Cassandra was sure that there was no one in Elemental Cottage who would stop until their high priest was safely back in their midst. And back in her arms, she thought. Fiori kissed her on the cheek as she set down a plate of pancakes in front of her. Beneath the table, Tara gave Cassandra's thigh a reassuring pat before digging into her own pancakes. And for the first time she could remember, Cassandra felt at home.

Away from the celebration, on the altar in the Room of Reflection, Deacon paced the length and breadth of his gilded mirror prison. It was his own little piece of the Ether, all that was allowed him. And it would be enough. For now.

Reviews for *Lakeland Heatwave*

"I am a huge fan of K.D. Grace's explicit, well-crafted writing (I've selected and published her work in multi-author "Best" collections), and this novel did not disappoint me. It's the first of a hardcore paranormal trilogy, and many readers think it is her best work to date." **Violet Blue**

*****

"Body Temperature and Rising is my favourite of K D Grace's books so far… So if you're looking for a well-written, pacy and smokin' hot paranormal romp, I'd point you towards this book. One warning, though. As soon as you've read it, you'll want to read the next book immediately. I know I do!" **5 out of 5,   Erotica For All**

*****

"This is powerful, sexy writing from the extremely competent K D Grace. The story contains a compelling narrative. And all of it is set in the most beautiful scenery in the natural world. You really will love this book." **Erotica Readers & Writers Association**

*****

"For the love of all things steamy, this is one HOT read. Steamy, sexy and some other words that start with S and mean hot things, Body Temperature and Rising is definitely a wild ride. If you don't like the sexy, stay out of the sex coven." **Reading the Paranormal**

*****

"Crossing my fingers that there is more to come in this series and soon! Body Temperature and Rising is steamy hot with an involved plot. Definitely give this paranormal erotica a try!" **BookingIt**